THE
PHANTOM HERD

B. M.Bower

1st WORLD
LIBRARY
Literary Society

The Phantom Herd

B. M. Bower

© 1st World Library – Literary Society, 2005
PO Box 2211
Fairfield, IA 52556
www.1stworldlibrary.org
First Edition

LCCN: 2004195584

Softcover ISBN: 1-4218-0405-0
Hardcover ISBN: 1-4218-0305-4
eBook ISBN: 1-4218-0505-7

Purchase *"The Phantom Herd"*
as a traditional bound book at:
www.1stWorldLibrary.org/purchase.asp?ISBN=1-4218-0405-0

1st World Library Literary Society is a nonprofit
organization dedicated to promoting literacy by:

- Creating a free internet library accessible from any
  computer worldwide.
- Hosting writing competitions and offering book
  publishing scholarships.

Readers interested in supporting literacy
through sponsorship, donations or
membership please contact:
literacy@1stworldlibrary.org
Check us out at: www.1stworldlibrary.ORG
and start downloading free ebooks today.

The Phantom Herd
contributed by Tim, Ed & Rodney
in support of
1st World Library Literary Society

FOREWORD

For the accuracy of certain parts of this story which deal most intimately with the business of making motion pictures, I am indebted to Buck Connor. whose name is a sufficient guarantee that all technical points are correct. His criticism, advice and other assistance have been invaluable, and I take this opportunity of expressing my appreciation and thanks for the help he has given me.

B.M.BOWER.

CONTENTS

I. THE INDIANS MUST GO ------------------------------------9

II. "WHERE THE CATTLE ROAMED IN
    THOUSANDS, A-MANY A HERD AND BRAND..." -- 18

III. AND THEY SIGN FOR THE DAYS THAT
    ARE GONE --- 37

IV. THE LITTLE DOCTOR PROTESTS ---------------------- 46

V. A BUNCH OF ONE-REELERS FROM
    BENTLY BROWN ------------------------------------- 58

VI. VILLAINS ALL AND PROUD OF IT -------------------- 68

VII. BENTLY BROWN DOES NOT APPRECIATE
    COMEDY--- 83

VIII. "THERE'S GOT TO BE A LINE DRAWN
    SOMEWHERES" ----------------------------------- 92

IX. LEAVE IT TO THE BUNCH ----------------------------107

X. UNEXPECTED GUESTS FOR APPLEHEAD----------- 124

XI. JUST A FEW UNFORESEEN OBSTACLES ----------- 138

XII. "I THINK YOU NEED INDIAN GIRL
    FOR PICTUE" ------------------------------------- 154

XIII. "PAM. BLEAK MESA - CATTLE DRIFTING
    BEFORE WIND - "-------------------------------------- 164

XIV. "PLUMB SPOILED, D'YUH MEAN?" ----------------179

XV. A LETTER FROM CHIEF BIG TURKEY-------------- 193

XVI. "THE CHANCES IS SLIM AND
      GITTIN' SLIMMER"------------------------------------203

XVII. THE STORM --212

XVIII. A FEW OF THE MINOR DIFFICULTIES ----------222

XIX. WHEREIN LUCK MAKES A SSPEECH--------------235

XX. "SHE'S SHAPING UP LIKE A BANK ROLL" --------245

CHAPTER ONE

THE INDIANS MUST GO

Luck Lindsay had convoyed his thirty-five actor-Indians to their reservation at Pine Ridge, and had turned them over to the agent in good condition and a fine humor and nice new hair hatbands and other fixings; while their pockets were heavy with dollars that you may be sure would not he spent very wisely. He had shaken hands with the braves, and had promised to let them know when there was another job in sight, and to speak a good word for them to other motion-picture companies who might want to hire real Indians. He had smiled at the fat old squaws who had waddled docilely in and out of the scenes and teetered tirelessly round and round in their queer native dances in the hot sun at his behest, when Luck wanted several rehearsals of "atmosphere" scenes before turning the camera on them.

They hated to go back to the tame life of the reservation and to stringing beads and sewing buckskin with sinew, and to gossiping among themselves of things their heavy-lidded black eyes had looked upon with such seeming apathy. They had given Luck an elaborately beaded buckskin vest that would photograph beautifully, and three pairs of heavy, beaded moccasins which he most solemnly assured them he would wear in his next picture. The smoke-smell of their tepee fires and perfumes still clung heavily to the Indian-tanned buckskin, so that Luck carried away with him an aroma indescribable and unmistakable to any one who has ever smelled it.

Just when he was leaving, a shy, big-eyed girl of ten had slid out from the shelter of her mother's poppy-patterned skirt, had proffered three strings of beads, and had fled. Luck had smiled his smile again - a smile of white, even teeth and so much good will that you immediately felt that he was your friend - and called her back to him. Luck was chief; and his commands were to be obeyed, instantly and implicitly; that much he had impressed deeply upon the least of these. While the squaws grinned and murmured Indian words to one another, the big-eye girl returned reluctantly; and Luck, dropping a hand to his coat pocket while he smiled reassurance, emptied that pocket of gum for her. His smile had lingered after he turned away; for like flies to an open syrup can the papooses had gathered around the girl.

Well, that job was done, and done well. Every one was satisfied save Luck himself. He swung up to the back of the Indian pony that would carry him through the Bad Lands to the railroad, and turned for a last look. The bucks stood hip-shot and with their arms folded, watching him gravely. The squaws pushed straggling locks from their eyes that they might watch him also. The papooses were chewing gum and staring at him solemnly. Old Mrs. Ghost-Dog, she of the ponderous form and plaid blanket that Luck had used with such good effect in the foreground of his atmosphere scenes, lifted up her voice suddenly, and wailed after him in high-keyed lament that she would see his face no

B. M. Bower

more; and Luck felt a sudden contraction of the throat while he waved his hand to them and rode away.

Well, now he must go on to the next job, which he hoped would be more pleasant than this one had been. Luck hated to give up those Indians. He liked them, and they liked him, - though that was not the point. He had done good work with them. When he directed the scenes, those Indians did just what he wanted, and just the way he wanted it done; Luck was too old a director not to know the full value of such workers.

But the Acme Film Company, caught with the rest of the world in the pressure of hard times, wanted to economize. The manager had pointed out to Luck, during the course of an evening's discussion, that these Indians were luxuries in the making of pictures, and must be taken off the payroll for the good of the dividends. The manager had contended that white men and women, properly made up, could play the part of Indians where Indians were needed; whereas Indians could never be made to play the part of white men and women. Therefore, since white men and women were absolutely necessary. Why keep a bunch of Indians around eating up profits? The manager had sense on his side, of course. Other companies were making Indian pictures occasionally with not a real Indian within miles of the camera, but Luck Lindsay groaned inwardly, and cursed the necessity of economizing. For Luck had one idol, and that idol was realism. When the scenario called for twenty or thirty Indians, Luck wanted *Indians*, - real, smoke-tanned, blanketed bucks and squaws and papooses; not made-up whites who looked like animated signs for cigarb stores and acted like, - well, never mind what Luck said they acted like.

"I can take the Injuns back," he conceded, "and worry along somehow without them. But if you want me to put on any more Western stuff, you'll have to let me weed out some of these Main Street cowboys that Clements wished on to me, and go out in the sagebrush and round up some that ain't all hair hatbands and high-heeled boots and bluff. I've got to have some whites to fill the foreground, if I give up the Injuns; or else I quit Western stuff altogether. I've been stalling along and keeping the best of the bucks in the foreground, and letting these said riders lope in and out of scenes and pile off and go to shooting soon as the camera picks them up, but with the Injuns gone, the whites won't get by.

"Maybe you have noticed that when there was any real riding, I've had the Injuns do it. And do you think I've been driving that stagecoach hell-bent from here to beyond because I'd no other way to kill time? Wasn't another darned man in the outfit I'd trust, that's why. If I take the Indians back, I've got to have some real boys." Luck's voice was plaintive, and a little bit desperate.

"Well, dammit, *have* your real boys! I never said you shouldn't. Weed out the company to suit yourself. You'll have to take the Injuns back; nobody else can handle the touch-me-not devils. You can lay off the company if you want to, and while you're up there pick up a bunch of cowboys to suit you. You're making good, Luck; don't take it that I'm criticizing anything you've done or the way you did it. You've been turning out the best Western stuff that goes on the screen; anybody knows that. That isn't the point. We just simply can't afford to keep those Indians any longer without retrenching on something else that's a lot more vital. You know what they cost as well as I do; you know what present conditions are. Figure it out for yourself."

"I don't have to," Luck retorted in a worried tone. "I know what we're up against. I know we ought to give them up - but I sure hate to do it! Lor-*dee*, but I can do things with that bunch! Remember Red Brother?" Luck was off on his hobby, the making of Indian pictures. "Remember the panoram effect I got on that massacre of the wagon train? Remember the council-of-war scene, and the close-up of Young-Dog-Howls-At-The-Moon making his plea for the lives of the prisoners? And the war dance with radium flares in the camp fires to give the light-effect? That film's in big demand yet, they tell me. I'll never be able to put over stuff like that with made-up actors, Martinson. You know I can't."

"I don't know; you're only just beginning to hit your gait, Luck," the manager soothed. "You have turned out some big stuff, - some awful big stuff; but at that you're just beginning to find yourself. Now, listen. You can have your 'real boys' you're always crying for. I can see what you mean when you pan these fellows you call Main Street cowboys. What you better do is this: Close down the company for two weeks, say. Keep on the ones you want, and let the rest out. And take these Injuns home, and then get out after your riders. Numbers and salaries we'll leave to you. Go as far as you like; it's a cinch you'll get what you want if you're allowed to go after it."

So here was Luck, arriving in due time at the railroad. He said good-by to Young-Dog-Howls-At-The-Moon who had ridden with him, and whose kingly bearing and clean-cut features and impressive pantomime made him a popular screen-Indian, and sat down upon a baggage truck to smoke a cigarette while he waited for the westbound train.

Young-Dog-Howls-At-The-Moon he watched meditatively until that young man had bobbed out of sight over a low hill, the pony Luck had ridden trailing after at the end of the lead-rope. Luck's face was sober, his eyes tired and unsmiling. He had done that much of his task: he had returned the Indians, and automatically wiped a very large item of expense from the accounts of the Acme Film Company. He did not like to dwell, however, on the cost to his own pride in his work.

The next job, now that he was actually face to face with it, looked not so simple. He was in a country where, a few years before, his quest for "real boys" - as he affectionately termed the type nearest his heart - would have been easy enough. But before the marching ranks of fence posts and barbed wire, the real boys had scattered. A more or less beneficent government had not gathered them together, and held them apart from the changing conditions, as it had done with the Indians. The real boys had either left the country, or had sold their riding outfits and gone into business in the little towns scattered hereabouts, or else they had taken to farming the land where the big herds had grazed while the real boys loafed on guard.

Luck admitted to himself that in the past two years, even, conditions had changed amazingly. Land was fenced that had been free. Even the reservation was changed a little. He threw away that cigarette and lighted another, and turned aggrievedly upon a dried little man who came up with the open expectation of

B. M. Bower

using the truck upon which Luck was sitting uncomfortably. There was the squint of long looking against sun and wind at a far skyline in the dried little man's face. There was a certain bow in his legs, and there were various other signs which Luck read instinctively as he got up. He smiled his smile, and the dried little man grinned back companionably.

"Say, old-timer, what's gone with all the cattle and all the punchers?" Luck demanded with a mild querulousness.

The dried little man straightened from the truck handles and regarded Luck strangely.

"My gorry, son, plumb hazed off'n this section the earth, I reckon. Farmers and punchers, they don't mix no better'n sheep and cattle. Why, I mind the time when - "

The train was late, anyway, and the dried little man sat down on the truck, and fumbled his cigarette book, and began to talk. Luck sat down beside him and listened, leaning forward with his elbows on his knees and a cold cigarette in his fingers. It was not of this part of the country that the dried little man talked, but of Montana, over there to the west. Of northern Montana in the days when it was cowman's paradise; the days when round-up wagons started out with the grass greening the hilltops, and swung from the Rockies to the Bear Paws and beyond in the wide arc that would cover their range; of the days of the Cross L and the Rocking R and the Lazy Eight, - every one of them brand names to glisten the eyes of old-time Montanans.

" Where would you go to find them boys now?" the

dried little man questioned mournfully. "The Rocking R's gone into sheep, and the old boys have all left. The Cross L moved up into Canada, Lord knows how they're making out; I don't. Only outfit in northern Montana I know that has hung together at all is the Flying U. Old man Whitmore, he's hangin' on by his eyewinkers to what little range he can, and is going in for thoroughbreds. Most of his boys is with him yet, they tell me - "

"What they doing? Still riding?" Luck let out a long breath and lighted his cigarette. A little flare of hope had come into his eyes.

"Riding - yes, what little there is to do. Ranching a little too, and kicking about changed times, same as I'm doing. Last time I saw that outfit they was riding, you bet!" The dried little man chuckled, "That was in Great Falls, some time back. They was all in a contest, and pulling down the money, too. I was talking to old man Whitmore all one evening. He was telling me - "

From away out yonder behind a hill came the throaty call of the coming train. The dried little man jumped up, mumbled that it did beat all how time went when yuh got to talking over old days, and hustled two trunks out of the baggage room. Luck got his grip out of the office, settled himself into his coat, and took a last, long pull at the cigarette stub before he threw it away. It was not much of a clue that he had fallen upon by chance, but Luck was not one to wait until he was slapped in the face with a fact. He had intended swinging back through Arizona, where in certain parts cattle still were wild enough to bunch up at sight of a man afoot. His questioning of the dried little man had not been born of any concrete purpose, but of the range

B. M. Bower

man's plaint in the abstract. Still –

"Say, brother, what's the Flying U's home town?" he called after the dried little man with his amiable, Southern drawl.

"Huh? Dry Lake. Yuh taking this train?"

"So long - taking it for a ways, yes." Luck hurried down to where a kinky-haired porter stood apathetically beside the steps of his coach. Dry Lake? He had never heard of the place, but he could find out from the railroad map or the conductor. He swung his grip into the waiting hand of the porter and went up the steps hurriedly. He meant to find out where Dry Lake was, and whether this train would take him there.

CHAPTER TWO

"WHERE THE CATTLE ROAMED IN THOU-SANDS, A-MANY A HERD AND BRAND ..."
- Old Range Song.

If you are at all curious over the name to which Luck Lindsay answered unhesitatingly, - his very acceptance of it proving his willingness to be so identified, - I can easily explain. Some nicknames have their origin in mystery; there was no mystery at all surrounding the name men had bestowed upon Lucas Justin Lindsay. In the first place, his legal cognomen being a mere pandering to the vanity of two grandfathers who had no love for each other and so must both be mollified, never had appealed to Luck or to any of his friends. Luck would have been grateful for any nickname that would have wiped Lucas Justin from the minds of men. But the real reason was a quirk in Luck's philosophy of life. Anything that he greatly desired to see accomplished, he professed to leave to chance. He would smile his smile, and lift his shoulders in the Spanish way he had learned in Mexico and the Philippines, and say: "That's as luck will have it. *Quien sabe?*" Then he would straightway go about bringing the thing to pass by his own dogged efforts. Men fell into the habit of calling him Luck, and they forgot that he had any other name; so there you have it, straight and easily understandable.

B. M. Bower

As luck would have it, then, - and no pun intended, please, - he found himself en route to Dry Lake without any trouble at all; a mere matter of one change of trains and very close connections, the conductor told him. So Luck went out and found a chair on the observation platform, and gave himself up to his cigar and to contemplation of the country they were gliding through. What he would find at Dry Lake to make the stop worth his while did not worry him; he left that to the future and to the god Chance whom he professed to serve. He was doing his part; he was going there to find out what the place held for him. If it held nothing but a half dozen ex-cow-punchers hopelessly tamed and turned farmers, why, there would probably be a train to carry him further in his quest. He would drop down into Wyoming and Arizona and New Mexico, - just keep going till he did find the men he wanted. That was Luck's way.

The shadows grew long and spread over the land until the whole vast country lay darkling under the coming night. Luck went in and ate his dinner, and came back again to smoke and stare and dream. There was a moon now that silvered the slopes and set wide expanses shimmering.

Luck, always more or less a dreamer, began to people the plain with the things that had been but were no more: with buffalo and with Indians who camped on the trail of the big herds. He saw their villages, the tepees smoke-grimed and painted with symbols, some of them, huddled upon a knoll out there near the timber line. He heard the tom-toms and he saw the rhythmic leaping and treading, the posing and gesturing of the braves who danced in the firelight the tribal Buffalo Dance.

After that he saw the coming of the cattle, driven up from the south by wind-browned, saddle-weary cowboys who sang endless chanteys to pass the time as they rode with their herds up the long trail. He saw the cattle humped and drifting before the wind in the first blizzards of winter, while gray wolves slunk watchfully here and there, their shaggy coats ruffled by the biting wind. He saw them when came the chinook, a howling, warm wind from out the southwest, cutting the snowbanks as with a knife that turned to water what it touched, and laying bare the brown grass beneath. He saw the riders go out with the wagons to gather the lank-bodied, big-kneed calves and set upon them the searing mark of their owner's iron.

Urged by the spell of the dried little man's plaintive monologue, the old range lived again for Luck, out there under the moon, while the train carried him on and on through the night.

What a picture it all would make - the story of those old days as they had been lived by men now growing old and bent. With all the cheap, stagy melodrama thrown to one side to make room for the march of that bigger drama, an epic of the range land that would be at once history, poetry, realism!

Luck's cigar went out while he sat there and wove scene after scene of that story which should breathe of the real range land as it once had been. It could be done - that picture. Months it would take in the making, for it would swing through summer and fall and winter and spring. With the trail-herd going north that picture should open - the trail-herd toiling over big, unpeopled plains, with the riders slouched in their saddles, hat brims pulled low over eyes that ached with

B. M. Bower

the glare of the sun and the sweep of wind, their throats parched in the dust cloud flung upward from the marching, cloven hoofs. Months it would take in the making, - but sitting there with the green tail-lights switching through cuts and around low hills and out over the level, Luck visioned it all, scene by scene. Visioned the herd huddled together in the night while the heavens were split with lightning, and the rain came down in white-lighted streamers of water. Visioned the cattle humped in the snow, tails to the biting wind, and the riders plodding with muffled heads bent to the drive of the blizzard, the fine snow packing full the wrinkles in their sourdough coats.

It could be done. He, Luck Lindsay, could do it; in his heart he knew that he could. In his heart he felt that all of these months - yes, and years - of picture-making had been but a preparation for this great picture of the range. All these one-reel pioneer pictures had been merely the feeble efforts of an apprentice learning to handle the tools of his craft, the mental gropings of his mind while waiting for this, his big idea. His work with the Indians was the mere testing and trying of certain photographic effects, certain camera limitations. He felt like an athlete taught and trained and tempered and just stepping out now for the big physical achievement of his life.

He grew chilled as the night advanced, but he did not know that he was cold. He was wondering, as a man always wonders in the face of an intellectual birth, why this picture had not come to him before; why he had gone on through these months and years of turning out reel upon reel of Western pictures, with never once a glimmering of this great epic of the range land; why he had clung to his Indians and his one-reel Indian pictures with now and then a three-reel feature to give him the elation of having achieved something; why he had left them feeling depressedly that his best work was in the past; why he had looked upon real range-men as a substitute only for those lean-bodied bucks and those fat, stupid-eyed squaws and dirty papooses.

With the spell of his vision deep upon his soul, Luck sat humiliated before his blindness. The picture he saw as he stared out across the moonlit plain was so clean-cut, so vivid, that he marvelled because he had never seen it until this night. Perhaps, if the dried little man had not talked of the old range -

Luck took a long breath and flung his cigar out over the platform rail. The dried little man? Why, just as he stood he was a type! He was the Old Man who owned this herd that should trail north and on through scene after scene of the picture! No make-up needed there to stamp the sense of reality upon the screen. Luck looked with the eye of his imagination and saw the dried little man climbing, with a stiffness that could not hide his accustomedness, into the saddle. He saw him ride out with his men, scattering his riders for the round-up; the old cowman making sharper the contrast of the younger men, fixing indelibly upon the consciousness of those who watched that this same dried little man had grown old in the saddle; fixing indelibly the fact that not in a day did the free ranging of cattle grow to be one of the nation's great industries.

Of a sudden Luck got up and stood swaying easily to the motion of the car while he took a long, last look at the moon-bathed plain where had been born his great, beautiful picture. He stretched his arms as does one who has slept heavily, and went inside and down to the

B. M. Bower

beginning of the narrow aisle where were kept
telegraph forms in their wooden-barred niches in the
wall. He went into the smoking compartment and
wrote, with a sureness that knew no crossed-out words,
a night letter to the dried little man who had sat on the
baggage truck and talked of the range. And this is what
went speeding back presently to the dried little man
who slept in a cabin near the track and dreamed,
perhaps, of following the big herds:

Baggageman,
Sioux, N.D.

Report at once to me at Dry Lake. Can offer you good
position Acme Film Company, good salary working in
big Western picture. Small part, some riding among
real boys who know range life. Want you bad as type
of cowman owning cattle in picture. Salary and
expenses begin when you show up. For references see
Indian Agent.

LUCK LINDSAY,
Dry Lake, Mont.

If you count, you will see that he ran eight words over
the limit of the flat rate on night letters, but he would
have over-run the limit by eighty words just as quickly
if he had wanted to say so much. That was Luck's way.
Be it a telegram, instructions to his company, or a
quarrel with some one who crossed him, Luck said
what he wanted to say - and paid the price without
blinking.

I don't know what the dried little man thought when
the operator handed him that message the next
morning; but I can tell you in a few words what he did:

He arrived in Dry Lake just two trains behind Luck.

Luck did not sleep that night. He lay in his berth with the shade pushed up as high as it would go, and stared out at the tamed plain, and perfected the details of his Big Picture. Into the spell of the range he wove a story of human love and human hate and danger and trouble. So it must be, to carry his message to the world who would look and marvel at what he would show them in the drama of silence. He had not named his picture yet. The name would come in its own good time, just as the picture had come when the time for its making was ripe.

The next day he did not talk with the men whose elbows he touched in the passing intimacy of travel; though Luck was a companionable soul who was much given to talking and to seeing his listeners grow to an audience, - an appreciative audience that laughed much while they listened and frowned upon interruption. Instead, he sat silent in his seat, since on this train there was no observation car, and he stared out of the window without seeing much of what passed before his eyes, and made notes now and then, and covered all the margins of his time-table with figures that had to do with film. Once, I know, he blackened his two front teeth with pencil tappings while he visualized a stampede and the probable amount of footage it would require, and debated whether it should be "shot" with two cameras or three to get scenes from different angles. A stampede it should be, - a real stampede of fear-frenzied range cattle in the mad flight of terror; not a bunch of galloping tame cows urged to foreground by shouting and rock-throwing from beyond the side lines of the scene. It would be hard to get, and it could not be rehearsed before the camera was turned on it. Luck decided that it should be shot from three angles, at least, and if he could manage it he would have a "panoram" of the whole thing from a height.

The porter came apologetically with his big whisk broom and told Luck that they would all presently be gazing at Dry Lake, or words which carried that meaning. So Luck permitted himself to be whisked from a half dollar while his thoughts were "in the field" with his camera men and company, shooting a real stampede from various angles and trying to manage so that the dust should not obscure the scene. After a rain - of course! Just after a soaking rain, he thought, while he gathered up his time-table and a magazine that held his precious figures, and followed the porter out to the vestibule while the train slowed.

It was in this mood that Luck descended to the Dry Lake depot platform and looked about him. He had no high expectation of finding here what he sought. He was simply making sure, before he left the country behind him, that he had not "overlooked any bets." His mind was open to conviction even while it was prepared against disappointment; therefore his eyes were as clear of any prejudice as they were of any glamour. He saw things as they were.

On the side track, then, stood a string of cars loaded with wool, as his nose told him promptly. Farms there were none, but that was because the soil was yellow and pebbly and barren where it showed in great bald spots here and there; you would not expect to raise cabbages where a prairie dog had to forage far for a living. Behind the depot, the prairie humped a huge, broad shoulder of bluff wrinkled along the forward slope of it like the folds of a full fashioned skirt. There, too, the soil was bare, - clipped to the very grass roots by hundreds upon hundreds of hungry sheep whose wool, very likely, was crowding those cars upon the siding. Luck wasted neither glances nor thought upon the scene. Dry Lake was like many, many other outworn "cow towns" through which he had passed; changed without being bettered; all of the old life taken out of it in the process of its taming.

He threw his grip into the waiting, three-seated spring wagon that served as a hotel bus, climbed briskly after it, and glanced ahead to where he saw the age-blackened boards of the stockyards. Cattle - and then came the sheep. So runs the epitaph of the range, and it was written plainly across Dry Lake and its surroundings.

They went up a dusty trail and past the yawning wings of the stockyards where a bunch of sheep blatted now in the thirst of mid-afternoon. They stopped before the hotel where, in the old days, many a town-hungry puncher had set his horse upon its haunches that he might dismount in a style to match his eagerness. Luck climbed out and stood for a minute looking up and down the sandy street that slept in the sun and dreamed, it may be, of rich, unforgotten moments when the cow-punchers had come in off the range and stirred the sluggish town to a full, brief life with their rollicking. Across the street was Rusty Brown's place, with its narrow porch deserted of loafers and its windows blinking at the street with a blankness that belied the things they had looked upon in bygone times.

A less experienced man than Luck would have been convinced by now that here was no place to go seeking

B. M. Bower

"real boys." But Luck had been a range man himself before he took to making motion pictures; he knew range towns as he knew men, - which was very well indeed. He looked, as he stood there, not disgusted but mildly speculative. Two horses were tied to the hitching rail before Rusty Brown's place. These horses bore saddles and bridles, and, if you know the earmarks, you can learn a good deal about a rider just by looking at his outfit. Neither saddle was new, but both gave evidence of a master's pride in his gear. They were well-preserved saddles. They had the conservative swell of fork that told Luck almost to a year how old they were. One, he judged, was of California make, or at least came from the extreme southwest of the cattle country. It had a good deal of silver on it, and the tapideros were almost Mexican in their elaborateness. The bridle on that horse matched the saddle, and the headstall was beautiful with silver kept white and clean. The rope coiled and tied beside the saddle fork was of rawhide. (Luck did not need to cross the street to be sure of these details; observation was a part of his profession.) The other saddle was the kind most favored on the northern range. Short, round skirts, open stirrups, narrow and rimmed with iron. Stamped with a two-inch border of wild rose design, it pleased Luck by its very simplicity. The rope was a good "grass" rope worn smooth and hard with much use.

Luck flipped a match stub out into the dust of the street, tilted his small Stetson at an angle over his eyes, went over to the horses, and looked at their brands which had been hidden from him. One was a Flying U, and the other bore a blurred monogram which he did not trouble to decipher. He turned on his heels and went into Rusty's place.

On his way to the bar he cast an appraising glance around the room and located his men. Here, too, a less experienced man might have blundered. One, known to his fellows as the Native Son, would scarcely be mistaken; his dress, too, evidently matched the silver-trimmed saddle outside. But Andy Green, in blue overalls turned up five inches at the bottom, and somewhat battered gray hat and gray chambray shirt, might have been almost any type of outdoor man. Certain it is that few strangers would have guessed that he was one of the best riders in that part of the State.

Luck bought a couple of good cigars, threw away his cigarette and lighted one, set the knuckles of his left hand upon his hip, and sauntered over to the pool table where the two men he wanted to meet were languidly playing out their third string. He watched them for a few minutes, smiled sympathetically when Andy Green made a scratch and swore over it, and backed out of the way of the Native Son, who sprawled himself over the table corner and did not seem to know or to care how far the end of his cue reached behind him.

Luck did not say a word to either; but Andy, noting the smile of sympathy, gave him a keenly attentive glance as he came up to that end of the table to empty a corner pocket. He fished out the four and the nine, juggled them absently in his hand, and turned and looked at Luck again, straight and close. Luck once more smiled his smile.

"No, I don't believe you know me, brother," he said, answering Andy's unspoken thought. "I'd have remembered you if I'd ever met you. You may have seen me in a picture somewhere."

"By gracious, are you the little fellow that drove a stage coach and six horses down off a grade - "

"That's my number, old-timer." Luck's smile widened to a grin. That had been a hair-lifting scene, and Andy Green was not the first stranger to walk up and ask him if he had driven that stage coach and six horses down off a mountain grade into a wide gulch to avoid being held up and the regulation box of gold stolen. It was probably the most spectacular thing Luck had ever done. "Got down that bank fine as silk," he volunteered companionably, "and then when I'd passed camera and was outa the scene, by thunder, I tangled up with a deep chuck-hole that was grown over with weeds, and like to have broken my fool neck. How's that for luck?" He took the cigar from his lips and smiled again with half-closed, measuring eyes. "Yes, sir, I just plumb spoiled one perfectly good Concord coach, and would have been playing leading corpse at a funeral, believe me, if I hadn't strapped myself to the seat for that drive off the grade. As it was, I hung head down and cussed till one of the boys cut me loose. Where did you see the picture?"

"Me? Up in the Falls. Say, I'm glad to meet you. Luck Lindsay's your name, ain't it? I remember you were called that in the picture. Mine's Green, Andy Green, - when folks don't call me something worse. And this is Miguel Rapponi, a whole lot whiter than he sounds. What, for Lordy sake, you wasting time on this little old hasbeen burg for? Take it from me, there ain't anything left here but dents in the road and a brimstone smell. We're all plumb halter-broke and so tame we - "
"You look all right to me, brother," Luck told him in that convincing tone he had.

"Well, same to you," Andy retorted with a frank heartiness he was not in the habit of bestowing upon strangers. "I feel as if I'd worked with you. Pink was with me when we saw that picture, and we both hollered 'Go to it!' right out loud, when you gathered up the ribbons and yanked off the brake and went off hell-popping and smiling back over your shoulder at us. It was your size and that smile of yours that made me remember you. You looked like a kid when you mounted to the boot; and you drove down off smiling, and you had one helanall of a trip, and you drove off that grade looking like you was trying to commit suicide and was smiling still when you pulled up at the post-office. By gracious, I - "

Luck gave a little chuckle deep in his throat. "I did all that smiling the day before I drove off the grade," he confessed, looking from one to the other. "I don't guess I'd have smiled quite so sweet, maybe, if I'd waited."

"Is that the way you make moving pictures, hind-side-foremost?" Andy, his back to the table, lifted himself over the rim to a comfortable seat and began to make himself a cigarette.

"Yes, or both ways from the middle, just as it happens." Luck was always ready to talk pictures. "In that stage-driver picture I made all the scenes before I made that drive, - for two reasons. Biggest one was that I wanted to be sure of having it all made, in case something went wrong on that feature drive; get me ? Other was plain, human bullheadedness. Some of the four-flushers I was cursed with in the company, - because they were cheap and I had to balance up what I was paying the Injuns, - they kept eyeing that bluff where I said I'd come down with the coach, and betting

I wouldn't, and talking off in corners about me just stalling. I just let 'em sweat. I made the start, and I made the finish. I drove right to where I looked down off the pinnacle - remember? - and saw the outlaw gang at the foot of the grade; I made all the 'dissolves,' and where I went back and captured 'em and brought 'em in to camp. But I didn't drive off the grade into the gulch till last thing, as luck would have it. Good thing, too. That old coach was sure some busted, and I wasn't doing any more smiles till I grew some hide."

Andy Green licked his cigarette and let his honest gray eyes wander from Luck to the darkly handsome face of the Native Son. "Sounds most as exciting as holding down a homestead, anyway. Don't you think so, Mig? And say! It's sure a pity we can't put off some things in real life till we get all set and ready to handle 'em!"

"That's right." Luck's face sobered as the idea caught his imagination. "That's dead right; how well I know it!"

Andy smoked and swung his feet and regarded Luck with interest. "It's against my religious principles to go poking my nose into the other fellow's business," he said after a minute, "but I'm wondering if there's anything in this God-forsaken country to bring a fellow like you here deliberate. I'm wondering if you meant to stop, or if you just leaned too far out the car window on your way through town."

For a half minute Luck looked up at him. He had expected a preparatory winning of the confidence of the men whom he sought. He had planned to lead up gradually to his mission, in case he found his men. But in that half minute he threw aside his plan as a weak, puerile wasting of time, and he answered Andy Green truthfully.

"No, I didn't fall off the train," he drawled. "I just grabbed my grip and beat it when they told me where I was. I'm out on a still hunt for some real boys. Some that can ride and shoot and that know cow-science so well they don't have to glad up in cowboy clothes and tie red bandanna bibs on to make folks think they're range broke."

"And yet you're wasting time in this tame little granger wart on the map!"

"No, not wasting time," smiled Luck serenely. "A little old trunk-juggler up the trail told me about the Flying U outfit that is still sending their wagons out when the grass gets green. I stopped off to give the high-sign to the boys, and say howdy, and swap yarns, and maybe haze some of 'em gently into camp. I wanted to see if the Flying U has got any real ones left."

Andy Green looked eloquently at the Native Son. "Now, what do you know about that, Mig?" he breathed softly behind a mouthful of smoke. "Wanting to rope him out a few from the Flying U bunch. Say! Have you got a real puncher amongst that outfit of long-haired hayseeds?"

The Native Son shook his head negligently and gave Luck a velvet-eyed glance of friendly pity.

"If there is, he's ranging deep in the breaks and never shows up at shipping time," he averred. "I've never seen one myself. They've got one that - what would you call Big Medicine, if you wanted to name him quick and easy, Andy?"

Andy frowned. "What I'd call him had best not be named in this God-fearing little hamlet," he responded gloomily. "I sure would never name him in the day I talked about cow-punchers that's ever dug sand outa their eyes on trail-herd."

The Native Son, still with the velvet-eyed look of pity, turned to Luck. "Andy's right," he sighed. "They've got one that takes spells of talking deliriously about when he punched cows in Coconino County; but I guess there's nothing to it."

"You say you was told that the Flying U outfit has got some real ones?" Andy eyed Luck curiously and with some of the Native Son's pity. "Just in a general way, what happens to folks that lie to you deliberate, when you meet 'em again? I'd like," he added, "to know about how sorry to feel for that baggage humper when you see him - after meeting the Flying U bunch."

The soul of Luck Lindsay was singing an impromptu doxology, but the face of him - so well was that face trained to do his bidding - became tinged with disgust and disappointment. With two "real boys" he was talking; he knew them by the unconscious range vernacular and the perfect candor with which they lied to him about themselves. But not so much as a gleam of the eye betrayed to them that he knew.

" So that's why he went off grinning so wide ," he mused aloud. "I was sure caught then with my gun at home on the piano. I might have known better than to look for the real thing here, though you fellows have a few little marks that haven't worn off yet."

"Me? Why, I'm a farmer, and I'm married, and I'm in a deuce of a stew because my spuds is drying up on me and no way to get water on 'em without I carry it to 'em in a jug," disclaimed Andy Green hastily. "All I know about punchers I learned from seeing picture shows when I go to town. Now, Mig, here - ".

"Oh, don't go and reveal all of my guilty past," protested the Native Son. "Those three days I spent at a wild-west carnival show have about worked outa my system. I'm still trying to wear out the clothes I won off some of the boys in a crap game," he explained to Luck apologetically, "but my earmarks won't outlast the clothes, believe me."

Luck thoughtfully flicked the ash collar off his cigar. "It won't be any use then to go out to the Flying U, I suppose," he observed tentatively, his eyes keen for their changing expressions. "I may as well take the next train out, I reckon, and drift on down into Arizona and New Mexico. I know about where some real punchers range - but I thought there was no harm in looking up the pedigree of this Flying U outfit. I'm sure some obliged to you boys for heading me off." Back of his eyes there was a laugh, but Andy Green and the Native Son were looking queerly at each other and did not see it there.

"Oh, well, now you're this close, you wouldn't be losing anything by going on out to the ranch, anyway," Andy recanted guardedly. "Come to think of it, there's one regular old-time ranger out there. They call him Slim. He's sure a devil on a horse - Slim is. I'd forgot about him when I spoke. He's a ranger, all right."

Luck knew very well that Andy Green had used the

B. M. Bower

word "ranger" with the deliberate attempt to appear ignorant of the terminology of the range. A cow-puncher comes a long way from being a ranger, as every one knows. A ranger is a man of another profession entirely.

"It used to be a real cattle ranch, they tell me," added the Native Son artfully. "We live out near there, and if you wanted to ride out - "

Luck appeared undecided. He sucked at his cigar, and he blew out the smoke thoughtfully, and contemplated the toe of one neat, tan shoe. Just plain acting, it was; just a playing of his part in the little game they had started. Better than if they had boasted of their range knowledge and their prowess in the saddle did Luck know that the dried little man had told him the truth. He knew that at the Flying U he would find a remnant of the old order of things. He would find some real boys, if these two were a fair sample of the bunch. That they lied to him about themselves and their fellows was but a sign that they accepted him as one of their breed. He looked them over with gladdened eyes. He listened to the unconscious tang of the range that was in their talk. These two farmers? He could have laughed aloud at the idea.

"Well, I might get some atmosphere ideas," he said at last. "If you don't mind having me trail along - "

"Glad to have yuh!" came an instant duet.
"And if I can scare up a horse - "

"Oh, we'll look after that. You can come right on out with us. The boys'll be plumb tickled to death to meet you."

"Are they all farmers, same as you - these boys you mention?" Luck looked up into Andy's eyes when he asked the question.

Andy grinned. "Farmers, yes - same as us!" he said ambiguously and picked up his gloves as he turned to lead the way out.

B. M. Bower

CHAPTER THREE

AND THEY SIGH FOR THE DAYS
THAT ARE GONE

Just when Luck's new acquaintances first forgot to carry on their whimsical pretense of knowing little of range matters, neither of them could have told afterwards. They left town with the tacit understanding between them that they were going to have some fun with the Happy Family and with this likable little man of the movies. They rode out between long lines of hated barbed wire stretched taut, and they lied systematically and consistently to Luck Lindsay about themselves and their fellows and their particular condition of servitude to fate.

But somewhere along the trail they forgot to carry on the deception; and only Luck could have told why they forgot, and when they forgot, and how it was that, ten miles or so out from town, the two were telling how the Flying U had fought to save itself from extinction; how the "bunch" had schemed and worked and had in a measure succeeded in turning aside the tide of immigration from the Flying U range. Big issues they talked of as they rode three abreast through the warm haze of early fall; and as they talked, Luck's mind visioned the tale vividly, and his eyes swept the fence-checkered upland with a sympathetic understanding.

"Right here," said Andy at last, when they came up to a gate set across the trail, "right here is where we drawed the line - and held it. Now, half of those shacks you see speckled around are empty. The rest hold nesters too poor to get outa the country. One or two, that had a little money, have stuck and gone into sheep. But from here on to Dry Creek there's nothing ranging but the Flying U brand. Not much - compared to what the old range used to be - but still it keeps things going. We throwed a dam across the coulee, up there next the hills, and there's some fair hay land we're putting water on. We have to winter-feed practically everything these days. The range just nicely keeps the stock from snow to snow. I've got pitchfork callouses on my hands I never will outgrow if I was to fall heir to a billion dollars and never use my hands again for fifty years except to feed myself. It takes work, believe me! And if there's anything on earth a puncher hates worse than work, it's some other kind of work.

"At the Flying U," he went on, looking at Luck pensively, "you'll see the effect of too many people moved into the range country. If there's anything more distressing than a baby left without a mother, it's a bunch of cow-punchers that's outlived their range. Ain't that right?"

"Sure it's right!" Luck's sympathy was absolutely sincere. "How well I know it! Barbed wire scraped me outa the saddle in Wyoming - barbed wire and sheep. All there is left for a fellow is to forget it and start a barber shop or a cigar stand, or else make pictures of the old days, the way I've been doing. You can get a little fun out of making pictures of what used to be your everyday life. You can step up on a horse and go whoopin' over the hills and kinda forget it ain't true." A wistfulness was in Luck's tone. "You pick out the big minutes from the old days - that had a whole lot of dust and sun and thirst and hunger in between, when all's said - you pick out the big minutes, and you bring them to life again, and sort of push them up close together and leave out most of the hardships. That's why so many of the old boys drift into pictures, I reckon. They try to forget themselves in the big minutes."

The two who rode with him were silent for a space. Then the Native Son spoke drily: "About the biggest minutes we get now come about meal times."

"Oh, we can get down in the breaks on round-up time and kinda forget the world's fenced clear 'way round it with barb-wire," Andy bettered the statement. "But round-up gets shorter every year."

"My next picture," Luck observed artfully and yet with a genuine desire to unbosom himself a little to these two who would understand, "my next picture is going to be different. It's going to have a crackajack story in it, of course, but it will have something more than a story. I'm going to start it off with a trail herd coming up from Texas. You know - like it was when we were kids. I'm going to show those cattle trailing along tired - and footsore, some of them - and a drag strung out behind for a mile. I'm going to show the punchers tired and hungry, and riding half asleep in the saddle. And with that for a starter, I'm going to show the real range; the *real* range - get that, boys? I'm going to cut clean away from regulation moving-picture West; clear out away from posses chasing outlaws all over a ten-acre location. I'm going to find me a real old cow-ranch; or if I can't find one, by thunder I'm going to *make* me one. I'm sick of piling into a machine and driving out into Griffith Park and hunting a location for shooting scrapes to take place in. I know a place where I could produce stuff that would make people talk about it for a month after. Maybe the buildings would need some doctoring, but there's sure some round-pole corrals that would make your mouth water."

"We used to have some," sighed Andy, "at the Flying U. But they kinda went to pieces, and Chip's been replacing them with plank. By gracious, you don't see many round-pole corrals any more, come to think of it. There's remains, scattered around over the country."

"The West - the real honest-to-goodness, twelve-months-in-the-year West," Luck went on riding his hobby, "has been mighty little used in films. Ever notice that? It's all gone to shooting, and stealing the full product of all the gold mines in the world, and killing off more bad men than the Lord ever sent a flood to punish. For film purposes, the West consists of one part beautiful maiden in distress, three parts bandit, and two parts hero. Mix these to taste with plenty of swift action and gun-smoke, and serve with bandits all dead or handcuffed and beautiful maiden and hero in lover's embrace on top. That's your film West, boys - and how well I know it!" Luck stopped to light a cigarette and to heave a sigh. "I've been building film West to order for four years now, and more. Only fun I've had, and the best work I've done, I did with a bunch of Indians I've just taken back to their reservation. For the rest, it's mostly bunk."

"Not that stage-driver picture," Andy dissented. "There wasn't any bunk about that, old-timer. That was some driving!"

40   B. M. Bower

"Some driving, yes. Sure, it was. It was darned good driving, but the same old story doctored up a little. Same old shipment of gold, same old bandits lying in wait, same old hero doing stunts. I ought to know," he added with a grin. "I wrote the story and did the stunts myself."

"Well, they were some stunts!" admired Andy with unusual sincerity.

Luck waved aside the compliment and went back to his hobby. "Yes, but the West isn't just a setting for stunts. I've got my story - here," and he tapped his forehead, which was broad and full and not too high. "I'm going to fire my camera man and get a better one, and I'm going to round me up a bunch of real boys that can get into the story and live it so well they won't need to do any acting, - boys that can stand a panoram on their work in the saddle. I've been getting by with a bunch of freaks that think they're real riders if they can lope a horse up-grade without falling off backwards. Most of my direction of those actorines has been knowing to a hair how much footage to give 'em without showing how raw their work is.

"They say the public demands a certain grade of rottenness in Western films, but I never believed that, down deep in my heart. I believe the public stands for that stuff because they don't see any better. This four-reeler I've got in mind will sure open the eyes of some producers - or I'll buy me a five-acre tract in Burbank and raise string beans for a living."

"I've got a patch of string beans," sighed the Native Son, "that I've been sitting up nights with. I don't know what ails the cussed things. Some kind of little green bug chews on them soon as my back is turned. They ought to be ripe by now - and they aren't through blossoming. Don't go into beans, *amigo*."

Luck looked at him and laughed. The Native Son, in black and white Angora chaps and cream-colored shirt and silver-filigreed hatband as ornamental touches to his attire, did not look like a man who was greatly worried over his crop of string beans while he rode with a negligent grace away from a glowing sunset. But in these days the West is full of incongruities.

"Oh, shut up about them beans!" implored Andy Green with a bored air. "It's water they want; and a touch of the hoe now and then. You leave 'em for a month at a time and then go back and wonder why you can't pick a hatful off 'em. Same as the rest of us have been ranching," he added ruefully, turning to Luck. "With the best intentions in the world, the Lord never meant us fellers for farmers, and that's a fact. We'll drop a hoe any time of day or night to get out riding after stock. Of course, we didn't take up our claims with the idea of settling down and riding a hoe handle the rest of our lives. If we had, I guess maybe we'd have done a little better at it."

"We did what we started out to do," the Native Son pointed out lazily: "We saved the range - what little there is to save - and we kept a lot of poor yaps from starving to death on that land, didn't we?" He smiled slowly. "If I hadn't gotten gay and planted those beans," he added, "I'd be feeling fine over it. A girl gave me a handful of pinto beans and asked me to plant them - I did hoe them," he defended tardily to Andy. "I hoed them the day before the Fourth. You know I did. Same time you hoed those lemon-colored spuds of yours."

Luck let them wrangle humorously over their agricultural deficiencies, and drifted off into open-eyed dreaming. Into his picture he began to fit these two speculatively, with a purely tentative adjustment of their personalities to his requirements. They were arguing about which of the two was the worst farmer; but Luck, riding alongside them, was seeing them slouched in their saddles and riding, bone-tired, with a shuffling trail-herd hurrying to the next watering place. He was seeing them galloping hard on the flanks of a storm-lashed stampede, with cunningly placed radium flares lighting the scene brilliantly now and then. He was seeing these two plodding, heads bent, into the teeth of a blizzard. He was seeing...

"I'll have to ride home to the missus now," Andy announced the second time before Luck heard him.

"Mig will take you on down to the home ranch, and after supper I'll ride over. So long."

He swung away from them upon a faintly beaten trail, looked back once to grin and wave his hand, and touched his horse with the spurs. Luck stared after him thoughtfully, but he did not put his thoughts into words. He had been trained in the hard school of pictures. He had learned to hold his tongue upon certain matters, such as his opinion of a man's personal attributes, or criticism of his appearance, or anything which might be repeated, maliciously or otherwise, to that man. He did not say to Miguel Rapponi, for instance, what he thought of Andy Green as a man or a rider. He did not mention him at all. He had learned in bitterness how idle gossip may eat away the efficiency of a whole company.

For that reason, and also because his mind was busy with his plans and the best means of carrying them out, the two rode almost in silence to the hill that shut the Flying U coulee away from the world. Luck gave a long sigh and muttered "Great!" when the whole coulee lay spread before them. Then his quick glances took in various details of the ranch and he sighed again, from a different emotion.

"It must have been a great place twenty years ago," he amended his first unqualified enthusiasm.

"Why twenty years ago?" The Native Son gave him a quick, half-resentful glance.

"Twenty years ago there wasn't so much barb-wire trimming," Luck explained from the viewpoint of the trained producer of Western pictures. "You couldn't place a camera anywhere now for a long shot across the coulee without bringing a fence into the scene. And the log stables are too old, and the new ones too new." He pulled up and stared long at the sweep of hills beyond, and the wide spread of the meadow and the big field farther up stream, and at the lazy meandering of Flying U creek with its willow fringe just turning yellow with the first touch of autumn. He looked at the buildings sprawled out below him.

"When that log house was headquarters for the ranch, and the round-pole corrals were the only fences on the place," he said; "when those old sheds held the saddle horses on cold nights, and the wagons were out from green grass to snowfall, and the boys laid around all winter, just reportin' regular at grub-pile and catching up on sleep they'd lost in the summer - Lor-dee, what a place it must have been!"

There was something in his tone that brought the Native Son for an instant face to face with the Flying U in the old days when all the range was free. So, with faces sober, because the old days were gone and would never any more return, they rode down the grade and up to the new stable that was a monument to the dead past, even though it might also be a sign-post pointing to present prosperity. And in this wise came Luck Lindsay to the Flying U and was made welcome.

CHAPTER FOUR

THE LITTLE DOCTOR PROTESTS

The Little Doctor stepped out upon the porch with the faint tracing of a frown upon her smooth forehead, and with that slight tightening of the lips which to her family meant determination; disapproval sometimes, tense moments always.

She stood for a minute looking down toward the stables, and the wind that blew down the coulee seized upon the scant folds of her skirt, and flapped them impishly against the silken-clad ankles that were exceedingly good to look upon, - since fashion has now made it quite permissible to look upon ankles. Her lips did not relax with the waiting. Her frown grew a trifle more pronounced.

"Mr. Lindsay?" with a rising inflection.

Luck turned his head, saw her standing there, waved his hand to show that he heard, and started toward her with that brisk, purposeful swing to his walk that goes with an energetic disposition. The Little Doctor waited, and watched him, and did not relax a muscle from her determined attitude. Poor little Luck Lindsay hurried, so as not to keep her standing there in the wind, and, not knowing just what was before him, he smiled his

B. M. Bower

smile as he came up to her.

I should have said, poor Little Doctor. She tried to keep her frown and the fixed idea that went with it, but she was foolish enough to look down into Luck's face and into his eyes with their sunny friendliness, and at the smile, where the friendliness was repeated and emphasized. Before she quite knew what she was doing, the Little Doctor smiled back. Still, she owned a fine quality of firmness.

"Come in here. I want to have it out with you, and be done," she said, and turned to open the door.

"Sounds bad, but I'm yours to command," Luck retorted cheerfully, and went up the steps still smiling. He liked the Little Doctor. She was his kind of woman. He felt that she would make a good pal, and he knew how few women are qualified for open comradeship. He cast a side glance at the kitchen window where the Kid stood with a large slice of bread and chokecherry jam balanced on his palm, and on his face a look of mental distress bordered with more jam. Luck nodded and waved his hand, and went in where the Little Doctor stood waiting for him with a certain ominous quiet in her manner. Luck shook back his heavy mane of hair that was graying prematurely, squared his shoulders, and then held out his hand meekly, palm upward. Boys learn that pose in school, you know.

"Oh, for pity's sake! If you go and make me laugh - and I am mad enough at you, Luck Lindsay, to - to blister that palm! If you weren't any bigger than Claude, I'd shake you and stand you in a corner on one foot."

"Listen. Shake me, anyway. I believe I'd kinda like it. And while I'm standing in the corner - on one foot - you can tell me all you're mad at me for."

The Little Doctor looked at him, bit her lip, and then found that her eyes were blurred so that his face seemed to waver and grow dim. And Luck Lindsay, because he saw the tears, laid a hand on her shoulder, and pushed her ever so gently into a chair.

"Tell me what's worrying you. If it's anything that I have done, I'll have one of the boys take me out and shoot me; it's what I would deserve. But I certainly can't think of anything - "

"Do you know that you have filled little Claude's mind up with stories about moving pictures till he's just crazy? He told me just now that he's going with you when you go back, and act in your company. And if I won't let him go, he said, he'd run away and 'hit a freight-train outa Dry Lake,' and get to California, anyway. And - he'd do it, too! He's perfectly awful when he gets an idea in his head. I know he's spoiled - all the boys pet him so - "

"Wait. Let's get this thing straight. Do you think for one minute, Mrs. Bennett, that I'd coax the Kid away? Say, that hurts - to have you believe that of me." There was no smile anywhere on Luck's face now. His eyes were as pained as his voice sounded.

Once more the Little Doctor weakened before him. She believed what he said, though five minutes before she had believed exactly the opposite. In her mind she had accused him of coaxing the Kid. She had fully intended accusing him of it to his face.

"I don't mean coax, perhaps. But - "

"Listen. If the Kid has got that notion, I'm more sorry than you can guess. Of course, I think pictures and I talk pictures; I admit I make them in my sleep. And the boys are interested. Those that are going back with me and those that are not are always sicking me at the subject. I admit that I sick easy," he added with a whimsical lightening of the eyes. "And the Kid and I are pals. I like him, Mrs. Bennett. He's got the stuff in him to make a real man - and I wouldn't call him spoiled, exactly. He's always been with grown-ups, and his mind has developed away ahead of the calendar; you see what I mean? He's nine, he tells me - "

"Only eight. He always tries to make himself older than he is," the Little Doctor corrected quickly.

"Well, he's some boy! And kids somehow take to me; I guess it's because I'm always chumming with them. He's been taking in everything that has been said; I could see that. But I surely never talked to him in the way you mean."

The Little Doctor looked at him and hesitated; but she was a frank young woman, and she could not help speaking her mind. "You mustn't take it personally at all," she said, "if I tell you that I am disappointed in the boys; in Andy and Rosemary especially, because they ought to appreciate the little home they have made, and stay with it. One sort of expects Pink and Big Medicine and Weary to do outlandish things. They haven't really grown up, and they never will. But I am disappointed, just the same, that they should want to go performing around and shooting blank cartridges and making clowns of themselves for moving pictures. Still, that's their own business, of course, if they want to be silly enough to do it. But now little Claude has taken the fever - and I wish, Mr. Lindsay, you could do something to - " She stopped, but not because what she said was hurting Luck's feelings. She did not know that she hurt him at all.

"It seems to be worse, in your estimation, than exposing the Kid to yellow fever," Luck observed quietly.

"Well, of course you can understand that I should not want a boy of mine to - to be all taken up with the idea of acting cowboy parts for a moving picture."

"Still, there are some fairly decent people in the business," Luck pointed out still more quietly, and got upon his feet. He had no smile now for the Little Doctor, though he was still gentle in his manner. "I see what you mean, Mrs. Bennett. I understand you perfectly. I shall do what I can to repair the damage to the Kid's character and ideals, and I want to thank you for coming to me in this matter. Otherwise I might have gone against your wishes without knowing that I was doing so." For two breaths or three he held her glance with something that looked out of his eyes; the Little Doctor did not know what it was. "You see, Mrs. Bennett, you don't quite understand what you are talking about," he added. "You have not had the opportunity to understand, of course. But I agree with you that the Kid's place is at home, and I shall certainly have a talk with him."

He moved to the door, laid a fine, well-kept hand upon the knob, and looked at her with a faint smile that had behind it a good deal that puzzled the Little Doctor.

"Don't worry one minute," he said, dropping his punctilious politeness of the minute before, and becoming again the intensely human Luck Lindsay. "I 'heap sabe.' I've certainly corrupted the morals and ambitions of some of the boys - looking at it the way you do - but I promise to check the devastation right where it's at, and save your only son." He turned then and went out.

The Little Doctor paid him the tribute of hurrying to the window where she could watch him go down the path. In his walk, in the set of his head, there was still something that puzzled her. She hoped that he was not offended, and she thankfully remembered a good deal that she had left unsaid. She saw him turn and beckon, and then wait until the Kid had joined him from the kitchen. She saw the greeting he gave the Kid, and the adoration on the Kid's face when he looked up at Luck. The two went away together, and the Little Doctor watched them dubiously. What if the Kid should run away? He had done it once, and it was well within the probabilities that he might do it again, if this present obsession of his were not handled just right. The Kid, she had long ago discovered, could not be driven, - and there were times when he could not be coaxed.

Luck had been just three days at the Flying U. In those three days he had fitted himself into the place so well that even old Patsy, the cook, called him "Look" as easily as though he had been doing it for years; and Patsy, you must know, was fast acquiring the querulousness of an old age that does not sweeten with the passing years. Patsy had discovered that Luck liked his eggs fried on both sides, and thereafter he painstakingly turned three eggs bottomside up in the frying pan every morning; three and no more, though Cal

Emmett remarked pointedly that he had always liked his eggs fried and flopped.

Three days, and the Old Man frequently left his big, soft-cushioned chair, and went slowly down to the bunk-house whence came much laughter, and listened to the stories that Luck told so well, - with one arm around the unashamed Kid, very likely, while he talked.

True, they had ranches of their own, those boys of the Flying U. But if you wanted to find them in a hurry, it were wise to ride first into Flying U coulee. That was headquarters, and that was home and always would be; even Andy Green, who was happily married, brought his wife and stayed there days at a time, with small excuse for the coming.

In three days, then, Luck had chosen his men from among the Happy Family, and had convinced them that their future welfare and happiness depended upon their going back with him to Los Angeles. In three days he had accomplished a good deal; but then, Luck was in the habit of crowding his days with achievement of one sort or another. As a matter of fact, the third day he had looked upon as one given solely to the pleasure of staying at the Flying U while the boys completed their arrangements for leaving with him. He had done all that he had planned to do, and he was in a very good humor with the world, or he had been until the Little Doctor had made his pride writhe under her innocent belittlement of his vocation. To have her boy work in pictures would be a calamity in her eyes; in Luck's eyes it would be an honor, provided he did the right kind of work in the right kind of pictures.

Luck's own personal opinion, however, did not weigh in this case. He had promised the Little Doctor that he would erase the impression he had made upon the Kid's too vivid imagination; so he led him to a retired place where they would be sheltered from the wind by a great stack of alfalfa hay, and he began in this wise:

"Old-timer, you're the luckiest boy I've seen in all my travels, - growing up here on the Flying U, with a mother like you've got, and a dad like Chip, and a ranch like this to get the swing of while you're growing; so that in another five years I expect you'll be running it yourself, and your folks will be larking around having the good time they've earned while they were raising you. I'll bet - "

"So Doctor Dell went and got around you, did she? I knew that was why she called you into the sett'n room. Forget it, Luck." The Kid spat manfully into the trodden hay, and pushed his small-size Stetson back so that his curls showed, and set his feet as far apart as was comfortable. "I knew she would," he added with weary wisdom in his tone. "Doctor Dell can get around anybody when she takes a notion."

Luck held his face from smiling. He looked surprised, and disappointed in the Kid, and sorry for the Kid's parents. At least, he made the Kid feel that he was thinking all these things, which proves how well one may master the art of facial expression. He did not say a word; therefore he put the Kid upon the defensive and set his young wits to devising arguments in his favor.

"A woman never knows when a fellow begins to grow up. Doctor Dell is the nicest girl in the world, but she needn't think I'm a baby yet. I can ride a buckin' horse, and I went on round-up last spring - and made a hand, too! I can swing a rope as good as any of the bunch; you seen me whirl a loop and jump through it, and there's more stunts than that I can do - it was dinner time, so I had to quit before I showed you." The Kid paused. He had not yet produced any effect whatever upon that surprised, pitying, disappointed look in Luck's face, and the Kid began to feel worried.

"Well, I was just bluffing when I said I'd run away - if she told you that." He stopped; the look was still there, only it now seemed to have contempt added to it. "I don't say I know more'n anybody on the ranch, and I don't say I'm boss of the ranch yet. I do what they tell me, even when I know there ain't any sense in it. I humor Doctor Dell a whole lot!" Could he never get that look off Luck's face? The Kid searched his soul anxiously. You couldn't go on arguing with that kind of a look; it made you feel like you'd been stealing sheep. "Oh, well, if you won't talk to a feller - " The Kid did not turn away quite soon enough to hide the quiver of his lips. Luck reached out and took a small, grimy hand and pulled the Kid nearer; near enough so that his arm could go around the Kid's quivering body. He held him close, and the Kid did not struggle. He dropped his face against Luck's shoulder, and began to fight back his tears.

"Listen, pardner," said Luck softly, one hand caressing the Kid's cheek. "You and I ought to sabe each other better than most folks, because we're pals. Now, I want you to go with me a heap more than you want to go; just tuck that away in your mind where you won't lose it. I want you, but I wouldn't have you without Doctor Dell's free and willing consent. I need you for my pal;

and I could teach you a lot that would be useful to you. But they need you a whole lot worse than I do. They've been taking care of you and loving you and planning for you all these eight years, just watching you grow, and being proud of you because you're what they want you to be: husky and healthy and good all the way through. You couldn't go off and leave them now; it wouldn't be right. And, pard, you need them even worse than they need you. I know, - because I had to grow up without any one to love me and look after me; and believe me, old pal, it isn't any cinch. It's just pure luck that I didn't get killed off or go bad. Now, I'd be good to you, if I had you with me, and so would the boys; but we couldn't take the place of Doctor Dell and Daddy Chip.

"I've talked pictures too much to you. I didn't know how it was hitting you, or how much you wanted to go. But listen. If I had the chance you've got here, - if I had a ranch like this, and cattle, and horses, and a father and mother and uncle like you've got, - I never would look a camera in the eye again as long as I live. That's straight, old-timer. Why, I'm working my head off trying to get enough ahead so that I can have a ranch of my own! So I can slap a saddle on a horse that carries my brand, and ride out after my cattle, and haze them into my corral; so I can have a home that is mine. I never did have one, pardner, - not since I was a heap smaller than you are now, - and a home of his own is what every man wants most, down deep in his heart.

"It looks fine to be traveling around, and making moving pictures. It is fine if you are cut out for that kind of work, and have got to be working for somebody else to get your start. But remember, pard, I am working and scheming and planning to get just what you've got already. You, a kid eight years old, stand right where I'd give all I've got to stand. You'll own your own ranch and your own home. You've got folks that love you - not because you hand out the pay envelope on a certain day of the week, but because you belong to them, and they belong to you. Kid, I'm thirty-two years old - and I've never known what that felt like. I have never known what it was like to have some one plan for me and with me, unless they were paid for it."

The Kid stood very still. "You could live here," he lifted his head to say gravely after a little silence that was full of thought. "This can be your home. You can be one of the Happy Family. We'd like to have you."

There was something queer in Luck's voice when he murmured a reply. There was something in his face which no one but the Kid had ever seen. The Kid's arm crept around Luck's neck, and tightened there and stayed. Luck's hand went up to the curls and hovered there caressingly. And they talked, in tones lowered to the cadence of deep-hidden hopes and longings revealed in sacred confidence.

The Little Doctor, shamelessly eavesdropping because she was a mother fighting for her fledgling, tiptoed away from the corner of the stack, and went back to the house, wiping her eyes frequently with the corner of her handkerchief that was not embroidered. She went into her room and stayed there a long while, and before she came out she had recourse to rosewater and talcum and other first aids to swollen eyelids.

Whatever she may have thought, whatever she may have overheard beyond what has been recorded, her manner toward Luck was so unobtrusively tender that Chip looked at her once or twice with a puzzled, husbandly frown. Also, the Kid felt something special in his Doctor Dell's good-night kiss; something he did not understand at all, since he had not yet told her that he was going to be a good boy and stay at home and take care of her and the ranch.

CHAPTER FIVE

A BUNCH OF ONE-REELERS
FROM BENTLY BROWN

The Manager of the Acme Film Company cleared his throat with a rasping noise that sounded very loud, coming as it did after fifteen minutes of complete silence. Luck, smoking a cigarette absent-mindedly by the window while he stared out across two vacant lots to a tawdry apartment house, - and saw a sage-covered plain instead of what was before his eyes, - started from his daydream and glanced at Martinson inquiringly. "Well, what do you think of it?" he asked.

Martinson cleared his throat again, and shuffled the typed sheets in his hands. "Seems to lack action, don't it?" he hazarded reluctantly. "Of course, this is a rough draft; I realize that. I suppose you'll strengthen up the plot, later on. Chance for some good cattle-stealing complications, I should think. But I'd boil it down to two reels, Luck, if I were you. There's a lot of atmosphere you couldn't get, anyway - "

"I can get every foot of that atmosphere," Luck put in crisply.

"Oh, I suppose - but you don't want that much. Too expensive, where it doesn't carry the action along. I'd put in some dance-hall scenes; you haven't enough interiors. Make your lead a victim of card sharps, why don't you, and have his sister come there after him? You could get some great dramatic action - have her meet the heavy there - "

"After the tried-and-tested recipe. Sure, Mart! We can take the middle out of that *Her-Brother's-Honor* film and use that; and if you're afraid the public may recognize it, we'll run it backwards. Or we can mix it with some *Western-Girl's-Romance* film, or take - "

"Now, Luck, wait a minute. Wait-a-minute!" Martinson's hand went up in the approved gesture of stopping another's speech. "You can give it an original twist. You know you can; you always have."

Luck swore, accustomed though he was to the makeshifts of the business. The street cars had stopped running the night before, while he was still hammering that scenario out on the typewriter; the street cars had stopped running, and the steam heat had been turned off in the hotel where he lived, and he had finished with an old Mexican *serape* draped about his person for warmth. But his enthusiasm had not cooled, though his room grew chill. He had gone to bed when the typing was done, and had dreamed scene after scene vividly while he slept. Still glowing with the pride of creation, he had read the script while his breakfast coffee had cooled, and he had been the first man in the office, so eager was he to share his secret and see Martinson's eyes gleam with impatience to have the story filmed.

Knowing this, you will know also why he swore. Martinson thrust out his under lip at the oath, and tossed the script neatly into the clear space on the desk. "Oh, if that's the way you feel about it!" His tone was trenchant. "Sorry I offered any suggestions. There are some good bits, if they're worked up right, and I naturally supposed you wanted my opinion."

"I did. I never saw you square up to anything but the same old dime-novel West before. I wanted to see how it would hit you."

"Well, it don't." Martinson waited a minute while that sunk in. When he spoke again, his manner was that of a man who has dismissed a disagreeable subject, and has taken up important business.

"We've made quite a haul since you left. A bunch of one-reelers from Bently Brown. You'll eat 'em up, Luck, - all those stories of his featuring the adventures of the XY cowboys. You've read 'em; everybody has, according to him. They'll be cheap to put on, because the same sets and the same locations will do for the lot. Same cast, too. He blew in here temporarily hard up and wanting to unload, and we got the whole series for next to nothing." He opened a desk drawer, and took out a bundle of folded scripts tied with a dingy blue tape. Martinson was a matter-of-fact man; he really did not understand just how much Luck's new story meant to its author. If he had, he surely would not have been quite so brisk and so frankly elated over that untidy lot of Bently Brown scenarios.

"I had all the synopses numbered and put on top here," he went on, "so you can run them over and see what they're like. A small company will do, Luck. That's one point that struck me. Two or three die, on an average, in the first four hundred feet of every story; so you can double a lot. I've had Clements go over them and start the carpenters on the street set where most of the exterior action takes place; we're behind on releases, you know, and these ought to be rushed. You'd better go over and see how he's making out; you may want to make some changes."

Luck hesitated so long that Martinson was on the edge of withdrawing the proffered scripts. But he took them finally, and ran his eye disparagingly over the titles. "Bently Brown!" he said, as though he were naming something disagreeable. "I'm to film Bently Brown's blood-and-battle stuff, am I?" He grinned, with the corners of his mouth tipped downward so that you never would have suspected it of ever producing Luck's famous smile. "I might turn them into comedy," he suggested. "I expect I could get a punch by burlesquing - "

"Punch!" Martinson pushed his chair back impetuously. "Punch? Why, my godfrey, man, that stuff's all punch!"

Luck curved a palm over his too-expressive mouth while he skimmed the central idea from two or three synopses. Martinson watched him uneasily. Martinson claimed to keep one finger pressed firmly upon the public pulse - wherever that may be found - and to be ever alert for its warning flutterings. Martinson claimed to know a great deal about what the public liked in the way of moving pictures. He believed in Luck's knowledge of the West, but he did not believe that the public would stand for the real West at all; the public, he maintained, wanted its West served hot and strong and reeking with the smoke of black powder. So -

"Well, the market demands that sort of thing," he declared, arguing against that curved palm and the telltale wrinkles around Luck's eyes. "It's all tommyrot, of course. I don't say it's good; I say it's the stuff that goes. We're here to make what the public will pay to look at." Martinson, besides keeping his finger on the public pulse and attending to the marketing of the Acme wares and watching that expenses did not run too high, found a little time in which to be human. "I know, Luck," the human side of him observed sympathetically; "it's just made-to-order melodrama, but business is simply rotten, old man. We've just got to release films the market calls for. There's no art-for-art's-sake in the movie business, and you know it. Now, personally, I like that scenario of yours - "

"Forget it!" said Luck crisply, warning him off the subject. To make the warning keener-edged, he lifted the typed sheets over which he had worked so late the night before, glanced at the top one, gave a snort, and tore them twice down the length of them with vicious twists of his fingers. He did not mean to be spectacular; he simply felt that way at that particular moment, and he indulged the impulse to destroy something. He dropped the fragments into Martinson's waste basket, picked up the bundle of scripts and his hat, and went out with his mouth pulled down at the corners and with his neck pretty stiff.

He went swinging across the studio yard and on past the great stage where the carpenters halted their work while they greeted him, and looked after him and spoke of him when he had passed. Early idlers - extras with high hopes and empty pockets - sent him wistful glances which he did not see at all; though he did see Andy Green and his wife (who had been Rosemary

Allen). These two stood hesitating just within the half-open, high board gate fifty yards away. Luck waved his hand and swerved toward them.

"Howdy! Where's the rest of the bunch?" he called out as they hurried up to him. Whereupon the group of extras were sharp bitten by the envy of these two strangers, spoken to so familiarly by Luck Lindsay.

"Do you know, I feel sure the boys are being held in the lost-child place at the police station!" Rosemary Green, twinkled her brown eyes at him from between strands of crinkly brown hair. "I had tags all fixed, with name, age, owner's address and all that, and I was going to hang them around the boys' necks with pale blue ribbon - pale blue would be so becoming! But do you know, I couldn't find them! I feel worried. I should hate to waste thirty-nine cents worth of pale blue ribbon. I can't wear it myself; it makes me look positively swarthy." Rosemary Green had a most captivating way of saying swarthy.

The corners of Luck's mouth came up instantly. "We'll have to send out scouting parties. I need that bunch of desperadoes. Let's look over by the corrals. I've got to go over and see what kind of a street set they're knocking together, anyway.

"Hello! I have sure-enough crying need for all you strays," he exclaimed five minutes later, when they came upon the Flying TJ boys standing disconsolately at the head of the street "set" upon which carpenters were hammering and sawing and painters were daubing. Luck's eyes chilled as he took in the stereotyped "Western" crudeness of the set.

"Well, we sure need you - and need you bad," Pink retorted. "We want to know what town was peeled so they could set the rind up like that and call it a street? Between you and me, Luck, it don't look good to me, back or front. You walk into what claims to be a saloon, and come out on a view of the hills. They tell me the bar of that imitation saloon is away over there on that platform, and they say the bottles are all full of tea. That right?"

Luck nodded gloomily. "Soon as they get the set up, it's going to be your privilege to come boiling out of that saloon, shooting two guns, Pink," he prophesied. "You'll have the fun of killing half a dozen boys that come down from this end shooting as they ride." He put his cigarette between his lips and began to untie the dingy blue tape that bound the scenarios together.

"Ever read any of Bently Brown's stories? They wished a bunch of them on to me while I was gone and couldn't defend myself," he said, as one who breaks bad news. "I'm certainly sorry about this, boys. It's a long way from what I brought you out here to do; and if you want to, you can call the deal off and go home. Rip-snorting, rotten melodrama - cheap as ice in Alaska. Stuff I hate - because it's the stuff that cheapens the West in pictures."

"What about our range picture?" Andy Green began anxiously.

Luck choked back an oath because of Andy's wife. "Ah - they're married to the idea that this rot is what sells best. They don't know what a *real* Western picture is: they never saw one. And they're afraid to take a chance. I was in hopes - but Mart's the big chief, you know. He'd gone and loaded up with this trash, and so he couldn't see my story at all. I get his viewpoint, all right; he's keen to pry off some real money, and he's afraid to experiment with new tools. But it does seem pretty raw to put you boys working on this cheap studio stuff after getting you out here to do something worth while."

"We're to stay right here, then?" Weary spoke the question that was in the minds of all of them.

"That's the present outlook," Luck confessed with bitterness. "I don't need real country for this junk. I was all primed to show him where I'd have to take my company to New Mexico, but I didn't say anything about it when he sprung this Bently Brown business. This will all be made right here at the studio and out in Griffith Park."

Down deep in Luck's heart there was a hurt he would not reveal to any one. It was built partly of disappointment and an honest dislike for doing unworthy work; it had in it also some personal chagrin at being compelled to put the Happy Family at work in the very class of pictures he had often ridiculed in his talk with them, after bringing them all the way from Montana so that he might produce his big range picture. He stood looking somberly at the set which Clements had planned to save time - and therefore dollars - for the Acme Company. He thought of his range story, as it had first grown out of the night away up there in the plains country; he thought of how he had hurried so that he might the sooner make the vision a reality; how he had talked of it confidently to these men who had listened with growing enthusiasm and interest, until his vision had become their vision, his hopes their hopes.

They had left the Flying U and come with him to help make that big picture of the range. By their eager talk they had helped him to strengthen certain scenes; they had even suggested new, original material as they told of this adventure and that accident, and argued - as was their habit - ever scenes and situations. That was why Andy had spoken of it as *their* picture. That was why they were here; that was what had brought them early to the studio. And in his hand he held a half dozen or more of those cheap, lurid stories he had always despised; they must let the public see their faces in these impossible, illogical situations, or they must go back and call Luck Lindsay names to salve their disappointment.

The dried little man - whose name was Dave Wiswell - came walking curiously up the fresh-made "street," his sharp eyes taking in the falsity of the whole row of shack-houses that had no backs; bald behind as board fences, save where two-by-fours braced them from falling. He saw the group standing before a wall that purported to be the front of a bank (which would be robbed with much bloodshed in the second scenario) and he hurried a little. Luck scowled at him preoccupiedly, nodded a good morning, and turned abruptly to the others.

"Listen. If you boys are game for this melodrama, I'd like to use you, all right. You'll get experience in the business, anyway, so maybe it won't do you any harm. And if the weather holds good, we'll just make a long hard drive of this bunch of drivel; we'll rush 'em through - sabe? And I'll make it my business to see that Mart doesn't unload any more of the same. You may even get some fun out of it, seeing you're not fed up on this said Western drama, the way I am. Anyway, what's the word? Shall I hop into the machine and go down and buy you fellows a bunch of return tickets, or shall I assign you your parts and wade into this blood and bullets business?"

Weary folded his arms and grinned down at Luck. "I'm all for the blood and bullets, myself," he said promptly. "I'm just crazy to come shooting and yelling down this little imitation street and do things that are bold and bad."

"I should think," interjected Rosemary Green, with a pretty viciousness, "that you'd be ashamed, Luck Lindsay! Do you think we are a bunch of quitters? Give me a part - and a gun - and I'll stand on a ladder behind that hotel window and shoot 'em as fast as they can turn the corner down there." Her brown eyes twinkled hearteningly at him. "I'll pull my hair down, and yell and shoot and wring my hands - Pink, you keep still! I'm positive I can shoot and wring my hands at the same time in a Bently Brown story, can't I, Luck?"

"You certainly can," Luck told her grimly. "You can do worse than that and get by. Well, all right, folks. You prowl around and kill time while I get ready to start. There won't be anything doing till after lunch, at the earliest, so make yourselves at home. I'd introduce you to some of these folks if it was worth while, but it ain't. You'll know them soon enough - most of them to your sorrow, at that." He turned on his heel with a hasty "See yuh later," and plunged into the work before him just as energetically as though his heart were in it.

CHAPTER SIX

VILLAINS ALL AND PROUD OF IT

"Day's work, boys!" called Luck through his little megaphone at three o'clock one day, and doubled up his working script that was much crumpled and scribbled with hasty pencil marks. "No use spoiling good film," he remarked to his assistant, glancing up at the sweeping fog bank, off to the west. "By the time we rehearse the next scene, she'll be too dark to shoot. You go and order these cavalry costumes, Beckitt; and, say! You tell them down there that if they're shy on the number, they better set down and make enough, because they won't see a cent of our money if there's so much as a canteen lacking. And tell 'em to send army guns. That last assortment of junk they sent out was pathetic. I want equipment for fifty U.S. Cavalry, time of the early eighties. That don't mean forty-nine - get me? You're inclined to let those fellows have it their own way too much. I want this cavalry - "

"There ain't any close-ups of cavalry, are there?" Beckitt demurred. "I told them last time I thought those guns would do, because I knew the detail wouldn't - "

"Listen." Luck's tone was deliberately tolerant. "That's maybe the reason you've been searching your soul for all along - the reason why you can't get past the

B. M. Bower

assistant-director stage. I want those fifty cavalrymen equipped! Do you get that?" While his eyes held Beckitt uncomfortably with their stern steadfastness, Luck thrust the script into his coat pocket that had a permanent, motion-picture-director sag to it. "If I meant that any old gun would do, I'd give my orders that way. Now, remember, there isn't going to be any waiting around while you go back and argue, nor any makeshifts, nor anything but fifty cavalrymen fully equipped. Here's the list complete for to-morrow's order. You see that it's filled!"

Beckitt took the list which he should have made himself, since that was what he was paid for doing, and went off in the sulks and the company machine. Luck pulled a solacing cigar from an inner pocket and licked down the roughened outer leaves, and scowled thoughtfully across the studio yard. The camera man was figuring up footage or something, and his assistant was hurrying to get the tripod folded and put away. There was a new briskness in the movements of every one save Luck himself, after he spoke that last sentence through the megaphone.

The Happy Family - or that part of it which had thrown away pitchforks and taken to the pictures - came clanking across the stage toward Luck. You would never have known the Happy Family, unless it were the Native Son who wore his usual regalia in exaggerated form. The Happy Family had wide, flapping chaps that made them drag their feet they were so heavy and so long, and great Mexican spurs whose rowels dug tiny trenches in the ground when they walked. They wore the biggest Stetsons that famous hat brand ever was stamped upon. They had huge bandanas draped picturesquely over their chests, and their sleeves were rolled to the elbows and their eyes rimmed with deep pencil shadings. At their hips swung six-shooters of violent pattern and portent. Around their middles sagged belts filled with blank cartridges. A sack of tobacco was making the rounds as they came on, and Luck watched them through speculatively narrowed lids.

"Say, by cripes, that there saloon is the driest poison-palace I ever surged out of with two guns spittin' death and dumnation!" Big Medicine complained, coming up with the plain intention of lighting his cigarette from Luck's cigar. "How'd we stack up this time, boss? Bein' soused on cold tea, I couldn't rightly pass judgment. How many was it I murdered in cold blood, in that there scene where I laid 'em out with black powder? Four, or five? Pink, here, claims I killed him twicet, whereas he oughta be left alive enough to jump on his horse and ride three hundred and fifty miles to fall dead in his best girl's arms. He claims he made that ride day before yesterday, and done some pitiful weaving around in the saddle, out there in the hills, and that he died in that blond lady's arms first thing this morning, and I hadn't no right to kill him twicet afterwards in the saloon fight. Now I leave it to you, boss. How about this here killin' Pink off every oncet in a while?"

Deep in his throat Luck chuckled. "Well, Pink certainly does die pathetic," he soothed the perturbed murderer, dropping his professional brusqueness for frank comradeship. "He's about the best little close-up dier I ever worked with. He can get a sob anytime he rolls his eyes and gasps and falls backward." He clapped his hand down on Pink's shoulder and gave it a little shake.

"That's all right," drawled the Native Son, taking off his sombrero to deepen the crease and the dents, because three girls were coming across the lot. "But I've got a complaint of my own to make. When you holler for Bud to start the rough stuff, he just goes powder crazy. He shot me up four times in that scene! Twice he held the gun so close my scalp's all powder-marked, and by rights he should have blowed the top of my head plumb into the street. He gets so taken up with this slaughter-house business that he'll wind up by shooting himself a few times if you don't watch him."

"One thing," Weary put in mildly, "I want to speak about, Luck. We need more blood for those murders. I didn't have half enough for all the mortal wounds Bud gave me. By rights that saloon should be plumb reeking with gore when we're all killed off - the way Bud flies at it with those two six-shooters. No bullets hit the walls anywhere, so it stands to reason they all land in a soft spot on our persons. I needed a large bucket of blood - and I had about a half teacupful." He grinned. "Mamma! That was sure some slaughter, though!"

"Where's Tracy Gray Joyce?" Luck inquired irrelevantly, with a hasty glance around them. "To-morrow, he'll have to come into that same slaughter pen and seize the murderer and subdue him by the steely glint of his eye and by his unflinching demeanor." He pulled the corners of his mouth down expressively. "That's the way the scenario reads," he added defensively.

"Well, say, by cripes, he better amble down to the city and buy him some more glint!" Big Medicine bawled, and laughed afterwards with his big *haw-haw-haw*. "And I'll gamble there ain't enough unflinchin' demeanor on the Coast to put that boy through the scene. Honest-to-gran'-ma, Luck, that there Tracy Gray Joyce gits pale, and his Adam's apple pumps up and down when I come up and smile at him! What color do yuh reckon he'll turn to when he stands up to me right after me slaying all these innocent boys - and me a-foamin' at the mouth and gloatin' over the foul deed I've just did? Say? How's he going to keep that there Adam's apple from shootin' clean up through his hair, and his knees from wobblin'? How - "

"He won't," said Luck suddenly, with a brightening of his eyes. "He won't. I hope they do wobble. You go ahead, Bud, and foam at the mouth. You - you *look* at Tracy Gray Joyce. Not in the rehearsing, understand; leave out the foam and the gloating till we turn the camera on the scene. Sabe? On the quiet, boys."

"Sure," came the guarded chorus. It was remarkable what a complete understanding there was between Luck and the Happy Family. It was that complete understanding which had kept Luck's spirits up during his unloved task of producing Bently Brown stuff in film.

"Well, say!" Big Medicine leaned close and throttled his voice down to a hoarse whisper. "What kinda hee-ro will your Tracy Gray Joyce look like, when I start up foamin' and gloatin' at him?"

Luck smiled. "That," he said calmly, "is for the camera to find out." He was going to say something more on the subject, but some one called to him anxiously from over toward the office. So he told them *adios* hurriedly and went his busy way, and left the Happy Family discussing him gravely among themselves.

The Happy Family were so interested in this new work that they were ready to see the bright side even of these weird performances which purported to be Western drama. If you did not take it seriously, all this violence of dress and behavior was fun. The Happy Family was slipping into a rivalry of violence; and the strange part of it was that Luck Lindsay, stickler for realism, self-confessed enthusiast on the uplifting of motion pictures to a fine art, permitted their violence, - which was not as the violence of other, better trained Western actors. The Happy Family, after their first self-conscious tendency to duck behind something or somebody, had come to forget the merciless, recording eye of the camera. They had come to look upon their work as a game, played for the amusement of Luck Lindsay, who watched them always, and for the open ridicule of Bently Brown, writer of these tales of blood and heroics.

And Luck not only permitted but encouraged them in this exaggeration, - to the amazement of the camera man who had turned the crank on more Western dramas than he could remember. Scenes of violence - such as the saloon row in which Big Medicine had forgotten that Pink was to be left alive, and so had killed him twice - made the camera man and the assistant laugh when they should have shuddered; and to wonder why Luck Lindsay, wholly biased though he was in favor of the Happy Family, did not seem to realize that they were not getting the right punch into the pictures.

Luck was not behaving at all in his usual manner with his company. Evenings, instead of holding himself aloof from his subordinates, he would head straight for the furnished bungalow which the Flying U boys had taken possession of, with Rosemary Green to give the home atmosphere which saved the place from becoming a mere bunk-house de luxe. If he could possibly manage it, Luck would reach headquarters in time for dinner - the Happy Family blandly called it supper, of course - and would proceed to forget the day's irritations while he ate what he ambiguously called "real cookin'."

There was a fireplace in that bungalow, and a fairly large living-room surrounding the fireplace. The Happy Family extravagantly indulged themselves in wood, even at the unbelievable price they must pay for it; and after supper they would light the fire and hunt up chairs enough, and roll cigarettes, and talk themselves quite away from the present and into the past of glowing memory.

The horses they rode - before that fireplace - would have made any Frontier Day celebration famous enough to be mentioned in the next encyclopedia published. The herds they took through hard winters and summer droughts would have made them millionaires all, if they could only have turned them into flesh-and-blood animals. They talked of blizzards and of high water and of short grass and of thunderstorms. They added little touches to the big range picture Luck had planned to make. Starting off suddenly in this wise: "Say, Luck, why don't you have - ?" and the fires of enthusiasm would flare again in Luck's eyes, and the talk would grow eager.

But - and here was the key to the remarkable interpretation which Luck permitted the Happy Family to give the Bently Brown stories - some time before the evening was too old, Luck would swing the talk around to the work they were doing. He would pull a Bently Brown scenario from his pocket and read, with much sarcastic comment, the scenes they were later to enact. He would incite the Happy Family to poking fun at such lurid performances as Bently Brown described in all seriousness and in detail. He would encourage comment and argument and the play of their caustic imaginations upon the action of the story. He would gradually make them see the whole thing in the light of a huge joke; he would, without saying much himself, bring the Happy Family into the mood of wanting to make Bently Brown appear ridiculous to all beholders.

Is it any wonder, then, if the camera man and the assistants should exchange puzzled glances when Luck put the Happy Family through their scenes? Exits and entrances, the essential details of the action, Luck directed painstakingly, as always he had done. Why, then, said camera man to assistants, should he let those fellows go in and ball up the dramatic business and turn whole scenes into farce with their foolery? And why had he chosen Tracy Gray Joyce as leading man? And that eye-rolling, limp sentimentalist, Lenore Honiwell, as his leading woman? Luck was known to despise these two, personally and professionally. They could not, to save their lives, get through a dramatic scene together without giving the observers a sickish feeling. To see Tracy Gray Joyce lay his hand upon the left side of his cravat and cast his eyes upward always made Luck shiver; yet Tracy Gray Joyce would he have for leading man, and none other. To see Lenore Honiwell throw back her head, close her eyes, and heave one of those terrific motion-picture sighs always made the camera man snort; yet Luck, who before had considered her scarcely worth a civil bow when he met her, had actually coaxed her away from a director who really admired her style of acting.

And when Luck, who had always gone about his work impervious to curious onlookers, suddenly changed his method and ordered all interior sets screened in, and all bystanders away from the immediate vicinity of his exterior scenes, the Acme people began to call him "swell-headed" - when they did not call him worse. Even his excuse that he was working with boys new to the business and did not want them rattled failed to satisfy most of them.

The Happy Family, in the tiny, bare dressing rooms which they called box-stalls in merciless candor, were smearing their faces liberally with cold cream and still arguing among themselves over the doubtful blessing of owning as many lives as a cat, and bewailing the bruises they had received while sacrificing a few of their lives to the blood-lust of Big Medicine and Pink, the two official, Bently-Brown bad men. Outside their two connecting "stalls" a fine drizzle was making the studio yard an empty place of churchyard gloom and incidentally justifying Luck in quitting so early. Big Medicine was swabbing paint from his eyebrows and bellowing his opinion of a man that will keep a-comin', by cripes, after he's shot the third time at close range, and then kick because he takes so much killing off. This was aimed at the Native Son, who had evidently died hard, and who meant to retaliate as soon as he got that dab of paint out of his eye. But the door opened violently against his person and startled him into forgetting his next observation.

This was Luck, and he had the look of a man who owns a guilty secret, and is ready to be rather proud of his guilt, - providing society consents to wink at it with him. He was not smiling, exactly; he had a wicked kind of twinkle in his eyes.

"Hurry up, boys! My Lord, how you fellows do primp and jangle in here! They're going to run our first picture, *The Soul of Littlefoot Law*. Don't you fel - "

"The which?" Big Medicine whirled upon him, rubbing his left eye into a terrifying, bloodshot condition while he glared with the other.

"*The Soul of Littlefoot Law*," Luck repeated distinctly with a perfect neutrality of manner.

"'S that what you call all that ridin' and shootin' we done, that you said was by moonlight?" Pink inquired pugnaciously - for a young man who had died the death four different times that day.

"That's what it's called," Luck averred with firmness.

"Aw - where does Soul of Littlefoot Law come in at?" Happy Jack scoffed.

"It doesn't, so far as I know."

"Aw, there ain't no sense in such a name as that. Is that where I got shot off'n my horse, and Bud, here, done his best to run over me?"

"That's the one. My Lord, boys, how long does it take you fellows to get your make-up off? They'll have the film run and passed and released and out on the five-cent circuit on its fifteenth round before you - " Luck, director though he was, found it wise to pass out quickly and hold the door shut behind him for a minute. "Honest, boys, you want to hurry," he called through the closed door. He waited until the sounds within indicated that they were hurrying quite violently, and then he went his way; and he still had the look in his eyes of one who bears in his soul a secret guilt of which he is inclined to be proud.

When the Acme people gathered resignedly in the private projection room, however, Luck's wicked little twinkle had turned a shade anxious. He excused himself from the chair between Martinson and Mollie Ryan, the stenographer, and went over to confer with the Happy Family and the dried little man who kept clannishly together as usual, and he forgot to return to his place.

The Acme people, personally and individually, were sick and tired of all motion pictures that did not portray with vividness the beauty or the talents of themselves, or the faults of their acquaintances. No Acme people, save Lenore Honiwell and Tracy Gray Joyce and a phlegmatic character woman, were in this picture at all. The camera man who took it did not think highly of it and considered the wonderful photography as good as wasted, and he had said as much - and more - to his intimates. Beckitt, Luck's assistant, had privately announced it as the rottenest piece of cheese he had ever seen under a Wild-West label, and disclaimed all responsibility. They of the cutting and trimming clan had not said anything at all. Martinson, having heard the rumors, felt that they confirmed his own suspicion that Luck had made a big blunder in bringing those cowboys into the company. They were not actors. They did not pretend to be actors.

You will see that it was a critical audience indeed that

gathered there in the projection room that rainy afternoon to see the trial run of *The Soul of the Littlefoot Law*. It would take a good deal to win any approbation from that bunch.

And then they were looking at the first scene, which Was a night in Whoopalong, the fake town over there beyond the big stage. The Happy Family, all disguised as cowboys, came surging out of the darkness. H-m-m. That was the bunch that Luck Lindsay had done so much bragging about, and called "real boys," was it? silently commented the audience. No different from any other cowboys, as far as any one could see.

True, they used about half the usual amount of film footage in getting to foreground; probably underspeeded the camera, - an old, old trick which has helped to put the dash and ginger into many a poor horseman's act.

But the "XY cowboys" certainly surged up to foreground, and it was seen that they rode with reins in their teeth, and that each and every man fired two huge six-shooters straight up at the moon every time their horses hit the ground with forefeet. The Happy Family leaned forward and craned around the heads of those in front that they might see all of it. Luck had told them before making this scene to "eat 'em alive," and the Happy Family had very nearly done so. Andy Green nudged his wife, Rosemary, and whispered hurriedly that this was where the camera man had pulled up his tripod by the roots and beat it, thinking he was going to be run over; and that was why the scene was cut unexpectedly just where Andy set his horse on its haunches and posed, a heroic figure of a cowboy rampant, immediately before the lens.

Luck, glancing hurriedly to right and left, slid down and rested the nape of his neck on the back of his chair, slipped a fresh stick of gum between his teeth, hung his hat on his knee, and prepared to view his work with critical mind and impartial, and with his conscience like his body at ease. The thing had certainly started off with zip enough, since zip was what Mart claimed the Public demanded.

The next scene was a continuation of the one before, - the camera man having evidently recovered himself and gotten to work again. The Happy Family, still surging and still shooting two guns apiece at the pale moon, were shown entering the saloon door four abreast and with the rest crowding for place. Still there was zip; all kinds of zip. The Happy Family nudged and grinned in the dusk and were very much pleased with themselves as XY cowboys seeking mild entertainment in town.

Some one behind remarked upon the surging and the shooting, and Big Medicine turned his head quickly and sent a hoarse stage whisper in the general direction of the mumble.

"Ah-h, that there ain't anything! Luck never let us turn ourselves loose there a-tall. You wait, by cripes, till yuh see us where we git warmed up and strung out proper! You wait! Honest to gran' - " It was Luck's elbow that stopped him by the simple expedient of cutting off his wind. Big Medicine gave a grunt and said no more.

Thereafter, the Happy Family discovered that there was a certain continuity in the barbaric performances in which Luck had grinningly encouraged them to indulge themselves. They beheld themselves engaged in various questionable enterprises, and they laughed in naive enjoyment as certain bloodcurdling traits in their characters were depicted with startling vividness. Accented by make-up and magnified on the screen, the goggling, frog-like ugliness of Big Medicine became like unto ogres of childish memory; his smile was a thing to make one's back hair stand up with a cold, prickling sensation. Happy Jack stared at himself and his exaggerated awkwardness incredulously, with a sheepish grin of appreciation. The rest of them watched and missed no slightest gesture.

So they saw the plot of Bently Brown unfold, scene by scene; unfold in violence and malevolent intrigue and zip and much fighting. Also unfolded something of which Bently Brown had never dreamed; something which the audience, though greeting it with laughter, failed at first to recognize for what it was worth, because every one knew all about the Bently-Brown Western dramas, and every one believed that they were to be made after the usual recipe more elaborately stirred. So every one had been chortling through several scenes before the significance of their laughter occurred to them.

Comedy - that was it. Comedy, that had slipped in with cap and bells just when the door was flung open for black-robed Tragedy. But it was too late to stop laughing when they discovered the trick. They saw it now, in the very sub-titles which Luck had twisted impishly into sly humor that pointed to the laugh, in the deeds of blood that followed. They saw it in the goggling ferocity of Big Medicine; in the innocent-eyed, dimpled fiendishness of Pink; in the lank awkwardness of Happy Jack. They saw it in the sentimental mannerisms of Lenore Honiwell, whose sickish emotionalism slipped pat into the burlesque. They rocked in their seats at the heroics of Tracy Gray Joyce, who could never again be taken seriously, since Luck had tagged him mercilessly as an unconscious comedian.

Oh, yes, there was zip to the picture! But there was no explanation of the title. *The Soul of Littlefoot Law* remained as great a mystery when the picture was finished as it had been at the start. Littlefoot Law, by the way, was Pink. That much the audience discovered, and no more; for as to his soul, he did not seem to own one.

Luck, still hunched down so that his back hair rubbed against his chair back, was laughing with his jaws wide apart and his fine teeth still gleaming in the half darkness, when Ted, general errand boy at the office, came straddling over intervening laps and laid a compelling hand on his shoulder.

"Say, Luck," he whispered excitedly, "the audience author's with Mart, and they both want t' see you. And, say, I guess you're in Dutch, all right; the author's awful mad, and so is Mart. But say, no matter what they do to you, Luck, take it from me, that pit'cher's a humdinger! I like to died a-laughing!"

CHAPTER SEVEN

BENTLY BROWN DOES NOT
APPRECIATE COMEDY

Luck unhooked his hat from his knee, brought his laughing jaws together with that eloquent, downward tilt to the corners of his mouth, sat up straight, considered swiftly the possibilities of the next half hour, and paid tribute in one expressive word of four letters before he went crawling over half a dozen pairs of knees to do battle for his picture. His picture, you understand. For since he had made it irresistible comedy instead of very mediocre drama, he felt all the pride of creation in his work. That was his picture that had set the Acme people laughing, - they who had come to carp and to talk knowingly of continuity and of technique and dramatic values, and to criticize everything from the sets to the photography. It was his picture; he had made it what it was. So he went as a champion rather than as a culprit to face the powers above him.

Martinson and Bently Brown were waiting for him near the door. They were not going to stay and see the next picture run, and that, in Luck's opinion, was a bad-weather sign. But he came up to them cheerfully, turning his hat in his fingers to find the front of it before he set it on his head. (These limp, wool, knockabout hats are always more or less confusing, and Luck was fastidious about his apparel.)

"Ah - Mr. Brown, this is Mr. Lindsay, ah - director who is producing your stories." Martinson's tone was as neutral as he could make it.

Luck said that he was glad to meet Mr. Brown, which was a lie. At the same instant he found the stitched-down bow on his hat, and from there felt his way to the front. At the same time he decided that there was going to be something doing presently, if Mart's manner meant anything at all. Mart was a peaceable soul, and in the approaching crisis Luck knew he would climb hurriedly upon the fence of neutrality and stay there; and Luck could fight or climb a tree as he chose.

They went outside, and Luck turned his eyes sidewise and took a look at Bently Brown. He measured him mentally from pigskin puttees to rakish, stiff brimmed Stetson with careful dimples in the crown and a leather hatband stamped with horses' heads and his initials. In a picture, Luck would have cast Bently Brown, costume and all, for a comedy mining engineer or something of that sort. You know the type: He arrives on the stage that is held up, and is always in the employ of the monied octopus, and the cowboys who pursue and capture the bandits have fun afterwards with the engineer, - so much fun that he crawls out of an up-stairs window in the night and departs hastily and forever from that place. You are perfectly familiar with the character, I am sure.

Luck, after that swift, comprehensive glance, was not greatly alarmed. In that he made his greatest blunder. He should have reckoned with the wounded vanity of

B. M. Bower

the little author who believes himself great. He should have reminded himself that Bently Brown was not a comedy mining engineer, but that touchiest of all mortals, the nearly successful author. He should have taken warning from the stiff-necked, stiff-backed gait of Bently Brown on the short walk to the office. He should have read danger in the blinking lids of his pale eyes, and in his self-conscious manner of looking straight before him.

In the office, then, luck basely deserted one Luck Lindsay, and left him to fight a losing battle. For Bently Brown was incensed, insulted, and outraged over the manner in which *The Soul of Littlefoot Law* had been filmed. The story had been caricatured out of all semblance to its original self. Littlefoot Law had been shown as having no soul whatever. Instead of being permitted to make the final, supreme sacrifice of his life for the honor of his enemy, - which would have revealed to the audience his possession of a clean white soul in spite of his bad character, - he had been made out a little fiend who would shoot you on the slightest provocation. The girl had been thrust into the background, and the hero had been made into a coward and a paltry villain; they were all desperadoes upon the screen. Never in his life had Bently Brown been made to suffer such an affront. Never had he dreamed that his work would be made a thing to laugh at -

"They certainly did laugh," Luck lazily interrupted. "And believe me, Mr. Brown, it takes real stuff to collect a laugh out of that bunch. It will be a riot with the public; you can bank on that. By the time I get a few more made and released, you can expect to see your name in the papers without paying advertising rates." Whatever possessed Luck to talk that way to

Bently Brown, I cannot say. He surely must have seen that the little, over-costumed author was choking with spleen.

"It was a farce!" The small, yellow mustache of Bently Brown was twitching comically with the tremble of his lips beneath. "A bald, unmitigated farce!"

"Surest thing you know," Luck agreed, with that little chuckle of his. "At first I was afraid the crowd wouldn't get it; I didn't know but they might try to take it seriously. Now, I know for certain that it will get over. It will be the cleanest, funniest, farce-comedy series that has ever been filmed." Luck sat up straight and pulled a cigar from his pocket and looked at it absent-mindedly. "Say, those boys of mine are certainly real ones! I wouldn't trade that bunch for the highest-salaried actors you could hand me. Do you know what made that picture such a scream? It was because there wasn't a bit of made-to-order comedy business in the whole film. Those boys didn't think about acting funny just to make folks laugh. They were so doggoned busy having fun with the story and showing up its weak points that they forgot to be self-conscious. If I'd had a regular comedy company working on it, believe me, Mr. Brown, it might have turned out almost as rotten a farce as it would be as a drama!"

Had Bently Brown owned under his pink skin any of the primitive instincts which he was so fond of portraying in his characters, he would have killed Luck without any further argument or delay.

Instead of that he spluttered and stormed like a scolding woman. He lifted first one puttee and then the other, and he shook his fist, and he nodded his head violently, and finally was constrained to lift the leather-banded Stetson from his blond hair and wipe the perspiration from his brow with a lavender initialed handkerchief. He said a great deal in a very few minutes, but it was too involved, too incoherent to be repeated here. Luck gathered, however, that he meant to sue the Acme Company for about nine million dollars damages to his feelings and his reputation, if *The Soul of Littlefoot Law* was released in its present form. He battered at Luck's grinning composure with his full supply of invectives. When he perceived that Luck's eyes twinkled more and more while they watched him, and that Luck's smile was threatening to explode into laughter, Bently Brown shook his fist at the two of them, shrilled something about seeing his lawyer at once, and went out and slammed the door.

"Lor-dee! He'd make a hit in comedy, that fellow," Luck observed placidly, and lighted the cigar he had been holding. "What's he mean - 'sue the company'?"

"He means sue the company," Martinson retorted grimly. "That clause in the contract where we agree to produce his stories in a manner befitting the quality and fame of these several stories in fiction; he's got grounds for action there, and he's going to make the most of it. He's sore, anyway. Some one's been telling him he practically made us a present of his stuff."

"Hell!" said Luck. "Why didn't you say so?"

"Why didn't you say that you were turning that stuff into farce-comedy?" Martinson came back sharply. "I could have told you it wouldn't get by. I knew Brown wouldn't stand for anything like that; and I knew he could put the gaff into us on that 'manner befitting' clause."

"It's a wonder you wouldn't have jarred loose from some of that wisdom," Luck observed tartly. "You never gave me any dope at all on this Bently Brown person. You handed me the junk he stung you on - and believe me, as drama he'd have stung you with it as a present! - you handed it to me to film. I made the most of it."

"You made a mess of it," Martinson corrected peevishly.

"You laughed," Luck pointed out laconically. Then his eyes twinkled suddenly. "'Laugh and the world laughs with you,'" he quoted shamelessly, and took a long, satisfying suck at his cigar.

"The world won't step up and pay damages to Bently Brown," Martinson reminded him, "if that picture is released as it stands. How many have you made, so far?"

"I'm finishing the third; getting funnier, too, as they go along."

"You've got to cut out that funny business. You'll have to retake this whole thing, Luck; make it straight drama. We can't afford a lawsuit, these hard times - and injunctions tying up the releases, and damages to pay when the thing's thrashed out in court. You'll have to retake this whole picture. Nice bunch of useless expense, I must say, when I've been chasing nickels off the expense account of this company and sitting up nights nursing profits! We'll have to cut salaries now, to break even on this fluke. I've left the payroll alone so far. That's the worst of a break like this. The whole company has got to pay for every blunder from now on."

Luck's eyes hardened while he listened. He did not call his work a blunder, and the charge did not sit well coming from another.

"Buy off Bently Brown," he advised crisply. "Offer him a new contract, naming this stuff as comedy. Advertise them as the famous comedies of Bently Brown, the well-known author. Show him some good publicity dope along that line. Give him the credit of making the stories live ones. This series will be a money-maker, and a big one, if ever they reach the screen. You're old enough in the business to know that, Mart. You saw how this film hit the bunch, and you know what it takes to rouse any enthusiasm in the projection room. And take it from me, Mart - this is straight! - that's the only way in God's world to make that series take hold at all. As drama the stuff is hopeless. Absolutely hopeless. It's only by giving it the twist I gave it that it will get over. You do that, Mart. You kid this Bently Brown into being featured as the humorist of the age, and pay him a little something for swallowing his disappointment as a dramatic author. I'll go ahead with my boys, and we'll deliver the goods. You do that, and you'll be setting up nights counting profits instead of nursing them!"

Martinson began to stir up the litter on his desk, - another bad-weather sign. "I can't waste time talking nonsense," he snapped. "I've got plenty to do without that. That stuff has got to be retaken; every foot of it, if you've gone on burlesquing the action. I happen to know that Brown wouldn't consider such a compromise. You've made a bad break, and I believe you made the first one when you brought that bunch of cowboys back with you. If they can do straight dramatic acting, all right; if not, you'd better let them out and start over with professionals."

For a peaceable man, Martinson was angry. He had taken some trouble in smoothing down the ruffled temper of Bently Brown, even before viewing the trial run of the picture. Martinson hated disputes as a cat hates to walk in fresh-fallen snow, and the parting tirade of Bently Brown had affected him unpleasantly.

For a full two minutes Luck smoked and did not speak, and as he had done once before, Martinson repented his harshness when it was too late. "Personally, your version struck me as awfully funny," he began placatingly.

"Who gives a cuss how it struck you personally?" Luck stood up with unexpected haste. "You trim and truckle to every one that comes along with a gold brick, and that's why you have to sit up nights to nurse the profits. If you had a little stiffening in your back, the profits would show up better. You paid good money for this bunch of rot, and turned it over to me to whip into a profitable investment. You can make the rounds of the studio and get a vote on whether I've done it or not. Put it up to your Public; they'll mighty soon let you know whether the film's a money-getter. If it is, your business as general manager and president of the Acme Film Company is to get Bently Brown in line for the production to go on. A clause such as you mention in the agreement with him shows a bigger blunder on your part than anything I've done or ever will do. If you'd had as much sense as Ted, you'd have kept that clause out. If you'd had half as much brains as the comedy burro out in the corral you'd never have loaded up with that stuff, anyway; you'd have seen at a glance that it was rotten.

"Now, I've shown what I can do with those stories. I've taken your bad bargain and put it into a money-making shape. As to the break I made in getting those boys out here, you'll have to show me - that's all. They seem, to have made good all right, judging from the way that film took with the crowd. And if you ask my opinion as a director, they beat any near-professional on the Acme pay roll. My work, and their work, goes right along as it has started - or it stops. If you want those stories worked up in a lot of darned, sickly, slush melodrama, you can set some simp at it that don't know any better." Luck stopped and shut his teeth together against some personal remarks that he would later feel ashamed of having uttered. He turned to the door, swallowed hard, and forced himself to a dignified calm before he spoke again.

"You know my phone number, Mart. By seven in the morning I'll expect to hear from you. You can tell me then whether I'm to go ahead with these stories the way I've started, or whether to pull out of the Company altogether. One or the other. I'll want to know in the morning." Then he went out.

"Dammit, who's running this company - you or I?" Martinson called after him heatedly. But Luck was already standing on the steps and hoisting his umbrella against the drizzle, and he did not give any sign that he heard.

CHAPTER EIGHT

"THERE'S GOT TO BE A LINE DRAWED SOMEWHERES"

By seven o'clock in the morning, - since that was his ultimatum, - Luck was standing in his bare feet and pajamas, acrimoniously arguing with Martinson over the telephone. Usually he was up at six, but he was a stubborn young man, and the day promised much rainfall, anyway. He would have preferred sunshine; the stand he meant to take would have had more weight in working weather. But since he could not prevent the morning from being a rainy one, he permitted more determination to slip into his tones.

Martinson had spent an unpleasant evening with Bently Brown, or so he declared. He had called up several stockholders of the Acme, and had talked the matter over with them, and -

"Well, cut the preamble, Mart," snapped Luck, trying to warm one foot by rubbing it with the other one. "Do I go on with the work, or don't I?"

"From the looks of the weather - " Mart began to temporize.

" Weather cuts no figure with this matter. You know

what I mean. What's the decision?" Luck scowled at the pretty girl on his wall calendar, and began to rub his right foot with the left and to curse the janitor with that part of his brain not occupied with the conversation.

"Well, listen. You come out to the office, after awhile, and we'll go into this matter calmly," begged Martinson. "No use in letting that temper of yours run away with you, Luck. You know we all - "

"What did Bently Brown say? Did you put the proposition up to him as I suggested?"

" Luck, you know I told you Brown wouldn't consider - "

"Say, Mart, get all those rambling words out of your system, and then call me up and tell me what I want to know!" And Luck hung up the receiver and went shivering back to bed. From the things he said to himself, he was letting that temper of his run away with him in spite of Martinson's warning.

He had just ceased having spasms of shivering, and had found his warm nest of the night, and was feeling glad that it was raining so that he could stay in bed as long as he liked, when the phone jingled shrilly again. Had he been certain that it was Martinson, Luck would have lain there and let it ring itself tired. But there is always the doubt when a telephone bell calls peremptorily. He waited sulkily until the girl at the switchboard in the office below settled down to prolong the siege. Luck knew that girl would never quit now that she was sure he was in. He crawled out again, this time dragging the bedspread with him for drapery.

"H'l-lo!" There was no compromise in his voice, which was guttural.

"Luck? This is Martinson. You are to retake all of the Bently Brown pictures which you have made so far, under the personal supervision of Bently Brown himself, who will pass upon all film before accepted by the company. This is final."

"Martinson? This is Luck. You and Bently Brown and the Acme Film Company can go where the heat's never turned off. This is final."

Whereupon Luck slammed the receiver into its brackets, trailed over to a table and gleaned "the makings" from among the litter of papers, programs, "stills," and letters, and rolled himself a much-needed smoke. He was sorry chiefly because he had been compelled to use such mild language over the telephone. It would be almost worth a trip to the office just to tell Martinson without stint what he thought of him and all his works.

He crawled back into bed and smoked his cigarette with due regard for the bedclothes, and wondered what kind of a fool they took him for if they imagined for one minute that he would produce so much as a sub-title under the personal supervision of Bently Brown.

After awhile it occurred to him that, unless he relented from his final statement to Martinson, he was a young man out of a job, but that did not worry him much. Of course, if he left the Acme Company, he would have to look around for an opening somewhere else, where he could take his Happy Family and maybe produce....

Right there Luck got up and unlocked his trunk, which was also his chest of treasures, and found the carbon copy of his range scenario. He had not named it yet. In thinking of it and in talking about it with the boys he had been content to call it his Big Picture. If he could place himself and his Big Picture and his boys with some company that would appreciate the value of the combination, his rupture with the Acme Company would be simply a bit of good luck. While he huddled close to the radiator that was beginning to hiss and rumble encouragingly, he glanced rapidly over the meagerly described scenes which were to his imagination so full of color.

"Pam. bleak mesa - snow - cattle drifting before wind. Dale and Johnny dis. riding to foreground. Reg. cold - horses leg-weary - boys all in - "

To Luck, sitting there in his pajamas as close as he could get to a slow-warming steam radiator, those curtailed sentences projected his mental self into a land of cold and snow and biting wind, where the cattle drifted dismally before the storm. Andy Green and Miguel Rapponi were riding slowly toward him on shuffling horses as bone-weary as their masters. Snow was packed in the wrinkles of the boys' clothing. Snow was packed in the manes and tails of the horses that moved with their heads drooping in utter dejection. "Boys all in," said the script laconically. Luck, staring at the little thread of escaping steam from the radiator valve, saw Andy and the Native Son drooping in the saddles, swaying stiffly with the movements of their mounts. He saw them to the last little detail, - to the drift of snow on their hatbrims and the tiny icicles clinging to the high collars of their sourdough coats, where their breath had frozen.

If he could get a company to let him put that on, he would not care, he told himself, if he never made another picture in his life. If he could get a company to send him and the boys where that stuff could be found -

Well, it was only eight o'clock in the morning, a rainy morning at that, when all good movie people would lie late in bed for the pure luxury of taking their ease. But Luck, besides acting upon strong convictions and then paying the price without whimpering, never let an impulse grow stale from want of use. He reached for the fat telephone directory and searched out the numbers of those motion-picture companies which he did not remember readily. Then, beginning at the first number on his hastily compiled list, he woke five different managers out of their precious eight-o'clock sleep to answer his questions.

Whatever they may have thought of Luck Lindsay just then, they replied politely, and did not tell him offhand that there was no possible opening for him in their companies. Three of them made appointments with him at their offices. One promised to call him up just as soon as he "had a line on anything." One said that, with the rainy weather coming on, they were cutting down to straight studio stuff, but that he would keep Luck in mind if anything turned up.

Then I suppose the whole five called him names behind his back, figuratively speaking, for being such an early riser on such a day. Not one of them asked him any questions about his reasons for leaving the

Acme; reasons, in the motion-picture business, are generally invented upon demand and have but a fictitious value at best. And since it is never a matter of surprise when any director or any member of any company decides to try a new field, it would seem that change is one of the most unchanging features of the business.

Luck had no qualms of conscience, either for his treatment of Martinson and his overtures, or for his disturbances of five other perfectly inoffensive movie managers. He dressed with mechanical precision and with his mind shuttling back and forth from his Big Picture to the possibilities of his next position. He folded his scenario and placed it in a long envelope, hunted until he found his rubbers, took his raincoat over his arm and his umbrella in his hand, and went blithely to the elevator. It was too stormy for his machine, so he caught a street car and went straight to the bungalow where the Happy Family were still snoring at peace with the world and each other.

Still Luck had no qualms of conscience. He lingered in the kitchen just long enough to say howdy to Rosemary Green who was anxiously watching a new and much admired coffee percolator "to see if it were going to perk," she told him gravely. He assured Rosemary that he had come all the way out there in the hope of being invited to breakfast. Then he went into a sleep-charged atmosphere and gave a real, old-time range yell.

"Why, I saw that peaked little person with Mr. Martinson," Mrs. Andy remarked slightingly at the breakfast table. "Was that Bently Brown? And he has the nerve to want to stand around and boss you - oh, find, me an umbrella, somebody! I shall choke if I can't go and tell him to his silly, pink face what a conceited little idiot he is!" (You will see why it was that Rosemary Green had been adopted without question as a member of the Happy Family.) "I hope you told him straight out, Luck Lindsay, that these boys would simply tear him limb from limb if he ever dared to butt in on your work. Why, it's you that made the picture fit to look at!"

Luck let his eyes thank her for her loyalty, and held out his empty cup for more coffee. "I came out," he drawled quietly, "to find out what you fellows are going to do about it. Of course, they'll get somebody else to go ahead with the stuff, and you boys can stay with it - "

"Well, say! Did you come away out here in the rain to insult us fellers?" Big Medicine roared suddenly from the foot of the table. "I'll take a lot from you, but by cripes they's got to be a line drawed somewheres!"

"You bet. And right there's where we draw it, Luck," spoke up the dried little man who seldom spoke at the table, but concentrated his attention upon the joy of eating what Mrs. Andy set before him. "I come out here to work for you. That peters out, by gorry I'll go back to chufferin a baggage truck in Sioux, North Dakoty. Kin I have a drop more coffee, Mrs. Green?"

While Rosemary proudly brought her new percolator in from the kitchen and refilled his cup, Luck Lindsay sat and endured the greatest tongue-lashing of his life. Furthermore, he seemed to enjoy the chorus of reproaches and threats and recriminations. He chuckled over the eloquence of Andy Green, and he grinned at

B. M. Bower

the belligerence of Pink and the melancholy of Happy Jack.

"I don't guess you're crazy to work under Bently Brown," he finally managed to slide into the uproar. "Do I get you as meaning to stick with me - wherever I go?"

"You get us that way or you get licked," Weary, the mild-tempered one, stated flatly. "You can fire us and send us home, but you can't walk off and leave us with the Acme, 'cause we won't stay."

That was what Luck had ridden twelve cold, rainy miles to hear the Happy Family declare. He had expected them to take that stand, but it was good to hear it spoken in just that tone of finality. He stacked his cup and saucer in his plate, laid his knife and fork across them in the old range style, and began to roll a cigarette, - smoking at the table being another comfortable little bad habit which Rosemary Green wisely and smilingly permitted.

"That being the case," he began cheerfully, "you boys had best go over with me now and give in your two weeks' notice. I'm director of our company till I quit - see? I'll arrange for your transportation home - "

"Aw, gwan! Who said we was goin' home?" wailed Happy Jack distressfully.

"Now, listen! You're entitled to your transportation money. That doesn't mean you'll have to use it for that purpose - sabe? It's coming to you, and you get it. There's a week's salary due all around, too, besides the two weeks you'll get by giving notice. No use passing up any bets like that. So let's go, boys. I've got an appointment at one o'clock, and I may as well wipe the Acme slate clean this forenoon, so I can talk business without any come-back from Mart, or any tag ends to pick up. Grab your slickers and let's move."

That was a busy day for Luck Lindsay, in spite of the fact that it was a stormy one. His interview with Mart, which he endured mostly for the sake of the Happy Family, developed into a quarrel which severed beyond mending his connection with the Acme.

It was noon when he reached his hotel, and his wrath had not cooled with the trip into town. There were two 'phone calls in his mail, he discovered, and one bore an urgent request that he call Hollywood something-or-other the moment he returned. This was from the Great Western Film Company, and Luck's eyes brightened while he read it. He went straight to his room and called up the Great Western.

Presently he found himself speaking to the great Dewitt himself, and his blood was racing with the possibilities of the interview. Dewitt had heard that Luck was leaving the Acme - extras may be depended upon for carrying gossip from one studio to another, - and was wasting no time in offering him a position. His Western director, Robert Grant Burns whom Luck knew well, had been carried to the hospital with typhoid fever which he had contracted while out with his company in what is known as Nigger Sloughs, - a locality more picturesque than healthful. Dewitt feared that it was going to be a long illness at the very best. Would Luck consider taking the company and going on with the big five-reel feature which Burns had just begun? Dewitt was prepared to offer special inducements and to make the position a permanent one. He would give Burns a dramatic company to produce features at the studio, he said, and would give Luck the privilege of choosing his own scenarios and producing them in his own way. Could Luck arrange to meet Dewitt at four that afternoon?

Luck could, by cancelling his appointment with a smaller and less important company, which he did promptly and with no compunctions whatever. He did more than that; he postponed the other two appointments, knowing in his heart that his chances would not be lessened thereby. After that he built a castle or two while he waited for the appointment. The Great Western Company had been a step higher than he had hoped to reach. Robert Grant Burns he had considered a fixture with the company. It had never entered his mind that he might possibly land within the Great Western's high concrete wall, - and that other wall which was higher and had fewer gates, and which was invisible withal. That the great Dewitt himself should seek Luck out was just a bit staggering. He wanted to go out and tell the bunch about it, but he decided to wait until everything was settled. Most of all he wanted the Acme to know that Dewitt wanted him; that would be a real slap in the face of Mart's judgment, a vindication of Luck's abilities as a director.

What Luck did was to telephone the hospital and learn all he could about Burns' condition. He was genuinely sorry that Burns was sick, even though he was mightily proud of being chosen as Burns' successor. He even found himself thinking more about Burns, after the first inner excitement wore itself out, than about himself. Burns was a good old scout. Luck hated to think of him lying helpless in the grip of typhoid. So it was with mixed emotions that he went to see Dewitt.

Dewitt wanted Luck - wanted him badly. He was frank enough to let Luck see how much he wanted him. He even told Luck that, all things being equal, he considered Luck a better Western director than was Robert Grant Burns, in spite of the fact that Burns had scored a big success with his *Jean, of the Lazy A* serial. You cannot wonder that Luck's spirits rose to buoyancy when he heard that. Also, Dewitt named a salary bigger than Luck had ever received in his life, and nearly double what the Acme had paid him. Luck spoke of his Big Picture, and when he outlined it briefly, Dewitt did not say that it seemed to lack action.

Dewitt had watched Luck with his keen blue eyes, and had observed that Luck owned that priceless element of success, which is enthusiasm for his work. Dewitt had listened, and had told Luck that he would like to see the Big Picture go on the screen, and that he would be willing to pay him for the scenario and let him make it where and how he pleased. He even volunteered to try and persuade Jean Douglas, of *Lazy A* fame, to come back and play the leading woman's part.

"That's one thing that has been bothering me a little," Luck owned gratefully. "Of course I considered her absolutely out of reach. But with her for my leading woman, and the boys holding up the range end as they're capable of doing - "

Dewitt gave him a quick look. "Yes, my boys are able to do that," he said distinctly. "They have been well trained in Western dramatic work."

Luck braced himself. "When I mentioned the boys," he said, "I meant my boys that I brought from the Flying U outfit, up in Montana. They go with me."

Dewitt did not answer that statement immediately. He inspected his finger nails thoughtfully before he glanced up. "It's a pity, but I'm afraid that cannot be managed, Mr. Lindsay. The boys in my Western company have been with me, some of them, since the Independent Sales Company was organized. They worked for next to nothing till I got things started. Two or three are under contracts. You will understand me when I say that my boys must stay where they are." He waited for a minute, and watched Luck's face grow sober. "I have heard about your Happy Family," he added. "There has been a good deal of discussion, I imagine, among the studios about them. Ordinarily I should be glad to have you bring those boys with you; but as matters stand, it is impossible. Our Western Company is full, and I could not let these boys go to make room for strangers, - however good those strangers might be. You understand?"

"Certainly I understand." But Luck's face did not brighten.

"Can't they stay on with the Acme? From what I hear, the Acme's Western Company is not large at best."

"They can stay, yes. But they won't. The whole bunch gave in their two weeks' notice this morning." There was a grim satisfaction in Luck's tone.

"Left when you did, I suppose?"

" That's just exactly what they did. I told them they

better stay, and they nearly lynched me for it."

"Have you made any agreement with them in regard to placing them with another company - for instance?"

"Certainly not. Some things don't have to be set down in black and white."

"I - see." Dewitt did see. What he saw worried him, even though it increased his respect for Luck Lindsay. He studied his nails more critically than before.

"These boys - have they any resources at all, other than their work in pictures? Did they burn their bridges when they came with you?"

"Oh, far as that goes, they've all got ranches. They wouldn't starve." Luck's voice was inclined to gruffness under quizzing.

"As I see the situation," Dewitt went on evenly and with a logic that made Luck squirm with its very truthfulness, "they left their ranches and came with you to work in pictures in a spirit of adventure, we might say. There is a glamour; and your personal influence, your enthusiasm, had its effect. Should they go back to their ranches now, they would carry back a fresh outlook and a fund of experiences that would season conversation agreeably for months to come. They will not have lost financially, I take it. They will have had a vacation which has in many ways been a profitable one. Should the question be laid before them, I venture the assertion that they would urge you to take this position with us.

"They would feel some disappointment of course - just

as you would feel sorry not to be able to bring them with you. But no reasonable man would blame you or expect you to bear the handicap of six or seven inexperienced young fellows. You must see that your only hope of placing them would be with some new company just starting up. And this is not the season for young companies. Next spring you might stand a better chance."

"Yes, that's all true enough," Luck admitted, since Dewitt plainly expected some reply. " At the same time - "

"There is no immediate need of a decision," Dewitt hastily completed Luck's sentence. "From all weather reports, this storm is going to be a long one. I doubt very much if you could get to work for several days. I wish you would think it over from all sides before you accept or refuse the proposition, Mr. Lindsay. Lay the matter before your boys; tell them frankly just how things stand. I'll guarantee they will insist upon your accepting the position. I know, and you know, that it will give you a better opportunity than you have had in some time. And I am going to say candidly that I believe you need only the opportunity to make your work stand out above all the others. That is why I sent for you this morning. I believe you have big possibilities, and I want you with the Great Western."

There was that instant of silence which terminates all conferences. Then Luck rose, and Dewitt tilted back his office chair and swung it away from the desk so that he was still facing Luck. So the two looked at each other measuringly for a moment.

"I certainly appreciate your good opinion of me, Mr.

Dewitt," Luck said. "Whether I take the place or not, I want to thank you for offering it to me. It all looks fine - the chance of my life; but I can't - "

"No, don't say any more." Dewitt raised his hand. "You do as I suggest; tell the boys just what has passed, if you like. Let them decide for you."

"No, that wouldn't be fair. They'd decide for my interests and forget about their own. I know that."

"Well, let's just wait a day or two. You think it over. Think what you could do with Jean Douglas, for instance. I'll try and get her back; I think perhaps I can. She's married, but I think they'll both come if I make it worth their while. Come and see me day after to-morrow, will you? We'll say four o'clock again. Good-by."

So Luck went away with temptation whispering in his ear.

CHAPTER NINE

LEAVE IT TO THE BUNCH

Not a word did Luck say to the Happy Family about his big opportunity. Instead, he avoided them half guiltily, and he filled the next day and the one after that by seeing, or trying to see, the head of every motion picture company in that part of the State. He even sent a night letter to a big company at Santa Barbara. Always he stipulated that he must take his own cowboys with him and have a free hand in the production of Western pictures - since he did not mean to risk having another irate author descend upon him with threats of a lawsuit.

By three o'clock of the day when he was to give Dewitt his decision, Luck was convinced that the two conditions he never failed to mention were as two iron bars across every trail that might otherwise have been open to him. No motion picture company seemed to feel that it needed seven inexperienced men on its payroll. A few general managers suggested letting them work as extras, but the majority could not see the proposition at all. They were more willing to give Luck the free hand which he demanded, had negotiations ever reached that far, which they did not.

The Happy Family, Luck was forced to admit to

himself, was a very serious handicap for an out-of-work director to carry at the beginning of the rainy season. He did his best, and he spent two sleepless nights over the doing, but he simply could not land them anywhere. He talked himself hoarse for them, he painted them geniuses all; he declared that they would make themselves and their company - supposing they were accepted - famous for Western pictures. He worked harder to place them in the business than he would ever work to find himself a job, and he failed absolutely.

Dewitt's eyes questioned him the moment he stood inside the office. Dewitt had heard something of Luck's efforts since their last meeting; and although he admired Luck the more for his loyalty, he felt quite certain that now he was convinced of his defeat, Luck would hesitate no longer over stepping into the official shoes of Robert Grant Burns, who was lying on his broad back, and shouting pitifully futile commands to his company and asking an imaginary camera-man questions which were as Greek to the soft-footed nurse. Dewitt, having just come from a visit to Burns, had a vivid mental picture of that ward in the Sister's hospital. But alongside that picture was another, quite as vivid, of Luck Lindsay standing beside Pete Lowry's camera with a script in his hand, explaining to Jean Douglas the business of some particular scene.

"Well?" queried Dewitt, and motioned Luck to a chair.

"Well," Luck echoed, and stopped for a breath. "No use wasting time, Mr. Dewitt. I can't take any position that doesn't include the Flying U boys. I'm certainly sorry that prevents my accepting your offer. I appreciate all it would mean for me and for my Big Picture to be with you. But – some things mean more - "

"You're under no obligations to tie your own hands just because theirs are not free," Dewitt reminded him sharply.

"I know I'm not."

"Can you figure where it will be to their advantage for you to refuse a good position just because they happen to be out of work?"

"I'm not trying to figure anything like that. Some things don't have to be figured. Some things just are! Do you see what I mean? Those boys didn't wait to do any figuring. When I quit the Acme, they quit - just as a matter of course. If I were as loyal to them as they have been to me, Mr. Dewitt, I wouldn't have taken two days to give you my answer. I'd have told you day before yesterday what I'm telling you now."

Dewitt did not reply at once. When he did speak he seemed to be answering an argument within himself.

"I can't let my own boys go to make room for yours. That is absolutely out of the question. There is a little matter of loyalty there, also."

"I know there is. I don't know that I should want you to let them go. We're both in the same position almost. And we're at a deadlock, Mr. Dewitt. I'm certainly sorry that I can't sign up with you."

"So am I, young man. So am I. Come back if things shape themselves so you can see your way clear to directing my Western company. I've an idea your boys will be going back to their ranches before the holidays. In case they do, let me hear from you."

That was more than Luck had any right to expect, and he had the sense to realize it. He thanked Dewitt and promised, and went away with something of a load off his mind. He could go now and face the Happy Family without feeling himself another Judas.

He found them sitting around waiting for their supper and trying to invent new words to fit their disgust with the Acme Film Company. They greeted Luck as though they had not seen him for a month.

"Bully for you, Luck!" Andy shouted, and gave him an approving slap on the shoulder that sent him skating dangerously toward the table. "Best job in town just came a-running up to you and says, 'Please take me!' - so they say. That right?"

"Yeah - what about this here Great Western gitting its loop on you first thing?" bawled Big Medicine gleefully. "By cripes, that's sure one on the Acme bunch! They'll wisht they wasn't quite so fresh, givin' that little tin imitation of an author so much rope. Me 'n' Pink was over to the studio to-day; honest to grandma, they was a sick lookin' bunch around there. Me 'n' Pink sure threwed it into 'em too, about letting the only real man they had git away from 'em the way they done."

"My gorry, son, I sure am tickled to see yuh light with both feet under yuh, like they say you done. I heard tell the Great Western's going to let yuh put on your own pitcher; I guess them Acme folks'll feel kinda foolish when they see it , " declared the dried little man , grinning over his pipe.

Luck was fighting his bewilderment and framing a demand for explanations when Rosemary bustled in from the kitchen.

"Oh, but we're glad, Luck Lindsay!" she began in her quick, emphatic way. "We all feel like a million dollars over your good luck. We're going to have fried chicken and strawberry shortcake for supper, too, just for a celebration. I knew you'd come out and tell us all about it. So sit right down, everybody, and keep still so Luck can tell us just what everybody said to the other fellow, and how Dewitt happened to get hold of him so quickly. Is it true? The boys heard you were going to get two hundred dollars a week!"

"Not get it - no." Luck unfolded his napkin with fingers that shook a little. "I was offered it, but I'm not going to take it."

"Not - why, Luck Lindsay!" Rosemary very nearly dropped her new percolator.

"*Y' ain't?*"

"Aw, gwan! Only reason I wouldn't take two hundred a week would be because I'd drop dead at the chance and couldn't."

"Well, listen. There's one point that hasn't spilled into studio gossip yet," Luck managed to slip into the uproar. "I didn't take the place. There were some details we couldn't get together on, so I thanked him and turned it down."

There was silence, while the Happy Family stared at him.

"What dee-tails was them?" Big Medicine demanded belligerently. "Way I heard it - "

"Studio gossip," Luck interrupted hastily. "You can't depend on anything you hear passed around amongst the extras. We failed to agree on certain technical details. I haven't any more job than a jack rabbit; let it go at that. What have you fellows been doing?"

"Us? Why, the Acme's goin' to give us absent, treatment from now on," Andy stated cheerfully. "They're paying us thirty a week apiece to stay away from 'em - and I sure never earned money easier than that. Clements is going to take orders from that so-called author, and he told me straight out that they'll be using actors in those stories."

"They'll need 'em," Luck commented drily. "You're in luck that they don't want you to work. Any other news?"

"You bet they's other news!" roared Big Medicine, goggling across the table at Luck. "I rustled me a job, by cripes! Soon as this rain's over, I'm goin' to cash in my face fer two dollars a day with the Sunset. Feller over there wants me bad fer atmosphere in a pitcher he's goin' to make of the Figy Islands. Feller claims he can clothe me in a nigger wig and a handful of grass and get more atmosphere, by cripes, to the square inch - "

Rosemary gasped and bolted for the kitchen. When she came back, red-faced and still gurgling spasmodically,

Pink was relating his experiences with another company. He and the Native Son and Weary, it transpired, were duly enrolled upon the extra list and were reasonably sure of a day's work now and then. Rosemary had paid her Japanese maid and let her go, and Andy was going to help her with the housework until the industrial problem was solved. She listened for a minute and then made a suggestion of her own.

"We're all in the same boat," she said, "and by just sticking together, I know we'll come out swimmingly. Why don't you leave the hotel, and come out here and batch with us, Luck? It would be so much cheaper; and I can turn that couch in the kitchen into a bed, easy as anything. I'd like to shake that Great Western Company for acting the way they have with you. Think of offering a man a two-hundred-a-week position and then haggling - "

"Say, Luck," the dried little man spoke up suddenly, "how much does one of them there camaries cost? I'd be willin' to chip in and help buy one; and, by gorry, we could make some movin' pitchers of our own and sell 'em, if we caji't do no better." He craned his neck and peered the length of the table at Luck. "Ain't no law ag'in it, is there?" he challenged.

"No, there's no law against it." Luck closed his lips against further comment. The idea was like a sudden blow upon the door of his imagination.

The Happy Family looked at one another inquiringly. They had never thought of doing anything like that. The dried little man may have meditated much upon the subject, but he certainly had not given a hint of it to any of them.

"Oh, why couldn't you boys do that?" Rosemary exclaimed breathlessly.

Luck stirred his coffee carefully and did not look up. "Don't run away with the idea that you can buy a camera for twenty or thirty dollars," he quelled. "A camera, complete with tripod, lenses, magazines, and cases, would cost about fourteen hundred dollars - at least."

That, as he had expected it to do, rather feazed the Happy Family for a few minutes. They became interested in the food they were eating, and their eyes did not stray far from their plates.

"I can ante two hundred," Weary remarked at last with elaborate carelessness, reaching for more butter.

"See yuh and raise yuh fifty," Andy Green retorted briskly. "I've got a wife that's learning me to save money."

"You can count my chips for all I got." Pink's dimples showed briefly. "I'll go through my pockets when I get filled up, and see how rich I am. But, anyway, there's a couple of hundred I know I've got, - counting Acme handouts and all."

"We-ell - " the dried little man laid down his fork to rub his chin thoughtfully, "I never had much call to spend money in Sioux, North-Dakoty. I batched and lived savin'. I can put in half of that fourteen hundred - mebby a little mite more."

"Well, by cripes, I got a boy t' look out fer, and I ain't rich as some, but all I got goes in the pot!" cried Big

Medicine impulsively.

Luck leaned back in his chair and regarded the flushed faces enigmatically. "This is all good material for an argument on our financial standing," he said, "but if you're taking yourselves seriously, let me tell you something before you go any farther. Buying a camera is only a starter. Besides, I wouldn't play with little stuff and compete with these big, established companies releasing on regular programs. Say, for the sake of argument, that we cooperate and go into this; all I'd handle would be features, - State's rights stuff. (Make big four-or-five reelers, and sell the rights in as many States as possible; that's what it amounts to.) But it isn't a thing to play with, boys. Let's do our joking about something else."

Rosemary set her two elbows upon the table, clasped her hands together, and dropped her chin upon them so that she was looking at Luck from under her eyebrows. That pose meant determination and an argumentative mood.

"I've been doing a little mental arithmetic," she began. "Also I've done a little thinking. I know now what spoiled that Great Western offer for you, Luck Lindsay. It was because they wouldn't take the boys too. And you turned it down because you - oh, they're the 'technical details,' young man! You see? Your eyes give you away. I knew it, once the idea popped into my head. What do you think of a fellow like that, boys? Refused a two-hundred-a-week position because he couldn't get you fellows a job too."

"That two hundred seems to worry you a good deal," Luck muttered, crimson to his collar.

"Now don't interrupt, because I shall keep right on talking just the same. I've a lot more to say. Do you realize that the donations these boys have made already amounts to over fifteen hundred dollars? And that does not include Happy Jack or Miguel, because they haven't - "

"Aw, gwan! I never had a chanct to git a word in edgeways," Happy hurriedly defended his seeming parsimony. "I'm willin' to chip in."

"Well, the point is this: Why not all put in what you can, and just go out where there are cattle, and make your Big Picture, Luck Lindsay? We could live in the country cheaper than we can here: and there wouldn't be anything to buy but grub, - just a bag of beans and some flour and coffee. I'd be willing to starve for the sake of making that Big Picture!"

"By gracious, there's our transportation money, too!" Andy broke another short silence. "Three hundred and fifty, right there in a lump."

"Let it stay transportation money, too!" Rosemary advised quickly. "It can transport you fellows to where Luck wants to make his picture."

They waited then for Luck to speak, but he was too busy thinking. On his shoulders would rest the responsibility of the outfit. On his word they would rely absolutely and without question. It was no light matter to lead these men into a venture which would take their time, more hard, heart-breaking work than they could possibly foresee, and the last dollar they possessed. He was sorely tempted to try it, but for their sakes he knew he must not let their enthusiasm sweep away his sober judgment. Had they owned but half his experience it would be different; but their very ignorance of the game hampered his decision.

"Well, boss, how about it?" Andy urged. "Are yuh game to try her a whirl? We haven't got much, but what we've got is yours if you want to tackle it. We'll be right with you - till hell's no bigger than a bullet ladle."

"That's just what holds me back. I'd certainly hate to lead you up against a losing proposition, boys. And if I went into it, I'd go in over my eyebrows; if I didn't make good I wouldn't have the price of a tag on a ten-cent sack of Bull Durham when I quit; so I couldn't pay you back - "

"Aw, thunder! Think we never set into a poker game in our lives? Think we're in the habit of hollerin' for our chips back when we lose? What's the matter with yuh, anyway?" cried Big Medicine wrathfully.

"Why, of course we share the risk of losing!" Rosemary scowled at him indignantly. "We'll go in over our eyebrows, too, - and stand on our toes long as we can, to keep our scalp locks showing above water!" Her brown eyes twinkled a swift glance around the table. "If you think these boys are quitters, Luck Lindsay, you just ought to have been around when they were hanging on to their homesteads! I could tell you things - "

"You say buying a camera is just a starter. How much do you figure it would cost to make our Big Picture? Cutting out salaries and all such little luxuries, what would the actual expenses be - making a rough guess?"

Weary leaned forward over his plate and forgot all about his tempting wedge of shortcake.

Luck pushed back his plate and smiled his smile. "For the Big Picture," he began, while the Happy Family leaned to listen, "there'd be the camera and outfit, - I could pick up some things second hand, - we'll call that fourteen hundred and fifty. Then there would be at least five thousand feet of film: perforated raw stock I could get for about three and three quarter cents a foot. Say a couple, of hundred dollars for that. We'd need at least three dozen radium flares for our night scenes; they cost close around twenty dollars a dozen. And one or two light diffusers, - that's just to get us started with an outfit, remember. Then there'd be our transportation to Albuquerque, New Mexico. I know that country, and I know what I can do there. I'd hit straight for a ranch I know between Bear Canyon and Rincon Arroyo - belongs to an old fellow that sure is a character, too, in his way. Old bachelor, he is; got some cattle and horses, and round-pole corrals and the like of that. I know old Applehead Forrman like I know my right hand; we'd make Applehead's place our headquarters - see? Exterior stuff we'd have right there, ready to shoot without any expense. As for interiors, - say! any of you fellows handy with hammer and saw?"

"By gracious, we all are!" Andy declared quickly. "We learned our little lessons when we were building claim shacks for ourselves."

"Good enough! You boys could be stage mechanics as well as leading men," Luck grinned. "Add hammers and saws to the outfit. We'd have to build a few interior sets."

Rosemary had her eyebrows tied in little knots, she was thinking so fast. "I'll write the Little Doctor that she can have my silver teaset," she informed Andy impulsively. "She offered me fifty dollars for it, you know. That would buy lots of beans!"

Luck looked at her, but he did not say what was in his mind. Instead he reached into an inner pocket and drew out his passbook, "I've got eighteen hundred and ninety-five dollars in the bank," he announced, reading the figures aloud. "And my car ought to bring three or four thousand, - if I can find the man that tried to buy it a month or so before I took the Injuns back. She's a pippin, boys! - "

"Oh, your lovely, big, white machine!" wailed Rosemary. "Would you have to sell it, Luck? Couldn't we squeak along without that?"

"Aw, you don't want to sell your car!" Pink protested. "I know where I can borrow two or three hundred. Maybe the Old Man - "

"We'll put this thing through alone, if we do it at all," Luck told him bluntly. "Can't afford to work with borrowed capital; the risk is too great. Sure, I'll sell the car. I was thinking of it, anyway," he testified falsely but reassuringly. "We'll need every cent I can raise. There's chemicals and Lord knows what all; and when we come to making our prints and marketing, why - " he threw out both hands expressively. "If we land in Albuquerque with five thousand dollars and our outfit, we won't have a cent to throw away. At that, we'll have to squeeze every nickel till it hollers, before we're through. Believe me, boys, this is going to be some undertaking!"

"Nice, comfortable way you've got of painting things cheerful," the Native Son drawled ironically.

"That's all right. I want you to realize what it's going to be like before you get in so far you can't back out."

"Aw, who's said anything about backing out?" Happy Jack grumbled.

"Let's get right down to brass tacks and see how strong we can go on money," Andy suggested, pulling a pencil out of an inner pocket. "Here, girl, you do the bookkeeping while we call off the size of our pile. Put 'er down in this book till you can get another one. You can set me down for two seventy-five - or make it three hundred. I can scrape it up, all right. How about you, Pink? This is hard-boiled figures, now, and no guess work."

Pink blew a mouthful of smoke while he did a little mental calculation. Then he took his twisted-leather purse and emptied it into his saucer. He investigated all his pockets and added eighty-five cents in small change. Then he gravely began to count, not disdaining three pennies in the pile. "I've got seventy-five dollars in the bank," he said. "Add ninety dollars salary, and you have a hundred and sixty-five. Add six dollars and eighty-seven cents, and you have - my pile."

Rosemary twisted her lips and wrote the figures opposite Pink's name. Next came Weary, then Miguel and Big Medicine and the dried little man who chewed violently upon a wooden toothpick and said he was good for eight hundred, and mebby a little mite more.

They pushed their plates to the table's center to make

B. M. Bower

room for their gesticulating hands and uneasy elbows while they planned ways and means. They argued over trivial points and left the big ones for Luck to settle. They talked of light effects and wholesale grocery lists and ray filters and smoke pots and railroad fares and the problem of cutting down their baggage so as to avoid paying excess charges. Luck, once he had taken the mental plunge into the deep waters of so hazardous an enterprise, began to exhibit a most amazing knowledge of the details of picture making.

To save money, he told them, he would be his own camera man. He could do without a "still" camera, because he would enlarge clippings from the different scenes in the negative instead. They'd have to manage the range stuff with only one camera, which would mean more work to get the various effects. But with a telephoto lens and a wide angle lens he could come pretty near putting it over the way he wanted it. "And there'll be no more blank ammunition, boys," he told them. "So you want to fit yourselves out with real shells. I'm not going very strong on this foreground bullet-effect stuff; we can afford to leave that for the Western four-flushers that can't do anything else. But she's some wild down where we'll be located, so we'll not be packing empty guns, at that.

"And there's another thing," he went on, talking and making notes at the same time. "If we're going to do this, we can't get started any too soon. We may be able to hit a late round-up and get some scenes, which will save rounding up stock ourselves for it. And there's all that winter stuff to make, too; we haven't any more time to throw away than we have money."

"Well, we're ready to hit the trail any time you are,"

Andy declared. "To-morrow, if yuh say so. You go ahead with your end of it, Luck, and I'll be straw boss here in camp and get the outfit packed and ready to ship outa here on an hour's notice. I can do it, too - believe me!"

"Do you know," said Rosemary, "I'd let James and Weary buy our winter's supplies and have them sent by freight right on to where we're going. Things are awfully cheap here. I'll make out a list, and the boys can attend to that to-morrow. And I'll bake up a lot of stuff for lunches on the train, too. We're not going to squander money in the dining car."

"Say, we'll just borry one of them dray teams from the Acme corral, by cripes, and haul our own stuff to the depot!" Big Medicine exclaimed with enthusiasm. "Save us four or five dollars right there!"

Luck rose and reached for his umbrella as though he had just recalled an important engagement. "I think I know where to find a buyer for my machine," he said, "so I'll just get on his trail. To-morrow I'll start getting my camera outfit together. Andy, I'll turn this end of the expedition over to you; that idea of getting food supplies here is all right, within certain limits. Don't buy any cheap, weighty stuff here, because the freight will eat up all you save. But I'll leave that to you folks; I guess you've had experience enough - "

"Considering most of us learned our *a-b-c's* outa Montgomery-Ward catalogues," Weary observed with a quirk of the lips, "I guess you can safely leave it to the bunch. Range kids are brought up on them Wind-river bibles, as we call mail order catalogues. I'll bet you I can give offhand the freight on anything you can name, from a hair hackamore to a gang plow."

"Fly at it, then," laughed Luck, with his hand on the doorknob. "I am going to be some busy myself. I'll just turn over the transportation problem to you folks. *Adios*."

"Prepare to ride in the chair car," Rosemary called after him warningly. "Even a tourist sleeper is going to be too luxurious for us; we're going to squeeze nickels till they just squeal!"

Luck held the door open while he smiled approvingly at her. "That'll be playing the game right from the start. *Adios*, folks."

CHAPTER TEN

UNEXPECTED GUESTS FOR APPLEHEAD

Applehead Forrman was worried over his cat, Compadre, which is Spanish for comrade or something of that sort. It was a blue cat and it was a big cat, and it had a bellicose disposition, and Applehead was anxious because it had lately declared war on a neighboring coyote and had not come out of the battle unscathed. Applehead had heard the disturbance and had gone out with a rifle and dispersed the coyote, but not until Compadre had lost half of his tail and a good deal of his self-assurance. Since that night, almost a week ago, Compadre had been a changed cat. He had sought dark corners and had yowled when the best friend he had in the world tried to coax him out to his meals. Applehead was very patient and very sympathetic, and hunted small game with which to tempt the invalid's appetite.

On this day he had a fat prairie dog which he had shot, and he was carrying it around by a hind leg looking for Compadre and calling "Kitty, kitty, kitty," in the most seductive tones of which his desert-harshened vocal chords were capable. He looked under the squat adobe cabin which held all the odds and ends that had accumulated about the place, and which he called the "ketch-all." He went over and looked under the water

B. M. Bower

tank where there was shade and coolness. He went to the stable, and from there he returned to the adobe house, squat like the "ketch-all" but larger. There was a hole alongside the fireplace chimney at the end next the hill, and sometimes when Compadre was especially disenchanted with his world, he went into the hole and nursed his grievances in dark seclusion under the house.

Applehead got down upon all fours and called "Kitty, kitty, kitty," with his face close to the hole. It was past noon, and Compadre had not had anything to eat since the night before, when he had lapped up half a saucer of canned milk and had apathetically licked a slice of bacon. Applehead put his ear to the hole and imagined he heard a faint meow from a far corner. He pushed the prairie dog into the aperture and called "Kitty-kitty-kitty" again coaxingly.

He was so absorbed in his anxious quest that he did not hear the chuckle of two wagons coming up through the sand to the corral. He did not even hear the footsteps of men approaching the house. He did not hear anything at all except a dismal yowl now and then from the darkness. He contorted his long person that he might peer into the gloom. He pushed the prairie dog in as far as he could reach. "Come, kitty-kitty-kitty!" he coaxed. "Doggone your onery soul, I'm gitting tired of this kinda performance! You can tromp on me just so fur and no further, now I'm a-tellin' yuh. That there tail of yourn needs a fresh rag tied to it, and some salve. But I ain't the burrowin' kind of animal, and I ain't comin' in under there after yuh. Come, kitty-kitty-kitty! Come on outa there 'fore I send a charge of birdshot in after yuh!" His voice changed to a tremulous chant of rising anger. "You wall-eyed, mangy, rat-eatin' son of a gun,

what have I been feedin' yuh fur all these years? You
come outa there! If it wasn't for the love uh God I got
in my heart, I'll fill yuh so full of holes the coyotes'll
have to make soup of ye! I'll sure spread yuh out so
thin your hide'll measure up like a mountain lion!
Don't yuh yowl at me like that! Come, kitty-kitty-
kitty - ni-ice kitty! Come to your old pard what
ketched yuh the fattest young dog on the flat for your
dinner. Come on, now; you ain't skeered uh me,
shorely! Come on, Compadre - ni-ice kitty!"

"Let me try!" cried Rosemary behind him, her voice
startling old Applehead so that he knocked his head
painfully on the rock foundation as he jerked himself
into a more dignified posture. His eyes widened at the
size of the audience grouped behind him, but he had
faced more amazing sights than that in his eventful
career. He got stiffly to his feet and bowed, the prairie
dog dangling limply from his hand.

"Howdy! Howdy! Pleased to meet yuh," he greeted
them dazedly. Then he spied Luck standing half behind
Weary's tall form, and his embarrassed smile changed
to a joyful grin. "Well, danged if it ain't Luck! How are
yuh, boy? I was jest thinkin' about you right this
morning. What wind blowed you into camp? Come
right on in, folks. If you're friends of Luck's, yuh don't
need no interduction in this camp. Luck and me's et
outa the same skillet months on end together. Come on
in. I've et, but they's plenty left." His blue eyes
twinkled quizzically over the Happy Family and then
went to Luck. "What yuh up to this time, boy? 'Nother
wild-west show?"

While they were waiting for coffee to boil, Luck told
him what he was up to this time. Told him what it was

he meant to do in the way of making a Western picture that should be worthy the West. He did not say a word about needing Applehead's assistance; he did not need to say a word about that. Applehead himself saw where he would fit into the scheme, and he seemed to take it for granted that Luck saw it also.

"Got all your stuff out from town?" he asked, while he was hunting cups enough to go around. "If yuh ain't, you can send a couple of the boys in with a four-horse team after dinner. I d'no about beds, unless yuh got your own beddin'-rolls with yuh. The missus, she can have a room, and the rest of yuh will have to knock some bunks together. Mebby we can clean out the 'ketch-all' and turn that into a bunk house. One I had, it burnt down last winter; some darn-fool Mexicans got to fightin' in there and kicked the lamp over. It could have a new roof put on, I reckon; the walls is there yet. You can take a look around after you eat, and see what all there is to do. Well, set up, folks; ain't much, but I've throwed my feet under the table fer less and was thankful to git it, now I'm a-tellin' yuh!"

Big Medicine bethought him of the remains of the train lunch which they had frugally saved. He brought that and added it to Applehead's impromptu meal. The sandwiches were mashed flat, and the pickles were limp, and the cake much inclined to crumble, but Applehead gave one look and took off his hat.

"I've et, but I can shore eat again when I git my eyes on cake," he declared exuberantly, and pulled an empty box up to the table for a seat. "I wisht Compadre could git a smell uh that there fried chicken; it would put new life into him, which he needs after tangling with that there coyote 'tother night."

"We ought to unhitch and give the horses a feed," Luck suggested. "Any particular place?"

"Well, you know where to put them cayuses as well as I do," Applehead mumbled, with his mouth full of cake. "I don't care what yuh do around the danged place. Go along and don't bother me, boy; I'm busy."

"Didn't I tell you how it would be?" Luck reminded Andy and Weary when they were outside. "That old boy is tickled to death to have us here. He sure is a type, too. I'll be using him in the picture. And just tale a look at that corral down there! We'll set up camp this afternoon and round up some horses, - Applehead always keeps a bunch running back here on the mesa, - and to-morrow morning we'll get to work. A couple of you will have to take these teams back this afternoon, too. I'll let you drive the four-horse in, Weary, and lead the other behind. And I'll send the Native Son in with Applehead's team and wagon, so you can haul out a thousand feet of lumber for a stage. Get it surfaced one side, - fourteen-foot boards, sabe? And about twenty-five pounds of eight-penny nails. We've got the tools in our outfit. I wonder which pasture Applehead's team is running in. I'll have one of the boys get them up, unless - "

"Luck Lindsay!" came Rosemary's high, clear treble. "Aren't you boys going to eat any dinner?"

"We'll eat when we have more time!" Luck shouted back. "Send Applehead out here, will you?"

Presently Applehead appeared with a large piece of cake in one hand and a well-picked chicken wing in the other. "What yuh want?" he inquired lazily, in the tone that implies extreme physical comfort.

"I want your big team to haul some lumber out from town. Where are they? If you don't mind catching them up while I help get this stuff unloaded, we'll have things moving around here directly."

"Shore I'll ketch 'em up fur ye, soon as I find Compadre and give him this here bone. He's been kinda off his feed since that coyote clumb his frame. He was under the house, but I reckon so many strange voices kinda got his goat. There ain't ary yowl to be got outa that hole no more. Come, kitty-kitty-kitty!"

Luck threw out his hands despairingly, and then laughed. Applehead's tender solicitude for his cat was a fixed characteristic of the man, and Luck knew there was no profit in argument upon the subject. He began unloading the lighter pieces of baggage while the boys fed the livery teams. The others came straggling down from the house, lighting their after-dinner cigarettes and glancing curiously at the adobe out-buildings which were so different from anything in Montana. The sagebrush slopes wore a comfortable air of familiarity, even though the boys were more accustomed to bunch grass; but an adobe stable was a novelty.

Fast as they came near him, Luck put them to work. There was plenty to do before they could even begin work on the Big Picture, but Luck seemed to have thought out all the details of camp-setting with the same attention to trifles which he had shown in the making of a picture. In half an hour he had every one busy, including old Applehead, who, having located Compadre in the stable loft and left the chicken wing at the top of the ladder, had saddled his horse and gone off into a far pasture to bring in all the horses down there, so that Luck could choose whatever animals he wished to use. Dave Wiswell, the dried little man, was helping Rosemary wash the dishes and put away the food supplies they had brought out with them, as fast as Happy Jack could carry them up from the wagon. Andy Green was ruthlessly emptying the only closet - a roomy one, fortunately - in the house, and tacking up black paper which Luck had brought, so that it might serve as a dark room. Big Medicine and Pink were clearing out the one-roomed adobe cabin which Applehead called the "ketch-all," so that the boys could sleep there until the bunk-house was repaired.

Luck was unpacking his camera and swearing softly to himself while he set it up, and wishing that his experience as assistant camera-man was not quite so far in the past. He foresaw difficulties with that camera until he got in practice, but he did not say anything about it to the others. He got it together finally, put in the two-hundred-foot magazine of negative that he had brought with him to use while waiting for his big order to arrive, made a few light tests, and went up to the house to see if Andy had the dark room dark enough.

He found Andy defending himself as best he could from a small domestic storm. In his anxiety to have that dark room fixed just the way Luck wanted it, Andy had purloined a shelf which Rosemary needed, and which she meant to have, if words could restore it to its place behind the kitchen stove. Andy had the shelf down and was taking out bent nails with a new hammer when Luck came to the door with his arms full of packages of chemicals and a ruby lamp.

B. M. Bower

"What can a fellow do?" Andy was inquiring plaintively. "There ain't another board on the place that's the right width. I looked. Luck's got to have a shelf; you don't expect him to keep all his junk on the floor, do you? I'm sorry, but I've just got to have it, girl."

"You've just got to put that shelf back, Andy. Where do you expect me to put things? There isn't a pantry on the place, and only that one dinky little cupboard over there. I can't keep my dishes on the floor, and cooking is going to be pretty important, itself, around this camp!"

"Soon as the lumber gets here, I'll have Andy build you a cupboard," Luck soothed her. "You haven't got many conveniences here, and that's a fact. But we'll get things straightened out, *pronto*. Got any bones or scraps left, Mrs. Andy? That little black dog that followed us out is here yet. He didn't go back with the boys. I found him curled up in the wagon shed just now; poor little devil looks about starved. His ribs stand out worse than a cow that's wintered on a sheep range."

With Rosemary's attention diverted to the little black dog, Andy got the shelf nailed firmly upon the wall of the dark room. And immediately Luck proceeded to use it to its fullest capacity and announced that he needed another one, whereat Andy groaned.

"Say, I'm a brave man, all right, but I don't dare to swipe any more shelves," he protested. "Not from my wife, anyway. Timber must sure be scarce in this man's country. I never did see a place so shy of boards as this ranch is."

"Well, let's see if there are any barrels," said Luck. "I've been studying on how to rig up some way to develop my film. If we can find some half barrels and knock the heads out, I can wind the negative around them with the emulsion side out, and dip it in the bigger barrels of developer; see how I mean? Believe me, this laboratory problem is going to be a big one till I can see my way to getting tanks and film racks out here. But I believe barrels will work all right. And, say! There's some old hose I saw out by the windmill tank; you get that, and see if you can't run it under the house and up through a hole in the floor. I expect it leaks in forty places, but maybe you can mend it. And we ought to have some way to run the water out in a trough or something. You see what you can do about that, Andy, while I go and unpack the rest of my camera outfit. There's a garret up over the ceiling, here, and you'll have to see what shape it's in for drying film. Stop all the cracks so dust can't blow in. I want to start taking scenes to-morrow morning, you know. I've got two hundred feet of raw stock to work with till the other gets here. I've got to develop my tests before to-morrow so I'll know what I'm doing. I can't afford to spoil any film."

"Well, hardly," Andy agreed. "By gracious, I hope you're making the rest of the bunch hump themselves, too. Honest, I'd die if I saw anybody sitting around in the shade, right now!"

"Andy, did you go and take that shelf after all?" came the reproachful voice of Rosemary from the kitchen, and Luck retreated by way of the front door without telling Andy just how busy the other boys were.

The "ketch-all," where Big Medicine and Pink were

clearing out the accumulation of years, was enveloped in a cloud of dust. Down in the corral a dozen horses were circling, with Applehead moving cautiously about in the middle dragging his loop and making ready for a throw. There was one snuffy little bay gelding that he meant to turn over to Luck for a saddle horse, and he wanted to get him caught and in the stable before showing him to Luck. Happy Jack was wobbling up the path with an oversized sack of potatoes balanced on his shoulder, and his face a deep crimson from the heat and his exertions. Down in the stable the little black dog, enlivened by the plate of bones Rosemary had given him, had scented the cat in the loft and was barking hysterically up the ladder.

Luck stepped out briskly, cheered by the atmosphere of bustling preparation which surrounded him. That he was the moving spirit which directed all these activities stimulated him like good old wine. It was for his Big Picture that they were preparing. Already his brain was at work upon the technique of picture production, formulating a system which should as far as possible eliminate the risk of failure because of the handicaps under which he must work.

Having to be his own camera-man, and to work without an assistant, piled high the burden of work and responsibility; but he could not afford to pay the salaries such assistants would demand. He had a practical knowledge of camera craft, since he had worked his way up through all branches of the game, and he was sure that with practice he could do the photographic work. He hoped to teach Andy enough about it so that he could help; Andy seemed to have an adaptability superior to some of the others and would learn the rudiments readily, Luck believed.

The lack of a leading woman was another handicap. He could not afford to hire one, and he could not very well weave a love story into his plot without a woman. He was going to try Rosemary, since her part would consist mostly of riding in and out of scenes and looking pretty, - at least in the earlier portion. And by the time he was ready to produce the dramatic scenes, he hoped that she would be able to act the part. It was a risk, of course, and down deep in his heart he feared that much of her charm would never reach the screen; but he must manage somehow, since there would be no money to spend on salaries. He ought to have a character woman, too, - which he lacked.

But other things he did have, and they were the things that would count most for success or failure. He had his real boys, for instance; and he had his real country; and, last and most important of all, he had his story to tell. In spite of his weariness, Luck was almost happy that first afternoon at Applehead's ranch. He went whistling about his task of directing the others and doing two men's work himself, and he refused to worry about anything.

That evening after supper, when they were all smoking and resting before Applehead's big rock fireplace, Luck's energy would not let him dwell upon the trivial incidents of their trip, which the Happy Family were discussing with reminiscent enjoyment. Applehead's booming laugh was to Luck as a vague accompaniment to his own thoughts darting here and there among his plans.

"Aw, gwan!" Happy Jack was exclaiming in his habitual tone of protest. "Conductor lied to me, is how I come to be over to that place when the train started to pull out. I was buyin' something. I wasn't talking to no Mexican girl. I betche - "

"Now, while we're all together," Luck broke suddenly into Happy's explanation, "I'm just going over the scenario from start to finish and assign your parts. Applehead, I'm going to cast you for the sheriff. You won't need to do any acting at all - "

"We-ell, if I do, I calc'late I got some idee uh how a shurf had oughta ack," Applehead informed him with a boastful note in his voice, and pulled himself up straighter in his chair. "I was 'lected shurf uh this county four different terms right hand runnin', and if I do say it, they wasn't nobody ever said I didn't do my duty. Ary man I went after, I come purty near bringin' him into camp, now I'm tellin' ye! This here old girl has shore talked out in meetin', in her time, and there wasn't ary man wanted to face her down in an argument, now I'm tellin' ye." He got up and took his old six-shooter off the mantel and held it lovingly in his palm. Very solemnly he licked his thumb and polished a certain place along the edge of the yellow ivory handle, and held it so the Happy Family could see three tiny notches.

"Them's three argyments she shore settled," he stated grimly, and turned slowly upon Luck.

"Yes-s, I calc'late I can play shurf for ye, all right enough."

Luck looked up at him with his eyes shining, remembering how staunch a friend Applehead had been in times past, and how even his boastings were but a naive recognition of facts concerning himself.

Applehead Forrman was fifty-six years old, but Luck could not at that moment recall a man more dangerous to meet as an enemy or more loyal to have as a friend.

"I calc'late you can," he agreed in his soft, friendly drawl. "Sit down and turn your good ear this way, Applehead, so this story can soak in. You'll see where you come in as sheriff, and you'll sabe just what you'll have to do. Bud, here, will be the outlaw that blows into the cow-camp and begins to mix things. He's the one you'll have to settle. So here's the way the story runs:"

"Say, boss, make it short and sweet, can't you?" Andy begged. He was sitting on the floor with his head against Rosemary's knees, and his eyelids were drooping drowsily. "By gracious, nobody'll have to sing me to sleep to-night! I'm about ready to hit the hay right now."

"I'll cut out the atmosphere and just stick to the action, then," Luck conceded. "I want to get you all placed, so we can get to work in the morning without any delay. *Sabe*?"

"Shoot," murmured Pink, opening his eyes with some effort "I can listen for five minutes, maybe."

"I can't, I don't believe," the Native Son yawned. "But go ahead, *amigo*. My heart's with you, anyway, whether my eyes are open or shut."

Luck was pretty sleepy himself, after two nights and a day spent in a chair car, with another day of hard labor to finish the ordeal. But his enthusiasm had never been keener than when, in the land of sage and cactus, he first unfolded his precious scenario and bent forward to read by the light of the fire. He forgot to skip the "atmosphere." Scene by scene he lived the story through. Scene by scene he saw his Big Picture grow vivid as ever the reality would be. Once or twice he glanced up and saw Applehead leaning forward with his elbows on his knees and his pipe gone cold in his fingers, absorbed, living the story even as Luck lived it.

A long, rumbling snore stopped him with a mental jolt. He came back to reality and looked at the Happy Family. Every one of them, save Rosemary, was sound asleep; and even Rosemary was dreaming at the fire with her eyes half closed, and her fingers moving caressingly through the unconscious Andy's brown hair.

"Let 'em be. You go ahead and read it out," Applehead muttered, impatient of the pause.

So Luck, with his audience dwindled to one bald-headed old rangeman, read the story of what he meant to create out there in the wild spaces of New Mexico.

CHAPTER ELEVEN

JUST A FEW UNFORESEEN OBSTACLES

It is surprising how much time is consumed by the little things of life, - unimportant in themselves, yet absolutely necessary to a satisfactory accomplishment of the big things. Luck, looking ahead into the next day, confidently expected to be making scenes by the time the light was right, - say nine o'clock in the morning. He had chosen several short, unimportant scenes, such as the departure of old Dave Wiswell, his cattleman of the picture, from the ranch; his return, and the saddling of horses and riding away of the boys. Also he meant to make a scene of the arrival of the sheriff after having received word of the presence of Big Medicine, the outlaw, at the ranch. Rosemary, too, as the daughter of old Dave, must run down to the corral to meet her father. Scattered scenes they were, occurring in widely separated parts of the story. But they had to be made, and they required no especial "sets" of scenery; and other work, such as the building of the stage for interior sets, could go on with few interruptions. The boys would have to work in their make-up, but since the make-up was to be nothing more than a sharpening of the features to make them look absolutely natural upon the screen, it would not be uncomfortable. This was what Luck had planned for that day.

Before breakfast he had selected a site for his stage, on the sunny side of the hill back of the house, where it would be partially sheltered from the sweeping winds of New Mexico. All day he would have the sun behind him while he worked, and he considered the situation an ideal one. He had the lumber hauled up there and unloaded, while Rosemary and Applehead were cooking breakfast for ten hungry people. He laid out his foundation and explained to the boys just how it should be built, and even sacrificed his appetite to his impatience by going a quarter of a mile to where he remembered seeing some old barbed wire strung along a fence to keep it off the ground so that stock could not tangle in it. He got the wire and brought it back with him to guy out the uprights for the diffusers. So on the whole he began the day as well as even he could desire.

Then little hindrances began to creep in to delay him. For one thing, the Happy Family had only a comedy acquaintance with grease paint, and their make-up reminded Luck unpleasantly of Bently Brown's stories. As they appeared one by one, with their comically crooked eyebrows and their rouge-widened lips and staring, deep-shadowed eyes, Luck sent them back to take it all off and start over again under his supervision. The outcome was that he gave a full hour to making up the faces of his characters and telling them how to do it themselves. Even Rosemary made her brows too heavy and her lips too red, and her cheeks were flushed unevenly. Luck was a busy man that morning, but he was not taking scenes by nine o'clock, for all his haste.

With a kindly regard for Rosemary's nervousness lest she fail him, he set up his camera and told her to walk down part way to the corral, looking - supposedly - to see if her dad had come home. She must stand there irresolutely, then turn and walk back toward the camera, registering the fact that she was worried. That sounds simple enough, doesn't it?

What Luck most wanted was to satisfy himself as to whether Rosemary could possibly play the part of old Dave's daughter. If she could, he would sleep sounder that night; if she could not, - Luck was not at all clear as to what he should do if she failed. He told her just where to walk into the "scene," which is the range of the camera. He went down part way to the corral and drew a line with his toe, and told her to stop when she reached that line and to look away up the trail which wound down among the rocks and sage. When he called to her she was to turn and walk back, trying to imagine that she was much worried and disappointed.

"Your dad was to have come last night," Luck suggested. "You tried to keep him from going in the first place, and now we've got to establish the fact that he is away behind time getting home. You know, this is where his horse falls with him, and he lies out all night, and Big Medicine brings him in next day. You kind of have a hunch that something is wrong, and you keep looking for him. Sabe." He fussed with the camera, adjusting it to what seemed to him the right focus. "Want to rehearse it first?" he added considerately.

"No," Rosemary gasped, "I don't. I know how to walk, and how to turn around and come back. I've been doing those things for twenty-two years or so, but Luck Lindsay, if you don't let me do it right away quick, I just know I'll stub my toe and fall down, or something!" The worst of it was, she meant what she said. Rosemary, I am sorry to say, was so scared that her teeth chattered.

"All right, you go on and do it now," Luck permitted, and began to turn the crank at seventeen in order to hold her action slow, while he watched her. Groaning inwardly, he continued to turn, while Rosemary went primly down the winding trail, stood with her toes on the line Luck had marked for her, gazed stiffly off to the right, and then, when he called to her, turned and came back, staring fixedly over his head. You have seen little girls with an agonized self-consciousness walk up an aisle to a platform where they must bow to their fathers and mothers and their critical schoolmates and "speak a piece." Rosemary resembled the most bashful little girl that you can recall.

"All right," said Luck tonelessly, and placed his palm over the lens while he gave the crank another turn. "We'll try it again to-morrow. Don't worry. You'll get the hang of it all right."

His very smile, meant to encourage her, brought swift tears that rolled down and streaked the powder and rouge on her cheeks. She had made a mess of it all; she knew that just as well as Luck knew it. He gave her shoulder a reassuring pat as she went by, and that finished Rosemary. She retreated into the gloomy, one-windowed bedroom with its litter of half-unpacked suitcases and an overflowing trunk, and she cried heartbrokenly because she knew she would never in this world be able to forget that terrible, winking eye and the clicking whirr of Luck's camera. Just to think of facing it gave her a "goose-flesh" chill, - and she did so want to help Luck!

With the Happy Family and old Dave, Luck fared better. They, fortunately for him, were already what he called camera-broke. They could forget all about the camera while they caught and saddled their horses. They could mount and ride away unconcernedly without even thinking of trying to act. Luck's spirits rose a little while he turned the crank, and just for pure relief at the perfect naturalness of it, he gave that scene an extra ten feet of footage.

With Applehead he had some difficulty. Applehead looked the part of sheriff, all right. He wore his trousers tucked inside his boots because he always wore them so, especially when he rode. He wore his big six-shooter buckled snugly about his middle instead of dangling far down his thigh, because he had always worn it that way. He wore his sheriffs badge pinned on his vest and his coat unbuttoned, so that the wind blew it open now and then and revealed the star. Altogether he looked exactly as he had looked when he was serving one of his four terms of office. But when he faced the camera, he was inclined to strut, and Luck had no negative to waste. He resorted to strategy, which consisted of a little wholesome sarcasm.

"Listen, Applehead! the public is going to get the idea that you sure hate yourself!" he remarked, standing with his hands on his hips while Applehead came strutting into the foreground. "You'll never make any one believe you were ever a real, honest-to-God sheriff. They'll put you down as an extra picked up through a free employment agency and feeling like you owned the plant because you're earning a couple of dollars. Go back down there to your horse and wait till some of that importance evaporates!"

Applehead went off swearing to himself, and Luck got a fifteen-foot scene of the departure of a very indignant sheriff who is with difficulty holding his anger subordinate to his official dignity. Before he had time to recover his usual good humor, Luck with further disparaging comment called him back. Applehead, smarting under the sarcasm, came ready for war, and Luck turned the crank until the sheriff was almost within reach of him.

"Gol darn you, Luck, I'll take that there camery and bust it over your danged head!" he spluttered. "I'll show ye! Call me a bum that's wearin' a shurf's star fer the first time in his life, will ye! Why, I'll jest about wear ye out if - "

"All right, pard; I was just aiming to make you come up looking mad. You did fine." Luck stopped to roll a smoke as though nothing had occurred but tiresome routine.

Applehead looked down at him uncertainly. He looked at the Happy Family, saw them grinning, and gave a mollified chuckle. "We-ell, you was takin' a danged long chance, now I'm tellin' yuh, boy!" he warned. "I was all set to tangle with yuh; and if I had, I reckon I'd a spiled something 'fore I got through."

It was noon by the sun, and a film of haze was spreading across the sky. Luck shot another scene or two and shouldered his precious camera reluctantly, when Rosemary, red-lidded but elaborately cheerful in her manner, called them in to dinner.

"She's goin' to storm, shore's you live," Applehead predicted, sniffing into the wind like a dog confronted by a strange scent. A little later he looked up from his full plate with a worried air. "How's a storm goin' to hit ye, Luck?" he asked. "Kinda put a stop to the pitcher business, won't it?"

"Not if it snows, it won't," Luck answered calmly, helping himself to the brown beans boiled with bacon. "We'll round up a bunch of cattle, and I'll shoot my blizzard stuff. I'll need more negative, though, for that. If I knew for sure it's going to storm - "

"I'm tellin' yuh it is, ain't I?" Applehead blew into his saucer of coffee, - his table manners not being the nicest in the world. "I kin smell snow two days off, and that there wind comin' up the canyon has got snow behind it, now I'm tellin' ye. 'Nother thing, I kin tell by the way Compadre walks, liftin' his feet high and bushin' up what's left of his tail. That there cat's smarter'n some humans, and he shore kin smell snow comin', same's I do. He hates snow worse'n pizen." Applehead drank his coffee in great gulps. "I'll bet he's huntin' a warm corner somewheres, right now."

"No, he ain't, by cripes!" Big Medicine corrected him. "That there Come-Paddy cat of yourn has got worse troubles than snow! Dog's got him treed up the windmill. I seen - "

Applehead did not wait to hear what Big Medicine had seen. He drank the remainder of his coffee in one great, scalding gulp, and went out to rescue his cat and to put the fear of death into the little black dog. When he returned, puffing a little, to his interrupted meal and had told them a few of the things he meant to do to that dog if it refused to mend its ways, he declared again that he could "shore smell snow behind that wind."

"I wish it would hold off till that raw stock gets here," Luck observed anxiously. "I wired the order in, but at that I'm afraid it won't get here before the end of the week. I'll have one of you boys pack me some water into the dark room so I can develop negatives right after dinner. I want to see how she's coming out before I take any more."

"I thought Andy'd fixed a hose fer that dark room," Happy Jack said forebodingly. If there was water to be carried, Happy was pessimistically certain that he would have to carry it.

"I turned that hose over to the missus for a colander," Andy explained soberly. "By gracious, I couldn't figure out anything else it could be used for."

"Did you get the barrels fixed like I said?"

"I sure did. Applehead must have had a Dutch picnic or two out here, from the number of beer kegs scattered all over the place. And a couple of big whisky - "

"Them there whisky bar'ls I bought and used fer water bar'ls till I got my well bored. Luck kin mind the time when we hauled water on a sled outa the arroyo down below." Applehead's eyes turned anxiously to Rosemary, toward whom he was beginning to show a timidly worshipful attitude.

"You bet I can. Do you remember the time we hitched that big bronk up with old Wall-eye, to haul water? Got back here a little ways beyond the stable with two barrels sloshing over the top, and the cat - not this one, but a black-and-white cat, that was - the cat jumped out from behind a buck brush. *Hot dog!* That bronk went straight in the air! Remember that time?" Luck leaned back in his chair to laugh.

"I shore do," Applehead chuckled. "Luck, here, he was walkin' behind the sled and drivin', - and he wasn't as big as he is now, even. That was soon after he come out here to fatten up like. Little bit of a peaked - why, I bet he didn't weigh over a hundred pounds after a full meal! He was ridin' the lines an' steadyin' the bar'ls, busy as a dog at a badger hole, when the cat jumped out, an' that there bronk r'ared back and swung off short and hit fur the mesa; and Luck here a-hangin' and hollerin', an' me a-leggin' it to ketch up, and bar'ls teeterin' and - Mind how you was bound you'd kill that cat uh mine?" he asked Luck, tears of laughter dimming his eyes. "That was ole Leather Lungs. He tuk sick an' died, year after that. Luck shore was mad enough to eat that thar cat, now I'm tellin' yuh!"

The Happy Family laughed together over the picture Applehead had crudely painted for them. But Luck, although he had started the story, already was slipping away from the present and was trying to peer into the future. He did not even hear what Applehead was saying to keep the boys in a roar of mirth. He was mentally reckoning the number of days since he had wired his order for a C.O.D. shipment of negative to be rushed to Albuquerque. Two days in Los Angeles, getting ready for the venture; two days on the way to Applehead's ranch, one day here, - five days altogether. He had told them to rush the order. If they did, there was a chance that it might have arrived. He decided suddenly to make the trip and see; but first he would develop the exposed negative of the forenoon's work. He got up with that businesslike air which the Happy

B. M. Bower

Family had already begun to recognize as a signal for quick action, and took off his coat.

"Happy, I wish you and Bud would carry me some water," he said. "I'll show you where to put it; I'm going to need a lot. Will you help me wind the film on my patent rack, Andy? And I'll want that little team hitched to the buckboard so I can go to town after I'm through. I've got some hopes of my negative being there."

"Want the rest of us to work on that stage, don't you, boss?" Weary asked, pausing in the doorway to roll a smoke. "And please may I wipe off my eyebrows?"

"Why, sure! - to both questions," answered Luck, going over to his camera. "I can't do much more till I get more negative, even with the light right, which it isn't. You go ahead and finish the stage this afternoon. And be sure the uprights are guyed for a high wind; she sure can blow, in this man's country."

"You're danged right, she can blow!" Applehead testified emphatically. "She can blow, and she's goin' to blow. You want to take your overshoes and mittens, boy, when you start out fer town. You know how cold she can get on that mesa. Chances are you'll come back facin' a blizzard. And, say! I wisht you'd take that there dog back with yuh, Luck, 'cause if yuh don't, him and me's shore goin' to tangle, now I'm tellin' yuh! Mighty funny note when a cat dassent walk acrost his own dooryard in broad daylight, no more! Poor ole Compadre was shakin' like a leaf when I clumb up and got him down of'n the windmill. Way the wind was whistlin' up there, the chances are he's done ketched cold in 'is tail, and if he has, yuh better see to it that thar dog ain't within gunshot uh me, now I'm tellin' yuh!"

Luck did not hear half the tirade. He had gone into the dark room and was dissolving hypo for the fixing bath, while the boys tramped in with full water buckets and began to fill the barrels he had placed in a row along the wall. He was impatient to see how his work of the forenoon would come out of the developer, and he was quite as impatient to be on his way to town. Whether he admitted it or not, he had a good deal of faith in Applehead's weather forecasts; he remembered how often the old fellow had predicted storms in the past when Luck spent a long winter with him here in this same adobe dwelling. If it did snow, he must have plenty of negative for his winter scenes; for snow never laid long on the level here, and he had a full reel of winter stuff to make.

He called Andy to come and help him wind his exposed film on the crude, improvised film racks that had lately been beer kegs, and closed the dark room door upon the last empty bucket that had been carried in full. In the dull light of the ruby lamp he carefully wound his long strip of exposed negative, emulsion side out, around the keg which Andy held for him. His developer bath was ready, and he immersed the film-jacketed keg slowly, with due regard for bubbles of air.

"You may not know it, but right here in this dark room is where I look for the real test of success or failure," he confided to Andy, while he rocked the keg gently in the barrel. "I wish I could afford a good camera-man; but then, the most of them wouldn't work with this kind of an outfit; they'd demand all the laboratory conveniences, and that would run into money. Ever notice that when you can't get anything but the crudest kind of tools to work with, you generally have to use them yourself? But it will take more than - oh, *hell*!"

"What's wrong?" Andy Green bent his brown head anxiously down beside Luck's fast graying mop of hair, and peered at the images coming out of the yellowish veil that had hidden them. "Ain't they good?"

Luck reached into the water tank and splashed a little water on his film to check it while he looked. "Now, what in the name of - " He scowled perplexedly down at the streaked strips. "What do you suppose streaked it like that?" He lifted worried, gray eyes to Andy's apprehensive frown, and looked again disgustedly at the negative before he dropped it back with a splash into the developer.

"No good; she's ruined," he said in the flat tone of a great disappointment. "Eighty feet of film gone to granny. Well, that's luck for you!"

Andy reached gingerly into the barrel and brought up the keg so that he could take another look. He had owned a kodak for years and had done enough amateur developing to know that something had gone very wrong here.

"What ails the darned thing?" he asked fretfully, turning to Luck, who was scowling abstractedly into his barrels of "soup."

"You can search me," Luck replied dully. "Looks like I'd been stung with a bunch of bum chemicals. Either that, or something's wrong with our tanks here." He reached down and pulled up the keg by its hooped top, glimpsed a stain on his finger and thumb and let the keg slip hastily over into the pure water so that he could examine the stains.

"Iron! Iron, sure as thunder!" he exclaimed suddenly. "Those iron hoops are what did it." He rubbed his hand vexedly. "I knew better than that, too. I don't see why I didn't think about those hoops. Of all the idiotic, fool - "

"What kinda brain do you think you've got in your head, anyway?" Andy broke in spiritedly. "Way you've been working it lately, engineering every blamed detail yourself, you oughtn't to wonder if one little thing gets by you."

"Well, it's done now," Luck dismissed the accident stoically. "Lucky I started in on those costume and make-up tests of all you fellows, and that scene of your wife's. And if I'd used the other half barrel instead of this five-gallon keg for a start-off, I'd have spoiled the whole bunch. I'll have to throw out all that developer. Blast the luck! Well, let's get busy." He pulled out the keg and held it up for another disgusted look. "I won't bother fixing that at all. Call Happy and Bud back, will you, and have them roll this barrel of developer out and ditch it? And then take those two half barrels you were going to fix, and wrap them with clothesline, - that cotton line on one of the trunks, - and knock off all the hoops. I'm going to beat it to 'Querque and see if that stuff's there. We'll try developing the rest this evening, after I get back. Darn such luck!"

The five thousand feet of negative had not arrived, but there was a letter from the company saying that they had shipped it. Luck, bone-tired and cold from his fifteen-mile drive across the unsheltered mesa, turned away from the express office, debating whether to wait for the film or go back to the ranch. It would be a pretty cold drive back, in the edge of the evening and facing that raw wind; he decided that he would save time by waiting here in town, since he could not go on with his picture without more negative. He turned back impulsively, put his head in at the door of the express office, and called to the clerk:

"When do you get your next express from the East, brother? I'll wait for that negative if you think it's likely to come by to-morrow noon or there-abouts."

"Might come in on the eight o'clock train to-night, or to-morrow morning. You say it was shipped the sixteenth? Ought to be here by morning, sure."

"I'll take a chance," Luck said half to himself, and closed the door.

A round-shouldered, shivering youth, who had been leaning apathetically against the side of the building, moved hesitatingly up to him. "Say, do I get it right that you're in the movies?" he inquired anxiously. "Heard you mention looking for negative. Haven't got a job for a fellow, have you?"

Luck wheeled and looked him over, from his frowsy, soft green beaver hat with the bow at the back, to his tan pumps that a prosperous young man would have thrown back in the closet six weeks before, as being out of season. The young man grinned his understanding of the appraisement, and Luck saw that his teeth were well-kept, and that his nails were clean and trimmed carefully. He made a quick mental guess and hit very close to the fellow's proper station in life and his present predicament.

"What end of the business do you know?" he asked, turning his face toward the warmth of the hotel.

"Operator. Worked two years at the Bijou in Cleveland. I'm down on my luck now; thought I'd try the California studios, because I wanted to learn the camera, and I figured on getting a look at the Fair. I stalled around out there till my money gave out, and then I started back to God's country." He shrugged his shoulders cynically. "This is about as far as I'm likely to get, unless I can learn to do without eating and a few other little luxuries," he summed up the situation grimly.

"Well, it won't hurt you to skip a lesson and have dinner with me," Luck suggested in the offhand way that robbed the invitation of the sting of charity. "I always did hate to eat alone."

The upshot of the meeting was that, when Luck gathered up the lines, next day, and popped the short lash of Applehead's home-made whip over the backs of the little bay team, and told them to "Get outa town!" in a tone that had in it a boyish note of exultation, the thin youth hung to the seat of the bouncing buckboard and wondered if Luck really could drive, or if he was half "stewed" and only imagined he could. The thin youth had much to learn besides the science of photography and some of it he learned during that fifteen-mile drive. For one thing, he learned that really Luck could drive. Luck proved that by covering the fifteen miles in considerably less than an hour and a

B. M. Bower

half without losing any of his precious load of boxed negative and coiled garden hose and assistant camera-man, - since that was what he intended to make of the thin youth.

CHAPTER TWELVE

"I THINK YOU NEED INDIAN GIRL FOR PICTURE"

Still it did not snow, though the wind blew from the storm quarter, and Applehead sniffed it and made predictions, and Compadre went with his remnant of tail ruffed like a feather boa. Immediately after supper Luck attached his new hose to the tank faucet and developed the corral scenes which he had taken, with the thin youth taking his first lesson in the dark room. The thin youth, who said his name was Bill Holmes, did not have very much to say, but he seemed very quick to grasp all that Luck told him. That kept Luck whistling softly between sentences, while they wound the negative around the roped half barrel that had not so much as a six penny nail in it this time, so thoroughly did Andy do his work.

The whistling ceased abruptly when Luck examined his film by the light of the ruby lamp, however, for every scene was over-exposed and worthless. Luck realized when he looked at it that the light was much stronger than any he had ever before photographed by, and that he would have to "stop down" hereafter; the problem was, how much. His light tests, he remembered, had been made rather late in the afternoon, when the light was getting yellow, and he had blundered in forgetting that the forenoon light was not the same.

He went ahead and put the film through the fixing bath and afterwards washed it carefully, more for the practice and to show Bill Holmes how to handle the negative than for any value the film would have. He discovered that Andy had not unpacked the rewinding outfit, but since he would not need it until his negative was dry, he made no comment on the subject. Bill Holmes kept at his heels, helping when he knew what to do, asking a question now and then, but silent for the most part. Luck felt extremely optimistic about Bill Holmes, but for all that he was depressed by his second failure to produce good film. A camera-man, he felt in his heart, might be the determining factor for success; but he was too stubborn to admit it openly or even to consider sending for one, even if he could have managed to pay the seventy-five dollars a week salary for the time it would take to produce the Big Picture. He could easier afford to waste a few hundred feet of negative now, he argued to himself.

"Come on down, and I'll show you what I can about the camera," he said to Bill Holmes. "The light's too tricky to-day to work by, but I'll give you a few pointers that you'll have to keep in mind when I'm too busy to think about telling you. Once I get to directing a scene, I'm liable to be busy as a one-armed prospector fighting a she-bear with cubs. I'm counting on you to remember what all I'va told you, in case I forget to tell you again. You see, I've ruined a hundred and fifty feet of negative already, just by overlooking a couple of bets. You're here to help keep that from happening again. *Sabe*?"

"Well, there's one or two things I don't have to learn," Bill Holmes told him by way of encouragement. "You get the camera set and ready, and I can turn it any speed you want. I'll guarantee that much. I learned that all right in projection."

"That's exactly why I brought you out here, brother," Luck assured him. "That's why - "

"Oh, Luck Lindsay!" came Rosemary's voice excitedly. "Mr. Forrman wants you right away quick! Somebody's coming that he doesn't know, and he says it's up to you!"

"What's up to me?" Luck came hurrying down the ladder backwards. "Has Applehead gone as crazy as his cat? I've nothing to do with strangers coming to the ranch."

"Yes," said Rosemary, twinkling her brown eyes at him, "but this is a woman. Mr. Forrman refuses to take any responsibility - "

"So do I. I don't know of any woman that's liable to come trailing me up. Where is she?"

From the doorway Rosemary pointed dramatically, and Luck went up and stood beside her, rolling down his sleeves while he stared at the trail. Down the slope, head bent to the whooping wind, a woman came walking with a free, purposeful stride that spoke eloquently of accustomedness to the open land. Her skirts flapped but could not impede her movements. She seemed to be carrying some bright-hued burden upon her shoulders, and she was, without doubt, coming straight down to the ranch as to a much-desired goal.

"You can search me," he said emphatically in answer to Applehead's question. "Must be some *senora* away off the trail. I never saw her before in my life."

"We-ell, now, that there lady don't act like she's lost," Applehead declared, watching her intently as she came on. "Aims to git whar she's goin', if I'm any jedge of actions. An' she shore is hittin' fur here. Ain't been ary woman on this ranch in ten year, till Mrs. Green come t'other day."

"She's none of my funeral; I don't know her from Adam," Luck disclaimed, and went back into the dark room as though be had urgent business there, which he had not. In the back of his mind was an uneasy feeling that the newcomer was "some of his funeral," and yet he could not tell how or why she should be. In her walk there was a teasing sense of familiarity; he did not know who she was, but he felt uncomfortably that he ought to know. He fumbled among the litter on the shelf, putting things in order; and all the while his ears were sharpened to the sounds that came muffled through the closed door.

"Oh, Luck Lindsay!" came Rosemary's voice at last, with what Luck fancied was a malicious note in it. "You're wanted out here!"

Luck fumbled for a minute longer while he racked his brain for some clue to this woman's identity. For a man who has lived the varied life Luck had lived, his conscience was remarkably clean; but no one enjoys having mystery stalk unawares up to one's door. However, he opened the door and went out, feeling sensitively the curious expectancy of the Happy Family, and faced the woman who stood just beyond the doorway. One look, and he stopped dead still in the middle of the room. "Well, I'll be darned!" he said in a hushed tone of blank amazement.

The woman's black eyes lighted as though flames had darted up behind them. "How, *Cola*?" she greeted him in the soft, cooing tones of the younger Indians whose voices have not yet grown shrill and harsh. "Wagalexa Conka!" It was the tribal name given him in great honor by his Indians of Pine Ridge Agency.

Through his astonishment, Luck's face glowed at the words. He went up and put out his hand, impelled by the hospitality which is an unwritten law of the old West, and is not to be broken save for good cause.

"How! How!" he answered her greeting. "You long ways from home, Annie-Many-Ponies!"

Annie-Many-Ponies smiled in a way to make Happy Jack gulp with a sudden emotion he would have denied. She flashed a quick glance around at the curious faces that regarded her so intently, and she eased her shawl-wrapped burden to the ground with the air of one who has reached her journey's end.

"Yes, I plenty long ways," she assented placidly. "I don't stay by reservation no more. Too lonesome. One night I beat it. I work for you now."

"How you know you work for me?" Luck felt nine pairs of eyes trying to read his face. "That's bad, you run away. You better go back, Annie-Many-Ponies. Your father - "

"Nah!" Annie-Many-Ponies cried in swift rebellion. "I work for you all time, I no want monies. I got plenty wardrobe; you give me plenty grub; I work for you. I think you need him Indian girl in picture. I think you plenty sorry all Indians go by reservation. You no like for Indians go home," she stated with soft sympathy. "I sabe you not got monies for pay all thems Indians. I come be Indian girl for you; I not want monies. You let me stay - Wagalexa Conka!"

"You come in and eat, Annie-Many-Ponies," Luck commanded with more gentleness than he was accustomed to show. The girl must have followed him all the way from Los Angeles, and she must have walked all the way out from Albuquerque. All this she seemed to take for granted, a mere detail of no importance beside her certainty that although he had no money to pay the Indians, he must surely need an Indian girl in his pictures. Loyalty always touched Luck deeply. He had brought the little black dog back with him and hidden it in the stable, just because the dog had followed him all around town and had seemed so pleased when Luck was loading the buckboards for the return trip. He could not logically repulse the manifest friendliness of Annie-Many-Ponies.

He introduced her formally to Rosemary, and was pleased when Rosemary smiled and shook hands without the slightest hesitation. The Happy Family he lumped together in one sentence. "All these my company," he told her. "You eat now. By and by I think you better go home."

Annie-Many-Ponies looked at him with smoldering eyes, standing in the middle of the kitchen, refusing to sit down to the table until the main question was settled.

"Why you say that?" she demanded, drawing her brows down sullenly. "You got plenty more Indian girls?"

Luck shook his head.

"You think me not good-looking any more?" With her two slim brown hands she pushed back the shawl from her hair and challenged criticism of her beauty. She was beautiful, - there was no gain saying that; she was so beautiful that the sight of her, standing there like an indignant young Minnehaha, tingled the blood of more than one of the Happy Family. "You think I so homely I spoil your picture?"

"I think you must not run away from the reservation," Luck parried, refusing to be cajoled by her anger or her beauty. "You always were a good girl, Annie-Many-Ponies. Long time ago, when you were little girl with the Buffalo Bill show, you were good. You mind what Wagalexa Conka say?"

Annie-Many-Ponies bent her head. "I mind you now, Wagalexa Conka," she told him quickly. "You tell me ride down that big hill," she threw one hand out toward the bluff that sheltered the house. "I sure ride down like hell. I care not for break my neck, when you want big 'punch' in picture. You tell me be homely old squaw like Mrs. Ghost-Dog, I be homely so dogs yell to look on me. I mind you plenty - but I do not go by reservation no more."

"Yow father be mad - I let you stay, he maybe shoot me," Luck argued, secretly flattered by her persistence.

Annie-Many-Ponies smiled, - a slow, sphinx-like smile, mysteriously sweet and lingering. "Nah! Not shoot you. I write one letters, say I go work for you. Now you write one letter by Agent, say you let me stay, say I work for you, say I good girl, say I be Indian girl for your picture. I mind you plenty, Wagalexa Conka!" She smiled again coaxingly, like a child. "I like you," she stated simply. "You good man. You need Indian girl, I think. I work for you. My father not be mad; my father know you good man for Indians."

Luck turned from her and gave the Happy Family a pathetic, what's-a-fellow-going-to-do look that made Andy Green snort unexpectedly and go outside. One by one the others followed him, grinning shamelessly at Luck's helplessness. In a moment he overtook them, wanting the support of their judgment.

"The worst of it is," he confessed, after he had explained how he had known the girl since she was a barefooted papoose with the "Bill" show, and he was Indian Agent there; "the worst of it is, she's a humdinger in pictures. She gets over big in foreground stuff. Rides like a whirlwind, and as for dramatic work, she can put it over half the leading women in the business - that is, in her line of Pocohontas stuff."

"Well, why don't you let her stay?" Weary demanded. "She will anyway - mama! We're not what you can call over-run with women on this job."

"Why don't you make a squaw-man outa Dave?" Pink suggested boldly, "and let her be his daughter instead of Rosemary?"

"Say, what does that there walka-some-darn-thing mean, that she calls yuh?" Big Medicine wanted to know. "By cripes, I hate talk I don't savey."

"Wagalexa Conka?" Luck smiled shamefacedly. "Oh, that's just a name the Indians gave me. Means Big Turkey, in plain English. Her father, old Chief Big Turkey, adopted me into the tribe, and they call me by his name. Annie-Many-Ponies has heard it used ever since she was a kid. By tribal law I'm her brother. Well, what's the word, boys? Shall we let her stay or not? We could use her, all right, and put a dash of old-plains' color in the picture that I haven't got, as it stands. It's up to you to decide."

"You're wrong," Pink grinned. "She's decided that, herself. Gee, she's pretty!"

"Certainly she is; but get this, boys: She isn't going to stay just because she's pretty, and if I had a different bunch than you fellows, she'd have to go for that reason. I'm responsible for her - *sabe?* Bill Holmes, you get this; I saw you eyeing her pretty strong. That girl is the daughter of an influential chief, and she comes pretty near being the pride of the reservation. There can't be any romantic stuff, if they let her stay. Her father and the Agent will consent, if they do consent, on the strength of the confidence they have in me. They're going to keep that confidence. Get that, and get it strong, because I sure mean what I'm telling you." He eased the tenseness with a laugh. "I don't mean to offend anybody," he said, "and that's why I'm putting it straight before the play comes up. Annie-Many-Ponies has got a heart-twisting smile, but she's a squaw just the same. She's got the ways of the Injun to the marrow of her bones, and I'll bet right now if you

B. M. Bower

were to shake her hard enough, you'd jingle a knife out of her clothes." He stopped and lighted the cigarette he had been carefully rolling. "Well," he finished after the pause, "does she stay or go?"

The Happy Family answered him with, various phrases, the meaning of which was that he could suit himself about that; as far as they were concerned, she could stay and welcome.

So she stayed, and Rosemary hung up a calico curtain across the one bedroom, so that Annie-Many-Ponies might have a corner to call her own. She stayed; and Luck rewrote two reels of his scenario so that there should be a place in it for a beautiful Indian girl who rode like a whirlwind and did not know the meaning of fear, and who had a mind of her own, and who was just exactly as harmless in that camp as half a quart of nitroglycerine, and added thereby a good bit to the load of responsibility which Luck was shouldering.

CHAPTER THIRTEEN

"PAM. BLEAK MESA - CATTLE DRIFTING BEFORE WIND - "

"Pam. bleak mesa - snow - cattle drifting before wind. Dale and Johnny dis. riding to foreground. Reg. cold - horses leg-weary - boys all in - "

Out toward Bear Canyon, where the land to the north rose brokenly to the mountains, Luck found the bleak stretches of which he had dreamed that night on the observation platform of a train speeding through the night in North Dakota, - a great white wilderness unsheltered by friendly forests, uninhabited save by wild things that moved stealthily across its windswept ridges. Beyond, the mountains rose barrenly, more bleak than the land that lay at their feet.

"Pam. bleak mesa - snow - " With the camera set halfway up a gentle slope commanding a steeper hill beyond, down which the boys would send the cattle in a slow, uneasy march before the storm, Luck focused his telephoto lens upon bleakness enough to satisfy even his voracious appetite for realism. Bill Holmes, his tan pumps wrapped in gunny sacks for protection against the snow that was a foot deep on the level and still falling, thrashed his body with his arms, like a windmill whose paddles have suddenly gone limp in a

B. M. Bower

high wind. When he was ready, Luck stopped long enough to blow on his fingers and to turn and watch for the signal from Annie-Many-Ponies, stationed on a higher ridge to the right of him, - the signal that the cattle were coming.

Through the drive of the snowstorm he saw her tall, straight figure as through a thin, shifting, white veil. The little black dog, for whom she had conceived a fierce affection in defiance of Rosemary's tacit opposition, was lying with its tail curled tight around its feet and its nose, hunting warmth in the shelter of her flapping garments. Annie-Many-Ponies was staring away to the north, shielding her keen eyes from the snow with one slim, brown hand, while she watched for the coming of the herd.

Luck looked at her, silhouetted against the sky. He had no scene written in his script to match the picture she made; he had no negative to waste. But he swung his camera around and, using the telephoto lens he had adjusted for his cattle scenes, he called to her to hold that pose, and indulged his artistic sense in a ten-or-twelve foot scene which showed Annie-Many-Ponies wholly absorbed in gazing upon farther bleakness.

Annie-Many-Ponies was so keenly conscious of her duty to the camera that she dared not break her pose, even to give the signal, until he had yelled, "All right, Annie!" and swung the camera back with its recording eye fixed upon that narrow depression between two blunt ears of hilltop, through which the herd was to be sent down to the ridge and on past the camera to the flat, where other scenes were to be taken later on, when the cattle were hungry enough to browse miserably upon the bosquet of young cotton woods.

"Cows come!" she called out, because Luck had his back to her at the moment and did not see the wave of hand she had been told to give him.

Luck, squinting into the view-finder, caught the swaying vanguard of the herd and swore. He had meant to "pan. bleak mesa" for half a minute before those swaying heads and horns appeared over the brow of the ridge. Now, even though he began to turn the crank the instant he glimpsed them, he would not have quite the effect which he had meant to have. He would be compelled to make two scenes of it, and pan. his bleak mesa afterwards and trust to a "cut-in scene" to cover the break. He did not trust Bill Holmes to turn the crank on that slow, plodding march of misery. With his diaphragm of the camera wide open to get all the light possible, because the air was filled with falling snow, he followed the herd, as it wound snakelike down the easiest descents, making for the more sheltered small canyons that opened out upon the flat. "Cattle drifting before the wind," read the script; and now Luck saw them coming, their snow-whitened backs humped to the driving storm, heads lowered and swaying weakly from side to side with the shambling motion of their feet. They were drifting before the wind, just as he had planned that they should do. That they shuffled wearily down that hill with poor cows and unweaned calves straggling miserably behind the main body in "the drag herd," proved how well the boys had done the work which he had sent them out at daylight to do.

The boys had gone out, under the leadership of Applehead, who knew that range as he knew his own dooryard, just when daylight began to break coldly upon the storm that had come with the sunset. Luck had already ridden out with them and had chosen his location for the blizzard scenes.

He had gone with them over every foot of that drive, and had told them just where the main body of riders was to fall back behind the ridge that would hide them from the camera, leaving Andy Green and the Native Son - since these were the two whom he always visualized in the scene - to come on alone in the wake of the herd. Under the leadership of old Applehead, they had combed every draw that sheltered so much as a lone cow and calf.

Luck had told them to bring in every hoof they could spot and get over that ridge by ten o'clock. He had a nervous dread of the storm breaking before noon, and his heart was set on getting that never-to-be-success-fully-faked blizzard scene. Realism ruled him absolutely, now that he was actually producing some of the big scenes of this picture. He had told them just where to watch for Annie-Many-Ponies and the flag she would wave, - a black flag, so that the boys could not fail to see it in the vague whiteness of the storm. He had located the jutting ledge behind which Happy Jack was to sneak, that he might watch for the signal as an extra precaution against an unseasonable appea-rance of the two riders over the ridge.

When the herd straggled down in what seemed an endless stream of storm-driven animals, Luck knew that the boys had done their work well. He knew cattle as he knew pictures; he knew that a full two thousand came over that ridge through a shallow pass he had chosen, "'Every hoof' is right," he remarked to Bill Holmes with a dry approval. "I'd hate to go hunting meat where that bunch was gathered from. Looks like they'd combed the country for fifty miles around." He sent a quick glance to the pinnacle where Annie-Many-Ponies stood waiting to give the signal. He wished that she had realized the importance of these cattle scenes keenly enough to have given him the signal at the cost of breaking her pose. But he had only himself to blame. He should not have taken the risk, even though he had believed that the cattle would not arrive for another half hour. He should have been ready; he had told the boys to send them right over the ridge when they came up to it, because he wanted to preserve unbroken that indescribable atmosphere of a long, weary journey.

Still they came; a good twenty-five hundred, he was ready to wager, when the last few stragglers, so weak that they wobbled when they hesitated before descending a particularly steep place, came down the slope. It surely did eat up film to take the full magnitude of that march, but Luck turned and turned and gloated in the bigness of it all.

"All right, Annie," he called out when he had taken the last of the herd as they filed out of sight into the narrow gully that would lead them to the flat half a mile below, where he meant to get other scenes. "Wave flag now for boys to come!"

Annie-Many-Ponies lifted high the black flag and waved it in slow, sweeping half circles above her head. "Boys, come," she called, a moment after.

Luck, still not trusting the camera to Bill Holmes, swung back slowly to the pass and made a panorama of the desolate hillside and the chill, forbidding mountains behind. At the pass he stopped. "How close?" he shouted to Annie. "Come now," she called down to him, and Luck began to turn the crank again, watching like a hawk for the first bobbing black specks which would show that the boys were nearing the crest of the ridge.

They came, on the very instant that he would have chosen for their coming. Side by side they rode, drooping of shoulders, and yet with their bodies braced backward for the descent which at the top was rather steep. "Register cold - horses leg-weary - boys all in - " read the script which Luck knew by heart. It was cold enough, and the camera must have registered it in the way the snow was heaped upon their hatbrims, drifted upon their shoulders, packed in the wrinkles of their clothing and in the manes and tails of the horses. And the horses certainly were leg-weary; so weary that Luck knew how the boys must have ridden to gather the cattle and to put their mounts in that condition of realistic exhaustion. In the story they were supposed to have ridden nearly all night, - the night-guard who had been on duty when the storm struck and the cattle began to drift, and who had stuck to their posts even though they could not turn the herd.

That might be stretching the probabilities just a shade, but Luck felt that the effects he wanted to get justified the slight license he had used in his plot. The effects were there, in generous measure. He turned the crank on the whole of their descent and got them riding up into the foreground pinched with cold, miserable as men may be. They did not look at him - they dared not until he had given the word that the scene was ended.

"Ride on past, down into that gully where the cattle went," he directed them sharply. "I'll holler when you're outa sight. You can turn around and come back then; the scene ends where your hat-crowns bob outa sight. And listen! You're liable to lose your cattle if you don't spur up a little, so try and get a little speed into them cayuses of yours!"

Obediently Andy's quirt rose and descended on the flank of his horse. It started, broke into a shuffling trot, and slowed again to a walk. There was no speed to be gotten out of those cayuses, - which was what Luck meant to show on the screen; for this, you must know, was the painting of one grim phase of the range-man's life. The Native Son spurred his horse and got a lunge or two that settled presently to the same plodding walk. Luck pammed them out of sight, bethought him of the rest of the boys, and commanded Annie-Many-Ponies to call them in.

They came, half frozen, half starved, and so tired they did not know which discomfort irked them most. They found Luck; his nose purple with cold marking the footage on his working script with numbed fingers. He barely glanced at them, and turned away to tell Bill Holmes to take the camera on down the draw to where that huddle of rocks stood up on the hillside. Andy and Miguel came back and met the others halfway.

"Say, boss, when do we eat?" Big Medicine inquired anxiously. "By cripes, I'm holler plumb down to my toes, - and them's froze stiff."

"Eat? We eat when we get these storm scenes taken," Luck told him heartlessly. "I'm afraid it'll clear up."

"Afraid it'll clear up!" Pink burrowed his chin deeper into his breath-frosted collar and shivered.

"Oh, quit kicking," the Native Son advised ironically. "We're only living some of Luck's big minutes he used to tell about."

Luck looked around at them and grinned a little. "Part of the business, boys," he said. "Think of the picture stuff there is in this storm!"

"Why, sure!" Weary responded with exaggerated cheerfulness. "I've been freezing artistically ever since daylight. Darn me for leaving my old sourdough coat at home when I hit for the land of orange blossoms and singing birds and sunshine."

"Aw, gwan! I never was warm a minute in Los Angeles except when I got hot at the Acme. Montana never seen the day it was as cold as here."

"Come on, boys, let's get these dissolve scenes of cattle perishing in a blizzard. After that - hey, Annie! You come, make plenty fire, plenty coffee. I show you location."

Annie called gently to the little dog, and came striding down through the snow to fall in docilely three paces behind her adored "brother," Wagalexa Conka after the submissive manner of squaws toward the human male in authority over them.

"Coffee!" Weary murmured ecstatically. "Plenty fire, plenty coffee - oh, mama!"

Down in the flat where the bushes grew sparsely along the tiny arroyo now gone dry, the herd had stopped from sheer exhaustion, and were already nibbling desultorily upon the tenderest twigs. This was what

Luck wanted in his scene, though the cattle must be moved into the location he had chosen where was just the background effect he wanted to get, with the bare mesa showing in the far distance. There was a dreary interval of riding and shouting and urging the cattle up over a low spur of the bluff and down the other side, and the placing of them to Luck's satisfaction. I fear that more than one of the boys wondered why that first bit of the flat would not do, and why Luck insisted that they should bring the herd to one particular point and no other, and why they must wear out their horses, and themselves just fussing around among the cattle, scattering one bunch, bringing others closer together, and driving certain animals up to foreground, when they very much objected to going there.

Luck had concealed his camera behind the rocks so that he could get a "close shot" without registering the fact that the cattle were watching him. His commands to "Edge that black steer over about even with that white bank!" and later, "Put that cow and calf out this way and drive the others back a little, so she will have the immediate foreground to herself," were easier given than obeyed. The cow and calf, for instance, were much inclined to shamble back with the others, and did not show any appreciation for the foreground, wherein they were vastly unlike any other "extras" ever brought before a camera. Still, in spite of all these drawbacks, the moment arrived when Luck began to turn the crank with his eyes keen for every detail of that bunch of forlorn, hungry, range cattle huddled under the scant shelter of a ten-foot bank, while the snows fell steadily in great flakes which Luck knew would give a grand storm-effect on the screen. The Happy Family, free for the moment, crowded close to the fire of dead sagebrush which Annie-Many-Ponies

B. M. Bower

had lighted in the lee of a high rock, and sniffed longingly at the smell which came steaming up from the dented two-gallon coffee-boiler blackened from many a camp fire.

Luck was turning the crank and watching his "foreground stuff" so that he did not at first see the two riders who came loping down the hill which he was using for background. Whether he would or no, he had got them in several feet of good scene before he saw them and stopped his camera. He shouted, but they came on headlong, slipping and sliding in the loose snow. There could be no doubt that they were headed straight for the group and felt that their business was urgent, so Luck stepped out from behind the rocks and started toward them, motioning for them to keep out, away from the cattle.

"Better let me git in the lead right now," Applehead advised hastily, and jumped in front of Luck as the two came lunging up. "I know these here *hombres*, to my sorrer, too, now I'm tellin' yuh!"

But Luck, feeling that his leadership might as well be established then as any time, pushed the old man back.

"What you want?" he demanded of the foremost who rode up. "Didn't you hear me tell you to keep out around the cattle?"

"*Adonde va V con mi vaca?*" snapped the first rider in high-keyed Spanish.

"My brother say where you go with our cattle?" interrupted the other one, evidently proud of his English.

"I know what he said," Luck snubbed this one bluntly. "I don't know that they are your cattle. I don't care. We're using them to make motion pictures. Get outa the way so we can go on with our work." Had he not spoiled several feet of film because of their coming he might have been more inclined to placate them. As it was, he did not welcome their interference, he did not like their looks, and their tones were to his temper as tow would be to a fire. Their half Mexican, half American dress irritated him; the interruption exasperated him. He was hungry and cold and keyed to a high nervous tension in his anxiety to make the most of his present big opportunity; he knew too well that he might not have another chance all winter, with the snow falling as if under his direction.

"Get over there outa range of the camera!" he commanded them sharply, "then you can spout Mex. till you're black in the face, for all I care. I'm busy." To make himself absolutely understood he repeated the gist of his remarks in Spanish before he turned his back on them to finish his interrupted scene.

Whereupon one swore in Spanish and the other in English, and they both declared that they would take their cattle right now, and reined their horses toward the shifting herd.

"Hold on thar, Ramone Chavez!" shouted Applehead, striding forward. "Didn't you hear the boss tell ye to git outa the way, both of yuh? Yuh better do it, now I'm tellin' yuh, 'cause if yuh don't, they's goin' to be right smart of a runction around here! A good big share uh them thar cattle belongs to me. Don't ye go messin' in there amongst 'em; you jest ride back outa the way uh that thar camery. Git!"

At Applehead's command they "got," at least as far as the camp fire, where the bright shawl of Annie-Many-Ponies caught and held their interest. Annie-Many-Ponies, being a woman who had both youth and beauty and sensed instinctively the value of both, sent a slant-eyed glance and a half smile toward Ramone, who possessed more good looks and more English than his brother. The Happy Family eyed them with a tolerant indifference and moved aside with reluctant hospitality when Ramone dismounted shiveringly and came forward to warm his fingers over the blaze.

"She's cold day, you bet," Ramone remarked ingratiatingly.

"She ain't what you could call hot," Big Medicine conceded drily, since no one else showed any disposition to reply.

"We don't get much snow like this. You live in Albuquerque, perhaps?"

There was really no excuse for snubbing these two, who had been well within their rights in making an investigation of this unheralded and unauthorized gathering of all the cattle on this range. Andy told Ramone where they were staying and where they came from, and let it go at that. The less Americanized brother dismounted and joined the group with a nod of greeting.

"My brother Tomas," announced Ramone, with a flash of white teeth, his eyes shifting unobtrusively toward Annie-Many-Ponies, who wore a secret, half-smiling air of provocative interest in him. "Not spik much English, my brother. Always stay too much at home.

Me, I travel all over - Denver, Los Angeles, San Francisco. I ride in all contests - Pueblo, San Antonio - all over. Tomas, he go not so often. His head, all for business - making money - get rich some day. Me, I spend. My hand wide open always. Money slip fast."

"There's plenty of us marked that way," Weary made good-natured comment, turning so that his back might feel the heat of the fire.

"Shunka Chistala!" murmured Annie-Many-Ponies in her soft contralto to the little black dog, and moved away to the mountain wagon, with the dog following close to her moccasined heels.

Ramone looked after her with frank surprise at the strange words. "Not Spanish, then?" he ventured.

"Indian," the Native Son explained briefly, and added, perhaps for reasons of his own, "Sioux squaw."

Ramone very wisely let his curiosity rest there. He had a good excuse, for Luck, having finished work for the time being, came tramping over to the fire. At him Ramone glanced apologetically.

"We borrow comfort from your fire, *senor*," he said indifferently. "She's bad day for riding."

Luck nodded, already ashamed of having lost his temper, yet not at the point of yielding openly to any overtures for peace. "Soon as we eat," he said to Weary and those others who stood nearest, "I'll have you cut out that poor cow and calf and drive 'em down the flat here, so I can get that other scene I was telling you about."

"Wagalexa Conka, here is plenty hot coffee," came a soft voice at his elbow, and Luck turned with a smile to take the steaming cup from the hand of Annie-Many-Ponies.

The Native Son poured a cup and offered it to Tomas Chavez. "*Quire cafe?*" he asked.

"*Si, senor; Gracias.*" Tomas smiled, and took the cup and bowed. Annie-Many-Ponies herself, with a sidelong glance at Luck to see if she might dare, carried the biggest cup of coffee to Ramone, and smiled demurely when he took it and looked into her eyes and thanked her.

In this fashion did the social sky clear, even though the snow continued to drive against those who broke bread together out there in the dreary wastes, with the snow halfway to their knees. The Native Son, being half Spanish and knowing well the language of his father, talked a little with Tomas. Ramone made himself friendly with any one who would give him any attention. But Applehead scowled over his boiled-beef sandwich and his coffee, and kept his back turned upon the Chavez brothers, and would not talk at all. He eyed them sourly when they still loitered after the meal was over and the remains packed away in the box by Annie-Many-Ponies, and Luck had gone to work again with Bill Holmes at his heels and the boys helping to place the cattle to Luck's liking.

When the Chavez brothers finally did show symptoms of intending to leave, Luck beckoned to Tomas, whom he judged to be the leader. "Here," he said in Spanish, when Tomas had come close to him. "I will pay you for using your cattle. When I am through, my boys will drive them back to the mesa again. For my picture I may need them again, *senor*. I promise you they will not be harmed." And he charged in his expense book the sum, "to use of locations."

"*Gracias*," said Tomas, and took the five dollars which Luck could ill afford to give, but which he felt would smooth materially the trail to their future work. Cattle he must have for his picture; cattle he would have at any cost, - but it would be well to have them with the consent of their owners. So the Chavez brothers rode away with smiles for their neighbors instead of threats, and with five dollars which had come to them like a gift.

"Yuh might better uh kicked 'em outa here without no softsoapin' about it, now I'm tellin' yuh!" Applehead grumbled when they were out of earshot. "You may know your business better'n what I do, but by thunder I wouldn't uh give 'em no five dollars - ner five cents. 'S like feedin' a stray dog; yuh won't never git rid of 'em now. They'll be hangin' around under yer feet - "

"At that, I might have use for them," Luck retorted unmoved. "They're fine types."

"Types!" old Applehead exploded indignantly. "Types! They're sneak-thieves and cutthroats 't I wouldn't trust fur's I could throw a bull by the tail. That's what they be. Types, - my granny!"

B. M. Bower

CHAPTER FOURTEEN

"PLUMB SPOILED, D' YUH MEAN?"

Luck came out of the dark room with the still, frozen, look of a trouble that has gone too deep for words. Annie-Many-Ponies eyed him aslant and straightway placed the hottest, juiciest piece of steak on his plate, and poured his coffee even before she poured for old Dave Wiswell, whom she favored as being an old acquaintance of the Pine Ridge country.

Once when her father, old chief Big Turkey, had broken his leg and refused to have a doctor attend him, and had said that he would die if his "son" did not make his leg well, Luck had looked as he looked now. Still, he had set chief Big Turkey's leg so well that it grew straight and strong again. Annie-Many-Ponies might be primitive as to her nature and untutored as to her mind, but she could read the face of her brother Wagalexa Conka swiftly and surely. Something was very bad in his heart. Annie-Many-Ponies searched her soul for guilt, remembered the smile she had given to Ramone Chavez whom Wagalexa Conka did not like, and immediately she became humbled before her chief.

Shunka Chistala - which is Sioux for little dog - she banished into the cold, and hardened her heart, against his whining. It is true that Wagalexa Conka had not forbidden her to have the little dog in the house, but in his displeasure he might make the dog an excuse for scolding her and for taking the part of Rosemary, who hated dogs in the house, and who was trying, by every ingratiating means known to woman, to make a friend of Compadre. Rosemary was a white woman and the wife of Wagalexa Conka's friend; Annie-Many-Ponies was an Indian girl, not even of the same race as her brother Wagalexa Conka. And although her vanity might lead her to believe herself and her smile the cause of Luck's mask-like displeasure, she had no delusions as to which side he would take in an argument between herself and Shunka Chistala on the one side, and Rosemary and Compadre on the other; and in the back of her mind lived always the fear that Wagalexa Conka might refuse to let her stay and work for him in pictures.

Therefore Annie-Many-Ponies crouched humbly before the rock fireplace, until Luck missed her at the table and told her to come and eat; she came as comes a dog who has been beaten, and slid into her place as noiselessly as a shadow, - humility being the heritage of her sex and race.

No one talked at all. Even Rosemary seemed depressed and made no attempt to stir the Happy Family to their wonted cheerfulness. They were worn out from their long day that had been filled with real hardships as well as work. In the general silence, Luck's deeper gloom seemed consistent and only to be expected; for hard as the others had worked, he had worked harder. His had been the directing brain; his hand had turned the camera crank, lest Bill Holmes, not yet familiar with his duties, might fail where failure would be disaster. He had endured the cold and the storm, tramping back and forth in the snow, planning, directing, doing literally the work of two men. Annie-Many-Ponies alone knew that exhaustion never brought just that look into Luck's face. Annie-Many-Ponies knew that something was very bad in Luck's heart. She knew, and she trembled while she ate with a precise attention to her table manners lest he chide her openly before them all.

"How long do you think this storm will last, Applehead?" Luck asked, when he had walked heavily over to the fireplace for his smoke, and had drawn a match sharply along the rough face of a rock.

"We-ell, she's showin' some signs uh clearin' up to-night," Applehead stated with careful judgment, because he felt that Luck's question had much to do with Luck's plans, and was not a mere conversational bait. "Wind, she's shiftin', er was, when I come in to supper. She shore come down like all git-out ever since she started, and I calc'late she's about stormed out. I look fer sun all day to-morrer, boy." This last in a tone of such manifest encouragement that Luck snorted. (Back by the table in the kitchen, Annie-Many-Ponies paused in her piling of plates and listened breathlessly. She knew that particular sound. Wagalexa Conka would presently reveal what was bad in his heart.)

"That would be my luck, all right," her chief stated pessimistically.

"What's the matter with the sun, now?" Big Medicine boomed reprovingly. "Comin' in, you said you had your blizzard stuff, and now if the sun'd jest come out, by cripes, you'd be singin' songs uh thanksgivin' - er words to that effect. Honest to gran'ma, there's folks that'd kick if - "

"But I haven't got my blizzard stuff," Luck stated, harshly because of the effort to speak at all. "All that negative I took to-day is chuck full of 'static.'"

Annie-Many-Ponies, out in the kitchen, dropped a granite-iron plate, but the others merely stared at Luck uncomprehendingly.

"Well, say, by cripes! What's statics?" demanded Big Medicine pugnaciously, as though he meant to ward off from his mind the realization of some new misfortune.

Luck's lips twitched in the faint impulse toward a smile that would not come. "Statics," he explained, "is that branch of mechanics that relates to bodies held at rest by the forces acting on them. In other words, it is electricity in a stationary charge, the condition being produced by friction, or induction. In other words - "

"In other words," Big Medicine supplied glumly, "I can shut up and mind my own business. I get yuh, all right!"

"Nothing like that, Bud," Luck corrected more amiably, warmed a little by the sympathy he knew would follow close upon the heels of understanding. "Static is a technical word used a good deal in motion-picture photography. In this case it was caused, I think, by the difference of temperature in the metal parts of the camera and negative, and the weather outside the camera box. I've been keeping it here in the house where it's warm, and I took it out into the cold and started work - *sabe*? And the grinding of the bearings, and the action of the film on the race plate, generated static electricity in tiny flashes which lighted up the interior of the camera and light-exposed the negative, as it was passing from one magazine to another. When it's developed, these flashes show up in contrasty lights, like tiny grape vines; I can show you that part; I've got about a mile of it, more or less, there in the dark room."

"Plumb spoiled, d' yuh mean?" Big Medicine asked, his voice hushed before the catastrophe.

"Plumb spoiled." Luck threw his cigarette stub viciously into the blaze. "All that drifting herd, all that panoram of Andy and Miguel - all - everything I took to-day, with the exception of those last scenes with the cow and calf. The one where the cow is down and the snow drifting over her, and the calf huddled there by the carcass, - that's dandy. Camera and negative were cold as the outside air by that time. That one scene will stand out big; it's got an awful big punch, provided I had the stuff leading up to it, which I haven't got."

"Hell!" said Andy softly, voicing the dismay of them all.

Presently old Applehead unlimbered himself from his chair and went out into the cold and darkness. When he came back, ribbing his knuckles for warmth, he stood before the fireplace and ruminated dispiritedly before he spoke.

"Ain't ary hope of it blizzardin' to-morrer, boy," he broke his silence reluctantly, "'less the wind changes, which she don't act to me like she's got ary notion of doin'; she's shore goin' to blind ye with sun to-morrer, now I'm tellin' yuh."

"Well, there won't be any more static in my film," Luck declared with sudden decision, and carried his camera outside. When he returned Applehead eyed him solicitously.

"We-ell, this ain't but the middle uh November, yuh want to recollect," he said. "We're liable to have purtier storms 'n what this here one was, 'fore winter's over. Cattle'll be in worse condition, too, - ribs stickin' out so'st you kin count 'em a mile off 'n' more. Way winter's startin' in, wouldn't s'prise me a mite if we had storms all through till spring opens up."

Luck knew the old man was trying in his crude way to encourage him, but he made no reply, and Applehead relapsed into drowsy meditation over his pipe. The boys, yawning sleepily, trailed off to bed in the Ketch-all cabin. Rosemary and Annie-Many-Ponies, having finished washing the dishes and tidying the kitchen, came through the room on their way to bed, Annie-Many-Ponies cunningly hiding the little black dog behind her skirts. Rosemary frowned at the two and went to the door and called Compadre; but the blue cat, scenting a dog in the house, meowed his regrets and would not come.

"I'll take 'im down with me," said Applehead, rising stiffly. "He cain't take no comfort in the house no more - not till he spunks up and licks that thar dawg a time er two. Comin', Luck?" he added, waiting at the door. But Luck was staring into the fire and did not seem to hear him, so Applehead went off alone to where the Happy Family were already creeping thankfully into their hard bunks.

The house grew still; so still that Luck could hear the wind whispering in the chimney, coming from the quarter which meant clearing weather. He sighed, flung more wood on the coals to drive back the chill of the night, and got out his scenario and some sheets of blank paper and a pencil. He had sold his typewriter when he was raising money for this trip, and he was inclined now to regret it. But he sharpened the pencil, laid a large-surfaced "movie" magazine across his knees, and prepared to revise his scenario to meet his present limitations.

With a good thousand feet of film spoiled through no real fault of his own, and with the expenses he knew he must meet looming inexorably before him, he simply could not afford a leading woman. Therefore, he must change his story, making it a "character" lead instead of the conventional hero and heroine theme. Chance - he called it luck - had sent him Annie-Many-Ponies, who "Wants no monies." He must change his story so that she would fit into it as the necessary feminine element, but he was discouraged enough that night to tell himself that, just as he had her placed and working properly, the Indian Agent or her father, old Big Turkey, would probably demand her immediate return. In his despondent mood he had no faith in his standing with the Indians or in the letter he had written to the Agent. His "one best bet", as he put it, was to make her scenes as soon as possible, before they had time to reach him with a letter; therefore he must reconstruct his scenario immediately, so that he could get to work in the morning, whatever the weather.

He read the script through from beginning to end, and his heart went heavy in his chest. He did not want to change one scene of that Big Picture. Just as it stood it seemed to him perfect in its way. It had the bigness of the West when the West was young. It had the red blood of courage, the strength of achievement, the sweetness of a great love. It was, in short, Luck's biggest, best work. Still, without a woman to play that lead -

Luck sighed and dampened his pencil on his tongue and drew a heavy line through the scene where "Marian" first appeared in the story. It hurt him like drawing a hot wire across his hand. It was his first real compromise, his first step around an obstacle in his path rather than his usual bold jump over it. He looked at the pencil mark and considered whether he could not send for a girl young in the profession, who would be satisfied with her transportation and thirty or forty dollars a week while she stayed. He could make all her scenes and send her back. But a little mental arithmetic, coupled with the cold fact that he did not know of any young woman who was capable of doing the work he required and would yet be satisfied with a small salary, killed that new-born hope. He drew a line through the next scene where the girl appeared.

When he had quite blotted the girl from his story, he was appalled at the gap he must fill in the continuity and in the theme. He had left old Dave Wiswell, his dried little cattleman, a childless old man - or else a "squaw" man whose squaw has, presumably, died before the story began. Somehow he could not "see" his cattleman as one who would set aside the barrier of race and take a squaw for his wife. He could not see Annie-Many-Ponies as anything save what she was - a beautiful young savage with an odd adornment of civilized speech and some of the civilized customs, it is true, but a savage for all that. He did not want to spoil her by portraying her as a half-caste in his picture.

He must make his story a man's story, with the full interest centered about the man's hopes, his temptations, his achievements. The woman - Annie, as he saw the woman now - must be of secondary interest. He laid his head against the chair back in his favorite attitude for uninterrupted thought, and stared into the fire. In this way he had stared out into the night of the Dakota prairie; at first brooding in discontent because things were not as he would have them, then drifting into dreams of what he would like; then weaving his dreams together and creating a something complete in itself. So had he created his Big Picture, - the picture which was already beginning to live in the narrow strips of negative. A few hundred feet of that negative were even dry and filed away ready for cutting; unimportant scenes, to be sure, with all of his "big stuff" yet to be produced. His mind went methodically over the completed scenes, judging each one separately, seeking some change of plot that would yet permit these scenes to be used. From there his thought drifted to the day's work in the blizzard, - the day's work that had been lost because of atmospheric conditions. Blizzard stuff he must have, he told himself stubbornly. Not only was that a phase of the range which he must portray if his picture were to be complete; he must have it to lead the story up to that tragic, pitifully eloquent scene which had come out clear and photographically perfect, - the scene of the old cow's struggle against the storm and of her final surrender, too weak to match her puny strength against the furies of wind and snow and cold. That scene would live long in the minds of those who saw it; that scene alone would lift his picture above the dead level of mediocrity. But he must have another blizzard....

His eyelids drooped low over his tired eyes; through their narrowing opening he stared at the yellow glow of the fire. Only half awake, he dreamed of the herd drifting down that bleak hillside, with Andy and the Native Son riding doggedly after them. Only half awake, his story changed, grew indistinct, clarified in stray scenes, held aloof from him, grew and changed, and was another story. And always in the background of his mind went that drifting herd. Sometimes snow-whitened, their backs humped in the wind, their heads lowered and swaying weakly from side to side, the cattle marched and marched before him, sometimes obscured by the blackness of night, a vague procession of moving shadows; sometimes revealed suddenly when the lightning split the blackness. Like a phantom herd -

"The phantom herd!" Aloud he cried the words. "*The Phantom Herd*!" He sat up straight in his chair. Here was his title, for which his mind had groped so long and could not grasp. His title -

"What - that you, Luck?" Andy Green's voice came sleepily from the next room. "What yuh want?"

"I've got my title!" Luck called back, his voice exultant. "And I've got my story, too! Get up, Andy, and let me tell you the plot!"

Whereupon Andy proved himself a real friend and an unselfish one. He felt as if getting up out of bed was the final, supreme torture under which a man may live; but he got up, for there was something in Luck's voice that thrilled him even through the clogging sleep-hunger. Presently he was sitting in his trousers and socks and shirt, sleepy-eyed beside Luck.

"Shoot it outa your system," he mumbled, and began feeling stupidly for his cigarette papers. "*E - a-ough!*" he yawned, if so inarticulate a sound may be spelled. "I knew you'd have to work your story over," he said, more normal of tone after the yawn. And he added bluntly, "Rosemary's one grand little woman - but she couldn't act if you trained her a thousand years. What's your next best bet?"

"No next best; it's *the* picture this time. *The Phantom Herd*. Get that as a title?"

"Gee!" Andy softly paid tribute. Then he grinned. "By gracious, they sure didn't act to me like any phantom herd when we first headed 'em into that wind!"

"Them babies are going to march us up to a pile of real money, though," Luck asserted eagerly.

"Listen. Here's the story - the part I've changed; all the first part is the same - the trail-herd and all. You're old Dave's son, and you're wild. You quarrel, and he turns you out, thinking he'll let you rustle for yourself awhile, and maybe tame down and come back more like he wants you to be. But you don't tame that way. You throw in with Miguel, and you two turn rustlers. You hold a grudge against your dad, and you rustle from him mostly, on the plea that by rights what's his is yours - you know. Annie is Mig's sweetheart, and she's a kind of go-between - keeps you posted on what's taking place on the outside, and all that. I haven't," he explained hastily, "doped out the details yet. I'm giving you the main points I want to bring out.

Well, here's the big stuff; you get a big herd together. You're holding 'em in a box canyon, - I know the spot, all right, - waiting for a chance to drive them outa the country; see? This blizzard hits, and you take advantage of it to drive the herd out under cover of the storm. But the blizzard beats you. You trail 'em along, but there's only two of you, and you can't keep 'em from swinging away from the wind. You try to hold the herd into the storm, - that's where I'll get my big storm effects, - but they swing off in spite of you. Your horses get tired; all you can do is follow the herd. Lord! I wish that stuff I took to-day wasn't spoiled! I sure would have had some big stuff there. Well, Mig's horse goes down in a drifted wash. You're trying to point the herd then, and the storm's so thick you don't miss him at first, we'll say.

"Anyway, as I've doped it out, Mig loses his life. You find him dead - whether then or later I don't know yet. The punch is this: You have been getting pretty sick of the life, and wishing you had behaved yourself and stayed with your dad. But you've been afraid of Mig. You couldn't see any chance of taking the back trail as long as he was alive to tell on you. Now he's dead. I guess maybe you better find him right there in the blizzard - hurt maybe - anyway, just about all in. You try to save him, *sabe*? You can't, though."

"I still don't see no phantom herd," observed Andy, wriggling his toes luxuriously in the warmth of the fire.

"Well, listen. You'll see it in a minute. You go back home after your pard's dead. You have a close squeak yourself, see? And the thing works on your mind. Cutting out the frills, you see things. You see a herd

B. M. Bower

drifting before a storm, maybe, - a blizzard like yesterday, with your pal riding point. You try to come up with it - no herd there. You come to yourself and go back home. Then maybe some black night you're brooding before a fire like this - I can get a great firelight effect on your face, sitting like this" - Luck, actor that he was, made Andy see just how the scenes would look - "have a flare in the fire to throw the light back on you; see what I mean? And outside a thunderstorm is rolling up. A bright flash of lightning startles you. You go to the door and open it; you see the herd drifting past with Mig trailing along on his horse – black shadows, and then standing out clear in the lightning - "

"How the deuce - "

"I'll do that with 'lap dissolves' and double exposures. Lots of work that will be, and careful work, but the result will be - why, Lord! It will be immense! That herd and the lone rider haunt you till you're on the edge of being crazy. Then I'll bring out somehow that it's a nervous condition, which of course it is. And I'll bring old Dave in strong; he follows you some night, and he finds out what you're after. You tell him - make a clean breast of your rustling, see? Just unburden your mind to your dad. He's big enough to see that he isn't altogether clear of guilt himself, for sending you off the way he did. Anyway, that pulls you out of it. The phantom herd and rider pass over the sky line some night - Lord, I can see what a picture I can get out of that! - and out of your life."

"Unh-hunh - that's a heap better than your first story, Luck."

"Andy, are you boys going to talk all night?" the voice of Rosemary came plaintively from the next room.

"Here. You go back to bed," Luck generously commanded. "I just wanted to get your idea of what it sounds like. I'll block it out before I turn in. Go on, now."

So Luck wrote his new story of *The Phantom Herd* that night. He had a midnight supper of warmed-over coffee and cold bean sandwiches, but he did not have any sleep. When he had finished with a last big, artistic scene that made his pulse beat faster in the writing of it, the white world outside was growing faintly pink under the rising sun.

B. M. Bower

CHAPTER FIFTEEN

A LETTER FROM CHIEF BIG TURKEY

Annie-Many-Ponies, keen of eye when her heart directed her glances, saw the Kyle postmark on a letter while Applehead was sorting Luck's mail from the weekly batch he had just brought. Luck also spied the Kyle postmark and the familiar handwriting of George-Low-Cedar, who was a cousin of Annie-Many-Ponies and the most favored scribe of Big Turkey's numerous family. There was no mistaking those self-conscious shadings on the downward strokes of the pen, or the twice-curled tails of all the capitals. The capital M, for instance, very much resembled a dandelion stem split and curled by the tongue of a little girl.

George-Low-Cedar and none other had written that letter, and Big Turkey himself had probably composed it in great deliberation over his pipe, while the smoke of his *tepee* fire curled over his head, and his squaw crouched in the shadow listening stolidly while her heart ached with longing for the girl-child who had gone a-wandering. Annie-Many-Ponies slid unobtrusively to the door and flattened her back against the wall beside it, ready to slip out into the dusk if she read in Wagalexa Conka's face that the letter was unpleasant.

Luck did not say a word while he held the letter up and

looked at it; he did not say a word, but Annie-Many-Ponies knew, as well as though he had spoken, that he too feared what the contents might be. So she stood flat against the wall and watched his face, and saw how his fingers fumbled at the flap of the envelope, and how slowly he drew out the cheap, heavily ruled, glazed paper that is sold alongside plug tobacco and pearl buttons and safety pins in the Indian traders' stores. Staring from under her straight brows at that folded letter, Annie-Many-Ponies had a swift, clear vision of the little store set down in the midst of barrenness and dust, and of the squaws sitting wrapped in bright shawls upon the platform while their lords gravely purchased small luxuries within. As a slim, barefooted papoose, proud of her shapeless red calico slip buttoned unevenly up the back with huge white buttons, and of her hair braided in two sleek braids and tied with strips of the same red calico, she had stood flattened against the wall of the store while her father, Big Turkey, bought tobacco. She had hoped that the fates might be kind and send her a five-cent bag of red-and-white gum drops. Instead, Big Turkey had brought her a doll, - a pink-cheeked doll of the white people. In her cheap suitcase which she had carried wrapped in her shawl on her back to the ranch, Annie-Many-Ponies still had that doll. So with her eyes fixed upon the letter, her mind stared trance-like at the vision of that long-ago day which had been to her so wonderful.

Then Wagalexa Conka looked at her and smiled, and the vision of the store and the slim, barefooted papoose with her doll vanished. The smile meant that all was well, that she might stay with Wagalexa Conka and be his Indian girl in the picture of *The Phantom Herd*. Annie-Many-Ponies smiled back at him, - the slow, sweet, sphinx-like smile which Luck called "heart-twisting," - and slipped out into the night with her heart beating fast in a strange mixture of joy that she might stay, and of homesickness for the little store set down in the midst of barrenness and dust, and for that long-ago day that had been so wonderful.

"Read this," said Luck, still smiling, and gave the letter into the flour-dusted hands of Rosemary. "Ever see a real, dyed-in-the-wool, Indian letter? Sure takes a load off my mind, too; you never can tell how an idea is going to hit an Indian. Pass it on to the boys."

So Rosemary read, with the whole Happy Family crowding close to look over her shoulder:

> Kyle, P. Office
> Pine Ridge, So. D
> Monday, Nov.

Luck Lindsay
at Motion Pictures ranch,
Albequrqe, New M.

Friend son,

I this day gets letter from agent at agency who tell my girl you sisters are now at New mexicos with you pictures. shes go way one days at night times and to-morrow mornings i no find him. i am glad she sees you. You Take care same as with shows them Buffalo bill. all indians have hard times for cold and much hays and fires of prairies loses much. Them indians shake you hands with good hearts they have with you. send me blue silks ribbon send Me pictures so i can see you. Again i shake you by hand with good heart same as I see you. Speak one Letters quick again.

you father,
BIG TURKEY.

"Pretty good spelling, for an Indian letter," Rosemary commented suspiciously. "Are you sure an Indian wrote it, Luck Lindsay?"

"Why, certainly, I'm sure!" Luck was shuffling his other letters with the air of a man whose mind has for the moment lost its load of trouble. "George-Low-Cedar wrote it. I know his writing. He's Annie's cousin, and he thinks he's highly educated. Indians have great memories, and once they learn to spell a word, they never seem to forget it. They learn to spell in school. What they don't learn is how to put the words together the way we do. Cousin George is also shaky on capitals, you notice. Now to-morrow we can go ahead with that big cattle-stuff. I can take my time about making Annie's scenes; I was afraid I might have to rush them all through first thing, so as to send her back. I'm sure glad she can stay; she's good to have around, to help in the house."

Rosemary screwed up her lips and gave him a queer look, but Luck had turned his attention to another letter, and she did not say what was in her mind. Annie-Many-Ponies, speaking theoretically, was good to have around to help Rosemary. In actual practice, however, Rosemary found her not so good. Personally Annie was fastidiously tidy, which Rosemary ungenerously set down to youthful vanity rather than to innate cleanliness. When it came to washing dishes, however, Annie-Many-Ponies left much to be desired. She was prone to disappear about the time she reached the biscuit-basin and the frying-pan stage of the thrice-daily performance. She was prone to fancy she heard

B. M. Bower

Wagalexa Conka calling her, or Shunka Chistala barking in pursuit of the cat, or a hen cackling out in the weeds; whatever the sound, it invariably became a summons which Annie-Many-Ponies must instantly obey. Then she forgot to come back within the next two or three hours, and Rosemary must finish the dishes herself. But all this, as Rosemary well knew, was an unimportant detail of the general scheme of work going on at Applehead's ranch.

To her it seemed wonderful, the way Luck was pushing his picture to completion against long odds sometimes, fighting some difficulty always. Much as she secretly resented certain Indian traits in Annie-Many-Ponies, and pleased as she would secretly have been if the girl had been recalled to the reservation, she was generously relieved because Luck could now go ahead with his round-up and trail-herd scenes while the weather was mild and sunny, and need not hurry the Indian-girl scenes at all.

In the ten days since the blizzard, Luck had worked hard. Some night scenes in a cow-town he had already taken, driving late in the afternoon into Albuquerque with his radium flares and his full company. Rosemary's memory cherished those nights as rare and precious experiences. First there were the old-time scenes, half Mexican in their atmosphere, when the dried little man was young, and the trail-herd started north. For these scenes Luck himself played the part of Dave Wiswell, turning the camera work over to Bill Holmes. Then there were the scenes of a later period, - scenes of carousal which depicted her beloved Andy as a very wild young man who spent his nights riotously. One full day of sunshine had also been spent at the stockyards there, taking shipping scenes.

On this day the two women had stayed at home, and Rosemary had nearly quarreled with Annie-Many-Ponies because Annie would not mend her stockings, but had spent the whole afternoon teaching Shunka Chistala to chase prairie dogs, the game being to try and frighten them away from their holes and then catch them. Annie-Many-Ponies attended to the strategic direction of the enterprise and let Shunka Chistala do most of the running. The high, clear laughter of the girl and her unintelligible cries to the little black dog had irritated Rosemary to the point of tears.

There had been no more days wasted because of spoiled film, - Luck was carefully guarding against that, - and it seemed to Rosemary that there were miles of it developed and dried and pigeon-holed, ready for assembling. That part of the work she was especially interested in, because it was done in the house.

To her it might seem that miles of film had been made, but to Luck it seemed as though the work crawled with maddening deliberation. Delays fretted him. The mounting expense account worried him, though as a matter of fact it mounted slowly, considering the work he was doing and the size of the company he was maintaining. When he took film clippings to a town photographer to have enlargements made for "stills," - the pictures which must accompany each set of prints as advertising matter, - the cost of the work gave him the blues for the rest of that day. Then there were the Chavez boys, whom he had found it expedient to use occasionally in his big range scenes and in his "cow-town stuff." They had no conception of regular rates as extras, but Luck had a conscience, and he had also established a precedent. Whenever he used them in pictures, he gave Tomas five dollars and left it to

B. M. Bower

Tomas to divide with Ramone. And five dollars, added to other fives and tens and twenty-fives, soon amounts to an amazing whole when anxiety holds the pencil.

As his story had changed and developed into *The Phantom Herd* plot, it had lengthened appreciably, because he could not and would not sacrifice his big range stuff. And double exposures meant double work, of course. He found himself with a five-reel picture in the making instead of the four-reeler he had started to produce. Thus he was compelled to send for more "raw stock." Also, he soon ran out of lumber for his interior sets and must buy more. As the possibilities of his production grew plainer to him, Luck knew that he could not slight a single scene nor skimp it in the making. He could go hungry if it came to that, but he could not cheapen his story by using make-shift settings.

Thanksgiving came, and they scarcely knew it, for the weather was fine, and they spent the day far afield and came in after dark, too tired to be thankful for anything save the opportunity to sleep.

Christmas came so suddenly that they wondered where the month had gone. Christmas Eve the Happy Family spent in arranging a round-up camp out behind the house where the hill rose picturesquely, and in singeing themselves heroically in the heat of radium flares, while Luck took his camp-fire scenes that were triumphs of lighting-effects and photography, - scenes which he would later tone red with aniline dyes.

Annie-Many-Ponies and Rosemary brought out the two-gallon coffee boiler and a can of cream and a small lard pail of sugar, with cups and tin spoons and a pan of boiled-beef and cold-bean sandwiches. Rosemary called "Merry Christmas!" when the dying radium flares betrayed her approach, and the Happy Family jumped up and shouted "Merry Christmas!" to her and one another, just as exuberantly as though they had been celebrating instead of adding six hours or so to a hard day's work.

"That was beautiful, Luck Lindsay," Rosemary declared, giving him a bean sandwich for which he declared himself "strong," and holding the sugar bucket steady while he dipped into it three times.

"We were watching from the house; and the boys' faces, the way you had them placed, looked - oh, I don't know, but it just sent shivers all over me, it was so beautiful. I just hope it comes out that way in the picture!"

"Better," mumbled Luck, taking great, satisfying bites into the sandwich. "Wait till you see it - after it's colored - with the chuck-box end of the wagon showing, and the night horses standing back there in the shadows; she will sure look like a million dollars!"

"She'll shore depict me cookin' and the smoke bilin' up," poor old Applehead remarked lugubriously. "Last five minutes er so I could hear grease a-fryin' on my shins, now I'm tellin' yuh!"

"Well, they don't use radium flares in cold-storage plants," Luck admitted reflectively.

"I know, by cripes, I'm goin' to mend my ways," Big Medicine declared meaningly. "I never realized b'fore how fire 'n brimstone's goin' to feel!"

"Well, I've got to hand it to you, boys," Luck praised them with a smile. "You sat tight, and when I said 'Hold,' you sure held the pose. You dissolved perfectly - you'll see."

"Aw, gwan!" contradicted Happy Jack with his mouth full. "I never dissolved; I plumb melted!"

"If you boys could just see how beautiful you looked," Rosemary reproved, starting on her second round with the coffee boiler. "I saw it from behind the camera, and Luck had you sitting so the light was shining on your faces; honestly, you looked *beautiful*!"

"Aw, gwan!" gurgled Happy Jack, reddening uncomfortably.

"It's late," Luck broke in, emptying his cup the second time. "But I'm going to make that firelight scene of you, Annie. The wind happens to be just right for the flame effect I want. Did you make up, as I told you?"

For answer, Annie-Many-Ponies threw back her shrouding red shawl and stepped proudly out before him in the firelight. Her brown arms were bare and banded with bracelets of some dull metal. Her fringed dress of deerskin was heavily embroidered with stained porcupine quills. Her slim feet were clothed in beaded moccasins. It was the gala dress of the daughter of a chief, and as the daughter of a chief she stood straight and slender and haughty before him. The Happy Family stared at her, astonished. They had not even known that she possessed such a costume.

Ordinarily the Happy Family would have taken immediate advantage of their freedom and would have gone to bed and to the sleep for which their tired bodies hungered the more as the food and hot coffee filled them with a sense of well-being. But not even Rosemary wanted to go and miss any of that wonderful scene where Annie-Many-Ponies, young savage that she was, stood in the light of her flaming camp fire and prayed to her gods before she went to meet her lover. She rehearsed it once before Luck lighted the radium flares. Then, in the searing heat of that white-hot flame, which will melt rock as a candle melts, Annie-Many-Ponies crossed herself, and then lifted her young face and bare arms to the heavens and prayed as the priest in the mission school had taught her, - a real prayer in her own Indian tongue, while Luck turned the crank and gloated professionally in her beauty.

The Happy Family, watching her, remembered that it was Christmas morning; remembered oddly, in the midst of their work, the old, old story of the three Wise Men and the Star, and of the Wonder-Child in the manger. Something there was in the voice and the face of Annie-Many-Ponies that suggested it. Something there was of adoration in her upturned glance, as if she too were looking for the Star.

They did not talk much after that, and when they did, their voices were lower than usual. They banked the fire with sand, and Bill Holmes shouldered the camera with its precious store of scenes. As they trooped silently down to the house and to their beds, they felt something of the magnitude of life, something of the mystery. Behind them, treading noiselessly in her beaded deerskin moccasins, Annie-Many-Ponies followed like a houseless wraith of the plains, the little black dog at her heels.

CHAPTER SIXTEEN

"THE CHANCES IS SLIM AND GITTIN' SLIMMER"

"Must be going to snow," Weary observed with a sly twinkle, "'cause Paddy cat has got his tail brustled up bigger than a trapped coon."

"Aw, that's because Shunky Cheestely chased him all the way up from the corral a minute ago," Happy Jack explained the phenomenon. "I betcher he swaps ends some uh these times and gives that dog the s'prise of his life. He come purty near makin' a stand t'night."

"We-ell, when he does turn on that thar mongrel purp, they's goin' to be some dawg scattered around over the premises - now I'm tellin' yuh!" Applehead cocked his eye toward Annie-Many-Ponies and nodded his head in solemn warning. "He's takin' a mighty long chance, every time he turns that thar trick uh chasin' Compadre all over the place; and them that thinks anything uh that thar dawg - "

"I betcher it's goin' to snow, all right," Happy Jack interrupted the warning. "Chickydees was swarmin' all over the place, t'day."

"We-ell, now, yuh don't want to go too much on them

chickydees," Applehead dissented. "Change uh wind'll set them flockin' and chirpin'. Ain't ary flake uh snow in the wind t'day, fur's I kin smell - and I calc'late I kin smell snow fur's the next one."

"Oh, let's not talk about snow; that's getting to be a painful subject on this ranch," Rosemary pleaded, while she placed twelve pairs of steel knives and forks on the long, white-oilcloth-covered table.

"'Painful subject' is right," Luck stated grimly, glancing up from the endless figuring and scribbling which seemed to occupy all his time indoors that was not actually given over to eating and sleeping. "If you don't begin to smell snow pretty quick, Applehead, I can see where *The Phantom Herd* don't have any phantom herd." The corners of his mouth quirked upward, though his smile was becoming almost a stranger to his face.

"We-ell, I dunno's you can blame me because it don't snow. I can't make it snow if it takes a notion not to snow - "

"Oh, come and eat, and never mind the snow," called Rosemary impatiently.

"We've got to mind the snow - or we don't eat much longer!" Luck laid aside his papers with the tired gesture which betrays heavy anxiety. "The whole punch of the picture depends on that blizzard and what it leads up to. It's getting close to March, - this is the twentieth of February, - and the Texas Cattleman's Convention meets the first of April. I've got to have the picture done by then, so as to show it and get their endorsement as a body, in order to boost the sales up

B. M. Bower

where they belong."

"Mamma!" Weary looked up at him, open-eyed. "How long have you had that notion in your head, - showing the picture to the Cattlemen's Convention? I never heard of it."

"I might say quite a few things you haven't heard me say before," Luck retorted, so harassed that he never knew how sharp a snub he had given. "I've had that in mind from the start; ever since I read when and where the convention would meet this spring. We've got to have that blizzard, and we've got to have it before many more days."

"Oh, well, we'll have it," Rosemary soothed, as she would have comforted a child. "I just know March will come in like a roaring lion! Have some beans. They're different, to-night. I cooked them with plain salt pork instead of bacon. You can't imagine what a difference it makes!"

Luck was on the point of snapping out something that would have hurt her feelings. He did not want baby-soothing. It did not comfort him in the least to have her assure him that it would snow, when he knew she had absolutely no foundation for such an assurance. But just before he spoke, he remembered how bravely she had been smiling at hardships that would have broken the spirit of most women, so he took the beans and smiled at her, and did not speak at all.

Trouble, that month, was riding Luck hard. The blizzard that was absolutely vital to his picture-plot seemed as remote as in June. Other storms had come to delay his work without giving him the benefit of any spectacular effect. There had been days of whooping wind, when even the saddle strings popped in the air like whiplashes, and he could not "shoot" interior scenes because he could not shelter his stage from the wind, and everything blew about in a most maddening manner to one who is trying, for instance, to portray the calmness of a ranch-house kitchen at supper time.

There had been days of lowering clouds which brought nothing but exasperating little flurries of what Applehead called "spit snow," - flurries that passed before Luck could get ready for a scene. There had been one terrific sand storm which had nearly caught them in the open. But Applehead had warned them, and Luck, fortunately for them all, had heeded the warning. They had reached shelter just before the full force of the storm had struck them, and for six hours the air was a hell of sand in violent flight through the air. For six hours they could not see as far as the stable, and the rooms were filled with an impalpable haze of dust which filtered through minute crevices under the roof and around the doors and windows.

Luck, when that storm broke, was worried over his negative drying in the garret, until he had hurried up the ladder to see what might be done. He had found the film practically dry, and had carried it down in much relief to his dark room which, being light-proof, was also practically dust-proof.

There had been other vexations, but there had been fine, clear days as well. Luck had used those fine days to their full capacity for yielding him picture-light. Could he have been certain of getting his "blizzard stuff" now, he would have left but his one load of financial worry. That was a heavy one, but he felt he

B. M. Bower

could carry it with a better grace if only he could be sure that his picture would be completed in time.

"Pass the beans, Luck," Pink broke into his abstraction. "Seems like I've had beans before, this week, but I'll try them another whirl, anyway."

"Ever try syrup on 'em?" old Dave Wiswell looked up from his plate to inquire. "Once you git to likin' 'em that way, they go pretty good for a change."

Pink, anxious for variety in the monotonous menu, but doubtful of the experiment, poured a teaspoon of syrup over a teaspoon of beans, conveyed the mixture to his mouth, and made a hurried trip to the door. "Say! Was that a joke?" he demanded, when he returned grimacing to his place.

"Joke? No, ain't no joke about that," the dried little man testified earnestly. "Once you git to likin' 'em that way - "

Pink scowled suspiciously. "I'll take mine straight," he said, and sent a resentful glance at Annie-Many-Ponies who was tittering behind her palm.

"I calc'late I better beef another critter," Applehead suggested pacifically. "Worst of it is, the cattle's all so danged pore they ain't much pickin' left on their bones after the hide's skun off. If that blizzard ever does come, Luck's shore goin' to have all the pore-cow atmosphere he wants!"

To Luck their talk, good-humored though it was, hurt him like a blow upon bruised flesh. For their faith in him they were eating beans three times a day with laughter and jest to sweeten the fare. For their faith in him they were riding early and late, enduring hardships and laughing at them. If he failed, he knew that they would hide their disappointment under some humorous phase of the failure; - if they could find one. He could not tell them how close he was to failure. He could not tell them in plain words how much hung upon the coming of that storm in time for him to reach the cowmen at their convention. Their ignorance of the profession kept them from worrying much about it; their absolute confidence in his knowledge let them laugh at difficulties which held him awake when they were sleeping.

But for all that he went doggedly ahead, trusting in luck theoretically while he overlooked nothing that would make for success. While Applehead sniffed the air and shook his head, Luck was doing everything he could think of to keep things going steadily along to a completion of the production.

He made all of his "close-ups," his inserts, and sub-titles. He cut negative by his continuity sheet at night after the others were all in bed, and pigeon-holed the scenes ready for joining. He ordered what "positive" he would need, and he arranged for his advertising matter. All his interior scenes, save the double-exposure "vision" scenes, were done by the fifteenth of March, - March which had not come in like a roaring lion, as Rosemary had predicted with easy optimism, but which had been nerve-wrackingly lamblike to the very middle of the month.

With a dogged persistence in getting ready for the fulfilment of his hopes, he ordered tanks and printer for the final work of getting his stuff ready for the

B. M. Bower

market. He had at best a crudely primitive outfit, though he saw his bank balance dwindle and dwindle to a most despairingly small sum. And still it did not snow nor show any faint promise of snow.

"Well," he remarked grimly one morning, when the boys asked him at breakfast about his plans, "you can go back to bed, for all I care. I've done everything I can do - till we get that snowstorm. All we can do now is sit tight and trust to luck."

"What day uh the month is this?" Applehead wanted to know. His face was solemn with his responsibility as a weather prophet.

"The twentieth day of March," Luck replied, with the air of one who has the date branded deep on his consciousness.

"Twentieth uh March - hm-mm? We-ell, now, I have knowed it to storm, and storm hard, after this time uh year. But comin' the way she did last fall, 'n' all this here wind 'n' bluster 'n' snowin' on the Zandias and never comin' no further down, I calc'late the chances is slim, boy - 'n' gittin' slimmer every day, now I'm tellin' yuh!"

"Well, say! Ain't yuh got a purty fair pitcher the way she stands?" Big Medicine inquired aggressively. "Seems t' me we've done enough ridin' and actin', by cripes, t' make half a dozen pitchers better'n what I've ever saw."

"That isn't the point." Luck's voice was lifeless, with a certain dogged combativeness that had come into it during the last two months. "We've got to have that storm. This isn't going to be any make-shift affair. We've got some good film, yes. But it's like starting a funny story and being choked off before you get to the laugh in it. We've got to have that storm, I tell you!" His eyes challenged them harshly to dispute his statement.

"Well, darn it, have your storm, then. I'm willin'," Big Medicine bellowed with ill-timed facetiousness. "Pink, you run and git Luck a storm; git him a good big one, guaranteed to last 'im four days or money refunded. You git one - "

"Listen, Bud." Luck stood suddenly before Big Medicine, quivering with nervous rage. "Don't joke about this. There's no joke in this at all. No one with any brains can see anything funny in having failure stare him in the face. Twelve of us have put every ounce of our best work and our best patience and every dollar we possess in the world into this venture. I've worked day and night on this picture. I've worked you boys in weather that wasn't fit for a dog to be out in. I've seen Rosemary Green slaving in this dark little hole of a kitchen because we can't afford a cook for the outfit. You've all been dead game - I'll hand it to you for that - every white chip has gone into the pot. If we fail we'll have to borrow carfare to get outa here. And here's Applehead. We've used his ranch, we've used his house and his horses and himself; we've killed his cattle for beef, by - - ! And we've got just that one chance - the chance of a storm - for winning out. One chance, and that chance getting slimmer every day, as he says. No - there's no joke in this; or if there is, I've lost my appetite for comedy. I can't laugh." He stopped as suddenly as he had begun his rapid speech, caught up his hat, and went out alone into the soft morning sunlight. He left silence behind him, - a stunned silence that was awkward to break.

"It's a perfect shame!" Rosemary said at last, and her lips were trembling. "He's just about crazy - and I know he hasn't slept a wink, lately, just from worrying."

"I calc'late that's about the how of it," Applehead agreed, rubbing his chin nervously. "He lays awful still, last few weeks, and that thar's a bad sign fer him. And I ain't heerd 'im talkin' in his sleep lately, either. Up till lately he made more pitchers asleep than he done awake. Take it when things was movin' right along, Mis' Green, 'n' Luck was shore talkative, now I'm tellin' yuh!"

"My father, he got one oncle," Annie-Many-Ponies spoke up unexpectedly from her favorite corner. "Big Medicine man. Maybe I write one letter, maybe Noisy-Owl he come, make plenty storm. Noisy-Owl, he got awful strong medicine for make storm come."

"Well, by cripes, yuh better send for 'im then!" Big Medicine advised gruffly, and went out.

CHAPTER SEVENTEEN

THE STORM

The Phantom Herd, as the days slipped nearer and nearer to April, might almost have been christened *The Forlorn Hope*. On the twenty-first the sun was so hot that Luck rode in his shirt sleeves to Albuquerque, stubbornly intending to order more "positive" for his prints in the final work of putting his Big Picture into marketable form. He did not have the slightest idea of where the money to pay for the stuff was coming from, but he sent the letter ordering the stock sent C.O.D. He was playing for big results, and he had no intention of being balked at the last minute because of his timidity in assuming an ultimate success which was beginning to look extremely doubtful.

On the twenty-second, a lark flew impudently past his head and perched upon a bush near by and sang straight at him. As a general thing Luck loved to hear bird songs when he rode abroad on a fine morning; but he came very near taking a shot at that particular lark, as if it were personally responsible for the sunny days that had brought it out scouting ahead of its kind.

On the twenty-third the sky was a brassy blue, and Applehead won Luck's fierce enmity by remarking that he "calc'lated he'd better get his garden in." Luck went

B. M. Bower

away off somewhere on the snuffy little bay, that day, and did not return until after dark.

On the twenty-fourth he took the boys away back on the mesa, where the mountains shoulder the plain, and scattered them on a wide circle, rounding up the cattle that had been permitted to drift where they would in their famished search for the scant grass-growth. Bill Holmes and the camera followed him in the buckboard with the lunch, and Luck, when the boys had met with their gleanings, "shot" two or three short scenes of poor cows and their early calves, which would go to help along his range "atmosphere." To the Happy Family it seemed a waste of horseflesh to comb a twenty-mile radius of mesa to get a cow and calf which might have been duplicated within a mile of the ranch. The Happy Family knew that Luck was wading chin deep in the slough of despond, and they decided that he kept them riding all day just for pure cussedness.

I suppose they thought that his orders to range-herd the cattle they had gathered came from the same mood, but they did not seem to mind. They did whatever he told them to do, and they did it cheerfully, - which, in the circumstances, is saying a good deal for the Happy Family. So with the sun warm as early May, and the new grass showing tiny green blade-tips in the sheltered places, they began range-herding two thousand head of cattle that needed all the territory they could cover for their feeding grounds.

The twenty-fifth day of March brought no faintest promise of anything that looked like snow. Applehead sharpened his hoe and went pecking at the soil around the roots of his grape-vine arbor, thereby irritating Luck to the point of distraction. He had reached a nervous tension where he could not eat, and he could not sleep, and life looked a nightmare of hard work and disappointments, of hopes luring deceitfully only to crush one at the moment of fulfilment.

It was because he could not sleep, but spent the nights stretched upon his side with his wide-open eyes boring into vacancy and a drab future, that he heard the wind whine over the ridgepole of the squat bunk-house and knew that it had risen from a dead calm since bedtime. The languor of nervous exhaustion was pulling his eyelids down over his tired eyes, and he knew that it must be nearly morning; for sleep never came to him now until after Applehead's brown rooster had crowed for two o'clock.

He closed his eyes and dreamed that he was "shooting" blizzard scenes with the snow to his armpits. He was chilled to the middle of his bones, and his hand went down unconsciously and groped for the blankets he had pushed off in his restlessness. In his sleep he was yelling to the Cattlemen's Convention to wait, - not to adjourn yet, because he had something to show them.

"Well, show'em, dang it, an' shut up!" muttered Applehead crossly, and turned over on his good ear so that he could sleep undisturbed.

Luck, half awakened by the movement, curled up with his knees close to his chin and went on with his dream. With the wind still mooing lonesomely around the corners of the house, he slept more soundly than he had slept for weeks, impelled, I suppose, by a subconscious easement from his greatest anxiety.

A slow tap-tap-tapping on the closed door near his

B. M. Bower

head woke him just before dawn. The lightest sleeper of them all, Luck lifted his head with a start, and opened his sleep-blurred eyes upon blackness. He called out, and it was the voice of Annie-Many-Ponies that answered.

"Wagalexa Conka! You come quick. Plenty snow come. You be awful glad when you see. Soon day comes. You hurry. I make plenty breakfast, Wagalexa Conka."

As a soldier springs from sleep when calls the bugle, Luck jumped out into the icy darkness of the room. With one jerk he had the door open and stood glorying in the wild gust of snow that broke over him like a wave. In his bare feet he stood there, and felt the snow beat in his face, and said never a word, since big emotions never quite reached the surface of Luck's manner.

"Day come quick, Wagalexa Conka!" The voice of Annie-Many-Ponies urged him from without, like the voice of Opportunity calling from the storm.

"All right. You run now and have breakfast ready. We come quick." He held the door open another half minute, and he heard Annie-Many-Ponies laugh as she fought her way back to the house through the blinding blizzard. He saw a faint glow through the snow-whirl when she opened the kitchen door, and he shut out the storm with a certain vague reluctance, as though he half feared it might somehow escape into a warm, sunny morning and prove itself no more than a maddeningly vivid dream.

" Hey! Wake up!" he shouted while he groped for a

match and the lamp. "Roll into your sourdoughs, you sons-uh-guns - "

"Say, Applehead," came a plaintive voice from Pink's hunk, "make Luck turn over on the other side, can't yuh? Darn a man that talks in his sleep!"

"By cripes, Luck's got to sleep in the hay loft - er I will," Big Medicine growled, making the boards of his bunk squeak with the flop of his disturbed body.

Then Luck found the lamp and struck a match, and it was seen that he was very wide awake, and that his face had the look of a man intent upon accomplishment.

The Native Son sat up in one of the top bunks and looked down at Luck with a queer solemnity in his eyes. "What is this, *amigo*?" he asked with a stifled yawn. "Another one of your Big Minutes?"

"*Quien sabe?*" Luck retorted, reaching for his clothes as his small ebullition subsided to a misleading composure. "Storm's here at last, and we'll have to be moving. Roll out and saddle your ridge-runners; Annie's got breakfast all ready for us."

"Aw, gwan!" grumbled Happy Jack from sheer force of habit, and made haste to hit the floor with his feet before Luck replied to that apparent doubt of his authority.

"Dress warm as you can, boys," Luck advised curtly, lacing his own heavy buckskin moccasins over thick German socks, which formed his cold-weather footgear. "She's worse than that other one, if anything."

"Mamma!" Weary murmured, in a tone of thanks-giving. "She didn't come any too soon, did she?"

Luck did not reply. He pulled his hat down low over his forehead, opened the door and went out, and it was as though the wind and snow and darkness swallowed him bodily. The horses must first be fed, and he fought his way to the stables, where Applehead's precious hay was dwindling rapidly under Luck's system of keeping mounts and a four-horse team up and ready for just such an emergency. He labored through the darkness to the stable door, lighted the lantern which hung just inside, and went into the first stall. The manger was full, and the feed-box still moist from the lapping tongue of the gray horse that stood there munching industriously. Annie-Many-Ponies had evidently fed the horses before she called Luck, and he felt a warm glow of gratitude for her thoughtfulness.

He stopped at the bunk-house to tell the boys that they had nothing to do but eat breakfast before they saddled, and found them putting on overcoats and gloves and wrangling over the probable location of the herd that would have drifted in the night. So they ploughed in a straggling group to the house, where Annie-Many-Ponies was already pouring the coffee when they trooped in.

Day was just breaking when they rode out into the full force of the belated storm and up on the mesa where they had left the cattle scattered and feeding more or less contentedly at sundown. They had not gone a mile until their bodies began to shrink under the unaccustomed cold. Bill Holmes, town-bred and awkward in the open, thankfully resigned to the Indian girl the dignity of driving the mountain wagon with its four-horse team, and huddled under blankets, while Annie-Many-Ponies piloted them calmly straight across country in the wake of the riders whom her beloved Wagalexa Conka was leading on the snuffy bay. Save for the difference in his clothes, Annie-Many-Ponies thought that he much resembled that great little war-chief of the white people who rode ahead of his column in a picture hanging on the wall of the mission school. Napoleon was the great little war-chief's name, and her heart swelled with pride as she drove steadily through the storm and thought what a great war-chief her brother Wagalexa Conka might have made, were these but the days of much fighting.

There was to be no trouble with "static" this time, if Luck could help it. To be doubly safe from blurred film, he had brought his ray filter along, for the flakes of snow were large and falling fast. He had chosen a different location, because of the direction of the wind and the difficulty the boys would have had in driving the cattle back in the face of it to the side hill where he had first taken the scenes of the drifting herd.

To-day he "shot" them first as they were filing reluctantly out through a narrow pass which was supposed to be the entrance to the box canyon where the two rustlers, Andy and Miguel, had kept them hidden away. Artistically speaking, the cattle were in perfect condition for such a scene, every rib showing as they trooped past the clicking camera cleverly concealed in a clump of bushes; hip bones standing up, lean legs shambling slowly through the snow that was already a foot deep. Cattle hidden for days and days in a box canyon would not come out fat and sleek and stepping briskly, and Luck was well pleased with the realism of his picture, even while he pitied the

B. M. Bower

poor beasts.

Later he took the drifting of the herd, and he knew in his heart that the scenes were better than those he had lost. He took tragic scenes of the Native Son in his struggle to keep up and to keep going. He took him as he fell and lay prone in the snow beside his fallen horse while the blizzard whooped over him, and the snow fell upon his still face. In his zeal he nearly froze the Native Son, who must lie there during two or three "cut-back" scenes, and while Andy was coming up in search of him. When Andy lifted him and found him actually limp in his arms, the anxiety which a "close-up" revealed in his face was not all art. However, he did not say anything until Luck's voracious scene-appetite had been at least partially satisfied.

"By gracious, I believe the son-of-a-gun is about froze," he snapped out then; Luck grinned mirthlessly and called to Annie for the precious thermos bottle, and poured a cup of strong black coffee, added a generous dash of the apricot brandy which he spoke of familiarly as his "cure-all," and had the Native Son very much alive and tramping around to restore the circulation to his chilled limbs before Bill Holmes had carried the camera to the location of the next scene.

"By rights I should have left you the way you were till I got this last death scene where Andy buries you under the rock ledge so he can get home alive himself," Luck told Miguel heartlessly, when they were ready for work again. "You were in proper condition, brother. But I'm human. So you'll have to do a little more acting, from now on."

With his mats placed with careful precision, he took

his dissolve "vision stuff" of the blizzard and the death of Miguel, - scenes which were to torment the conscience of Andy the rustler into full repentance and confession to his father. While the boys huddled around Annie's camp fire and guzzled hot coffee and ate chilled sandwiches, Luck took some fine scenes of the phantom herd marching eerily along the skyline of a little slope.

He "shot" every effective blizzard scene he had dreamed of so despairingly when the weather was fine. Some scenes of especial importance to his picture he took twice, so as to have the "choice-of-action" so much prized by producers. This, you must know, was a luxury in which Luck had not often permitted himself to indulge. With raw negative at nearly four cents a foot, he had made it a point to shoot only such scenes as gave every promise of being exactly what he wanted. But with this precious blizzard that numbed his fingers most realistically while he worked, but never once worried him for fear the sun was going to shine before he had finished, he was as lavish of negative as though he had a million-dollar corporation at his back.

That evening, when they were luxuriating before the fireplace heaped with dry wood which the flames were licking greedily, Luck became, for the first time in months, the old Luck Lindsay who had fascinated them at the Flying U. He told them stories of his days with the "Bill show," and called upon the giggling Annie-Many-Ponies for proof of their truth; whereat Annie-Many-Ponies would nod her head vigorously and declare that it was "No lie. I see him plenty times do them thing. I know." He disputed energetically with Big Medicine over the hardships of the day's work; and

B. M. Bower

as a demonstration of the fact that he was perfectly able to go out right then and shoot another seven hundred feet of film, he seized upon the *tom-tom* which Annie-Many-Ponies had made from a green calf hide and an old cheese box, and in his moccasins he danced the Sioux Buffalo Dance and several other dances in which Annie-Many-Ponies finally joined and teetered around in the circle which the Happy Family enthusiastically widened for the performers.

Work there was yet to do, and plenty of it. Even if the weather came clear on the morrow as he desired, he must make every minute count, if he would take his picture to the Cattlemen's Convention. Work there was, and problems there were to be solved. But he had his big blizzard stuff, and he had his scenes of the phantom herd. So for an hour or two, on this evening of triumph, Luck Lindsay threw care into a far corner, and danced and sang as the Happy Family had never known he could do.

"Here, Annie, take the drum; it's 'call the dog and put out the fire and all go home.' If my luck stays with me, and the sun shines to-morrow, we'll take these interiors of the double-exposure stuff. And then we'll be eating on the run and sleeping as we ride, till that picture pops out on the screen for the old cattlemen to see. Good night, folks; I'm going to sleep to-night!"

He went out whistling like a schoolboy going fishing. For luck was with him once more, and his *Phantom Herd* was almost a reality as a picture.

CHAPTER EIGHTEEN

A FEW OF THE MINOR DIFFICULTIES

However obliging fate may desire to be, certain of nature's laws must be observed. Whether luck was disposed to stay with Luck Lindsay or not, a storm such as the fates had conjured for his needs could not well blow itself out as suddenly as it had blown itself in; so Luck did not get all of his interior double-exposure stuff done the next day, nor his remaining single-exposure stuff either. When his own reason and Applehead's earnest assurances convinced him that the day after the real blizzard day was going to be unfit for camera work, Luck took Weary, Pink, and the Native Son to Albuquerque, rented a little house he had discovered to be vacant, and set them to work building a drying drum for his prints, according to the specifications he furnished them. He hauled his tanks from the depot and showed the boys how to install them so as to have the benefit of the running water, and got his printer set up and ready to work; for he knew that he would have to make his first prints himself, with the help of the Happy Family, the photographer having neither the room nor the time for the work, and Luck having no more than barely money enough to pay house rent and the charges on his tanks and printer.

B. M. Bower

Then, being an obliging young man when the fates permitted him to indulge his natural tendencies, Luck made a hurried trip to a certain little shop that had dusty mandolins and watches and guns and a cheap kodak in the dingy window. He went in with his watch in his pocket ticking cheerfully the minutes and hours that were so full of work and worry. When he came out, the watch was ticking just as cheerfully in a drawer and the chain was looped prosperously across his vest from buttonhole to empty pocket. He went straight across to a grocery store and bought some salt pork and coffee and cornmeal and matches which Rosemary had timidly asked him if he could get. She explained apologetically that she was beginning to run out of things, and that she had no idea they were going to have such awful appetites, and that of course there were two extra people to feed, and that they certainly could dispose of their share three times a day, - meaning, of course, Annie-Many-Ponies and Bill Holmes.

Even while his brain was doing swift mental gymnastics in addition and subtraction, Luck had told her he would get whatever she wanted. His watch brought enough to buy everything she asked for except a can of syrup; and that, he told her, the groceryman must have overlooked, for he certainly had ordered it. He called the groceryman names enough to convince Rosemary that her list had not been too long for his purse, and that Luck's occasional statement that he was broke must be taken figuratively; Luck breathed a sigh of relief that Rosemary, at least, was once more spared the knowledge that all was not yet plain sailing to a smooth harbor.

The next day being sunny, Luck finished the actual

camera work on *The Phantom Herd*. That night he and Bill Holmes developed every foot of negative he had exposed since the storm began, and they finished just as Rosemary rapped on the darkroom door and called that breakfast was ready. Bill took it for granted that he could sleep, then, while the negative was drying; but Luck was merciless; that Cattlemen's Convention was only two days off, - counting that day which was already begun, - and there was also a twelve-hour train trip, more or less, between his picture and El Paso.

Bill Holmes had learned to join film in movie theaters, and Luck set him to work at it as soon as he had finished his breakfast. When Bill grumbled that there wasn't any film cement, Luck very calmly went to his trunk and brought some, thereby winning from Rosemary the admiring statement that she didn't believe Luck Lindsay ever forgot a single, solitary thing in his life! So Bill Holmes assembled the film, scene by scene, without even the comfort of cigarettes to keep awake. At his elbow Luck also joined film until the negative in the garret was dry enough to handle, when he began cutting it according to the continuity sheet, ready for Bill to assemble.

Luck's mood was changeable that day. He would glow with the pride of achievement when he held a yard or so of certain scenes to the light and knew that he had done something which no other producer had ever done, and that he had created a film story that would stand up like a lone peak above the level of all other Western pictures. When those night scenes were tinted - and that scene which had for its sub-title *Opening Exercises*, and which showed the Happy Family mounting Applehead's snakiest bronks and riding away from camp into what would be an orange sunrise after the positive had been through its dye bath -

And then discouragement would seize him, and he would wonder how he was going to get hold of money enough to take him to El Paso and the Convention. And how, in the name of destitution, was he going to pay for that stock of "positive" when it came? Applehead was dead willing to help him, - that went without saying; but Applehead was broke. That last load of horse-feed had cleaned his pockets, as he had cheerfully informed Luck over three weeks before. Applehead was not, and never would be by his own efforts, more than comfortably secure from having to get out and work for wages. He had cattle, but he let them run the range in season and out, and it was only in good years that he had fair beef to ship. He hated a gang of men hanging around the ranch and eating their fool heads off, he frequently declared. So he and Compadre had lived in unprosperous peace, with a little garden and a little grape arbor and a horse for Applehead in the corral, and teams in the pasture where they could feed and water themselves, and a month's supply of "grub" always in the house. Applehead called that comfort, and could not see the advantage of burdening himself with men and respon-sibilities that he might pile up money in the bank. You can easily see where the coming of Luck and his outfit might strain the financial resources of Applehead, even though Luck tried to bear all extra expense for him. No, thought Luck, Applehead would have to mortgage something if he were to attempt raising money then. And Luck would have taken a pack-outfit and made the trip to El Paso on horseback before he would see Applehead go in debt for him. As it was, he was seriously considering that pack-horse proposition as a last resort, and trying to invent some way of shaving his work down so that he would have time for the trip. But certain grim facts could not be twisted to meet his needs. He simply had to print his positive for projection on the screen. And that positive simply had to go through certain processes that took a certain amount of time; and it simply had to be dry and polished before he could wind it on his reels. Reels? Lord-ee! He didn't have any reels to wind it on!

"What's the matter? Spoil something?" Bill Holmes asked indifferently, pausing to look at Luck before he took up the next strip of celluloid ribbon with its perforated edges and its little squares of shadowlike pictures that to the unpractised eye looked all alike.

"No. What reel is that you're on now? We want to be in town before dark with this stuff, so as to start the printer going to-night." By printing, that night, and by hard riding, he might be able to make it, he was thinking.

"Think we'll be through in time?"

"Certainly, we'll be through in time." Luck held up another strip to see where to cut it. "We've got to be through!"

"I'm liable to be joining this junk by the sides instead of the ends, before long," Bill hinted.

"No, you won't do anything like that." Luck's voice had a disturbing note of absolute finality.

Bill looked at him sidelong. "A fellow can't work forever without sleep. My head's splitting right now. I can hardly see - "

"Yes, you can see well enough to do your work - and do it right! Get that?"

Bill grunted. Evidently he got it, for he said no more about his head, or about sleep. He did glance frequently out of the tail of his eye at Luck's absorbed face with his jaw set at a determined angle and his great mop of iron-gray hair looking like a heavy field of grain after a thunderstorm, standing out as it did in every direction. Now and then Luck pushed it back impatiently with the flat of his palm, but he showed no other sign of being conscious of anything at all save the picture; though he could have told you offhand just how many times Bill turned his eyes upon him.

At noon they were not through, and to Bill the attempt to finish that day seemed hopeless, not to say insane. But by four o'clock they were done with the cutting and joining, and had their film carefully packed and in the mountain wagon, and were ready to drive through the slushy mud which was the aftermath of the blizzard to the little house in Albuquerque which the boys had turned into a crude but efficient laboratory.

There Luck continued to be merciless in his driving energy. He canvassed the moving-picture theaters of the town and borrowed reels on which to wind his film when it was once ready for winding. He went back to the little house and set every one within it to work and kept them at it. He printed his positive, dissolved his aniline dye, which was to be firelight effect, in the bathtub, - and I should like to know what the landlord thought when next he viewed that tub! He made an orange bath for sunrise effects in one of the stationary tubs, and his light blue for night tints in the other. He buzzed around in that little house like a disturbed blue-bottle fly that cannot find an open window. He had his sleeves rolled to his shoulders and his hair more tousled than ever; he had blue circles under his eyes and dabs of dye distributed here and there on his face and his arms; he had in his eyes the glitter of a man who means to be obeyed instantly and implicitly, whatever his command may be, - and if you want to know, he was obeyed in just that manner.

Happy Jack and Big Medicine took turns at the crank of the big drying drum, around which Andy and Weary had carefully wound the wet film. Being a crude, home-made affair, the crank that kept that drum turning over and over did not work with the ease of ball-bearings. But Happy Jack, rolling his eyes up at Luck when he hurried past to attend to something somewhere, did not venture his opinion of the task. Nor did Big Medicine bellow any facetious remarks whatever, but turned and sweated, and used the other hand awhile, and turned and turned, and goggled at Luck whenever Luck came within his range of vision, and changed off to the other hand and turned and turned, and still said nothing at all.

Bill Holmes went to sleep about midnight and came near ruining a batch of firelight scenes in the analine bath, and after that Luck did all the technical part of the work himself. The Happy Family did what they could and wished they were not so ignorant and could do more. They could not, for instance, help Luck in the final assembling of the polished film and the putting in of the sub-titles and inserts. But they could polish that film, after he showed them how; so Pink and Weary did that. And at daylight Luck shook Bill Holmes awake and set him to work again.

Just to show that Luck was human, even though he was obsessed by a frenzy of work, he sent the boys outside, whenever one of them could be spared, for the smoke they craved and could not have among that five thousand feet of precious but highly inflammable film. But he did not treat himself to the luxury of a cigarette.

Luck had not yet solved the problem of meeting the expense of the trip to El Paso. Riding down with a pack-horse would take him too long; the best he could do would not be quick enough; for the Convention would be over before he got there, and his trip therefore useless. He worked just as fast, however, as though he had only to buy his ticket and take the train.

And then, when the last drumful was drying, he got his idea, and took Andy by the shoulder and led him out into the little front hall. "Boy," he said, "you hook up the team and drive like hell out to the ranch and get the camera and all the lenses. And right under the lid of my trunk you'll find a letter file marked Receipts. In the C pocket you'll find the sales slips of camera and so on; you bring them along. And bring my bag and any clean socks and handkerchiefs you can find, and my gray suit and some collars and ties. Oh, and my shoes. Make it back here by two o'clock if you can; before three at the latest."

"You bet yuh," assented Andy just as cheerfully as though he saw some sense in the order. Luck's clothes were a reasonable request, but Andy could not, for the life of him, figure any use for the camera and lenses; and as for the receipts, that sounded to him like plain delirium. Andy's brain, at that time, seemed to be revolving slowly round and round like the big drying drum, and his thoughts were tangled in exasperating visions of long, narrow strips of wet film.

However, at two-thirty he drove smartly up to the little house with the camera and Luck's brown leather bag packed with the small necessities of highly civilized journeying, and a large flat package wrapped in old newspapers. He had not set the brake that signalled the sweating horses to stop, before Luck was in the doorway with his hat on his head and the air of one whose business is both urgent and of large issues.

"Got the receipts? All right! Where are the things? This the lenses? All right! Put the team in the stable and go get yourself some rest."

"Where's your rest coming in at?" Andy flung back over his shoulder, as Luck turned away with the camera on his shoulder and the small case in his hands.

"Mine will come when I get through. I've got the last reel wound and packed, though. You bed down somewhere and sleep. I'll be back in a little. I'm going to catch that four o'clock train."

When you consider that Luck made that statement with about fifteen cents in his pocket and no ticket, you will understand why Andy gave him that queer look as he drove off to the stable. Luck might have climbed up beside Andy and ridden part of the way, but he was too preoccupied with larger matters to think of it until he found himself picking his footing around the mud through which Andy had splashed in comfort.

At the bank, Luck went in at the side door which gave

easy access to the office behind; and without any ceremony whatever he tapped on a certain glass-paneled door with a name printed across. He waited a second, and then turned the knob and walked briskly in, carrying camera, tripod, and the case of small attachments, and smiling his smile of white teeth and perfect assurance and much good will.

Now, the cashier whom he faced was a tall man worn thin with the worries of his position and the care of a family. He lived in a large white house, and his wife never seemed able to find a cook who could cook; so the cashier was troubled with indigestion that made his manner one of passive irritation with life. His children were for some reason forever "coming down" with colds or whooping-cough or measles or something (you have seen children like that), so his eyes were always tired with wakeful nights. It needed a Luck Lindsay smile to bring any answering light into the harassed face of that cashier, but it got there after the first surprised glance.

Luck stood his camera - screwed to its tripod - against the wall by the door. "I'm Luck Lindsay, Mr. White," he announced in his easy, Texas drawl. "I'm in a hurry, so I'll omit my full autobiography, if you don't mind, and let you draw your own conclusions about my reputation and character. I've a five-reel feature film called *The Phantom Herd* just completed, and I want to take it down to El Paso and show it before the Texas Cattlemen's Convention which meets there to-day. I want their endorsement of it as a Western film which really portrays the West, to incorporate in my advertisements in all the trade journals. But the production of the film took my last cent, and I've got to raise money on my camera for the trip down there.

You see what I mean. I'm broke, and I've got to catch that four o'clock train or the whole thing stops right here. This camera cost me close to fifteen hundred dollars. Here are the receipted sales slips to prove it. In Los Angeles I could easily get - " He caught the beginning of a denial in Mr. White's sidewise movement of the head - "ten times as much money on it as you can give me. You probably don't know anything at all about motion-picture cameras, but you can read these slips and find out how prices run."

Mr. White had in a measure recovered from the effects of Luck's smile. He picked up the slips and glanced at them indifferently. "There's a pawn-shop just down the street, I believe," he said. "Why - "

"I want to leave this camera here with you, anyway," Luck interrupted. "It's valuable - too valuable to take any risk of fire or burglary. I want to leave it in your vault. You've handled a good deal of my money, and you know who I am, and what my standing is, or else you aren't the right man for the position you occupy. It's your business to know these things. Now, I'm not asking you for any big loan. All I want is expense money for that trip. If you'll advance me seventy-five or a hundred dollars on my note, with this camera as security, I'll thank you and romp down to El Paso and get that endorsement before the convention adjourns till next year."

Mr. White looked at the camera strangely, as though he half expected it to explode. "I should have to take it up with the directors - "

"Directors! Hell, man, that train's due in an hour! What *are* you around here - a man in authority, or just a

B. M. Bower

dummy made up to look like one? Do you mean to tell me you're afraid to stake me to enough money to make El Paso and return? What, for the Lord's sake, do I look like, anyway, - a crook?"

Mr. White's head was more than six feet in the air when he stood up, and Luck Lindsay in his high-heeled boots lacked a good six inches of that altitude; but for all that, Luck Lindsay was a bigger man than Mr. White. He dominated the cashier; he made the cashier conscious of his dyspepsia and his thin hair and his flabby muscles and his lack of enthusiasm with life.

"The directors have to pass on all bank loans," he explained apologetically, "but I can lend you the money out of my personal account. If you will excuse me, I'll get the money before my assistant closes the vault. And shall I put these inside for you?" He rose and started for the inner door with a deprecating smile.

"Aren't you going to take a note?" Luck studied the man with sharpened glance.

"My check will be a sufficient record of the transaction, I think." And Mr. White, with two or three words scribbled at the bottom, proceeded to make the check a record. "I am glad to be able to stake you, Mr. Lindsay, and I hope your trip will be successful."

He got another Luck Lindsay smile for that, and the apology he had coming to him. And then in a very few minutes Luck hurried out and back to the little house on the edge of town.

"Where's my bag? So long, boys; I'm going to drift. I'll change clothes on the train - haven't got time now.

Here's five dollars, Andy, for the stable bill and so on. Bill, you're the only one of the bunch that shirked, so you can carry this box of reels to the depot for me. *Adios*, boys, I'm sure going to romp all over that Convention, believe me, if they don't swear *The Phantom Herd's* a winner from the first scene!"

B. M. Bower

CHAPTER NINETEEN

WHEREIN LUCK MAKES A SPEECH

Luck stood on the platform of the Texas Cattlemen's Convention and looked down upon the work-lined, brown faces of the men whose lives had for the most part been spent out of doors. Their sober attentiveness confused him for a minute so that he forgot what he wanted to say - he, Luck Lindsay, who had faced the great audiences of Madison Square Garden and had smiled his endearing smile and made his bow with perfect poise and an eye for pretty faces; who had without a quiver faced the camera, many's the time, in difficult scenes; who had faced death more times than he could count, and what was to him worse than death, - blank failure. But these old range-men with the wind-and-sun wrinkles around their eyes, and their ready-to-wear suits, and their judicial air of sober attention, - these were to him the jury that would weigh his work and say whether it was worthy. These men -

And then one of them suddenly cleared his throat with a rasping sound like old Dave Wiswell, his dried little cowman of the picture, and embarrassment dropped from Luck like a cloak flung aside. He was here to put his work to the test; to let these men say whether *The Phantom Herd* was worthy to be called a great picture, one of which the West could be proud. So he pushed back his mop of hair - grayer than the hair of many here old enough to be his father - with the fiat of his palm, and looked straight into the faces of these men and said what he had to say:

"Mr. Chairman, and gentlemen of this Convention, I consider it a great privilege to be able to stand here and speak to you - a greater privilege than any of you realize, perhaps. For my heart has always been in the range-land, my people have been the people of the plains. I have to-day been honored by the hand-grip of old-timers who were riding circle, trailing long-horns, and working cattle when I was a boy in short pants.

"I have trailed herds on the pay roll of one man who remembers me here to-day, and of others who have crossed the Big Divide. I have seen the open range shrink before the coming of barbed wire and settlers. I have watched the 'long shadow' fall across God's own cattle country.

"Since I entered the motion-picture business, my one great aim and my one great dream has been to produce one real Western picture. One picture that I could present with pride to such a convention as this, and have men who have spent their lives in the cattle industry give it the stamp of their approval; one picture that would make such men forget the present and relive the old days when they were punchers all and proud of it. Such an opportunity came to me last fall and I made the most of it. I got me a bunch of real boys, and went to work on the picture I have called *The Phantom Herd.* From the trail-herds going north I have tried to weave into my story a glimpse of the whole history of the range critter, from the shivering, new-born calf that hit the range along with a spring blizzard, to the big, four-year-old steer prodded up the chutes into the shipping cars.

"I want you, who know the false from the real, to see *The Phantom Herd* and say whether I have done my work well. I finished the picture yesterday, and I have brought it down here for the purpose of asking you to honor me by accepting an invitation to a private showing of the picture this evening, here in this hall. I want you to come and bring your wives and your children with you if you can. I want you to see *The Phantom Herd* before it goes to the public - and to-morrow I shall face you again and accept your verdict. You know the West. You will know a Western picture when you see it. I know you know, and I want you to tell me what you think of it. Your word will be final, as far as I am concerned. Gentlemen, I hope you will all be present here to-night at eight o'clock as my guests. I thank you for your attention."

Luck went away from there feeling, and telling himself emphatically, that he had made a "rotten" talk. He had not said what he had meant to say, or at least he had not said it the way he had meant to say it. But he was too busy to dwell much upon his deficiencies as an orator; he had yet to borrow a projection machine and operator from somewhere - for, as usual, he had issued his invitation before he had definitely arranged for the exhibition, and had trusted to luck and his own efforts to be able to keep his promise.

Luck (or his own efforts) landed him within easy conversational reach of a man who was preparing to open a little theater on a side street. The seats were not in yet, but he had his machine, and he meant to operate it himself, while his wife sold tickets and his boy acted as usher, - a family combination which to Luck seemed likely to be a success. This man, when Luck made known his needs, said he was perfectly willing to "limber up" his machine and himself on *The Phantom Herd*, if Luck would let his wife and boy see the picture, and would pay the slight operating expenses. So that was settled very easily.

At five minutes to eight that evening all of the cattlemen and a few favored, influential citizens of El Paso whom Luck had invited personally sat waiting before the blank screen. Up in the operator's cramped quarters Luck was having a nervous chill and trying his best not to show it, and he was telling the operator to give it time enough, for the Lord's sake, and to be sure he had everything ready before he started in, and so forth, until the operator was almost as nervous as Luck himself.

"Now, look here," he cried exasperatedly at last. "You know your business, and I know mine. You're going to have me named in your write-ups as the movie-man that run this show for the convention, ain't you? And I'm going to open up a picture house next week in this town, ain't I? And I ain't going to advertise myself as a bum operator, am I? Now you *vamos* outa here and get down there in the audience, if you don't want me to get the fidgets and spoil something. Go on - beat it!"

Luck must have been in a strange condition, for he beat it promptly and without any retort, and slid furtively into a chair between two old range-men just as the operator's boy-usher switched off the lights. Luck's heart began to pound so that he half expected his neighbors to tell him to close his muffler, - only they were of the saddle-horse fraternity and would not have known what the phrase meant.

The Phantom Herd flashed suddenly upon the screen and joggled there dizzily, away over to one side. Luck clapped his hand to his perspiring forehead and murmured "Oh, my Gawd!" like a prayer, and shut his eyes to hide from them the desecration. He opened them to find that the caste was just flicking off and the first scene dissolving in.

The man at his left gave a long sigh and crossed his knees, and leaned back and began to chew tobacco rapidly between his worn old molars.

"Oh, a ten dollar hoss and a forty dollar saddle,
I'm goin' to punchin' Texas cattle."

The sub-title dissolved slowly into a scene showing a cow-puncher (who was Weary) swinging on to his rangy cow-Horse and galloping away after the chuck-wagon just disappearing in the wake of the dust-flinging *remuda*. Back somewhere in the dusk of the audience, a man began to hum the tune that went with the words, and the heart of Luck Lindsay gave an exultant bound. He had used lines from "The Old Chisholm Trail" and other old-time range songs for his sub-titles, to keep the range atmosphere complete, and that cracked voice humming unconsciously told how it appealed to these men of the range.

Luck did not slide down in his seat so that his head rested on the chair-back while *The Phantom Herd* was being shown. Instead, he sat leaning forward, with his face white and strained, and watched for weak points and for bad photography and scenes that could have been bettered.

He saw the big trail-herd go winding away across the level, with Weary riding "point" and Happy Jack bringing up the "drag," and the others scattered along between; riding slouched in their saddles, hatbrims pulled low over eyes smarting with the dust that showed in a thin film at the head of the herd and grew thicker toward the drag, until riders and animals were seen dimly through a haze.

"My - I can just feel that dust in m' throat!" muttered the man at his right, and coughed.

Luck saw the storm come muttering up just as the cattle were bedding down for the night. He saw the lightning, and he knew that those who watched with him were straining forward. He heard some one say involuntarily: "They'll break and run, sure as hell!" and he knew that he had done that part of his work well.

He saw the night scenes he had taken in town. He almost forgot that all this was his work, so smoothly did the story steal across his senses and beguile him into half believing it was true and not a fabric which he had built with careful planning and much toil. He saw the round-up scenes; the day-herd, the cutting-out and the branding, the beef-herd driven to the shipping cars. True, those steers were not exactly prime beef, - he had caught the culls only, late in the season for these scenes - but they passed, with one audible comment that this was a poor season for beef!

"We rounded 'em up and we put 'em in the cars - "

The sub-title sang itself familiarly into the minds of the range men. More than one voice was heard to begin a surreptitious humming of the old tune, and to cease abruptly with the sudden self-consciousness of the singer.

But there was the story, growing insensibly out of the range work. Luck, more at ease now in his mind, studied it critically. There was the quarrel between old Dave and Andy, his son. He saw the old man out with his men, standing his shift of night-guard, stubbornly resisting the creeping years and his load of trouble; riding around the sleeping herd with his head sunk on his chest, meeting the younger guard twice on each complete circle, and yet never seeming to see him at all.

"Sing low to your cattle, sing low to your steers - "

The words and the scene opened wide the door of memory and let whole troops of ghosts come drifting in out of the past. The hall, Luck roused himself to notice, was very, very still; so still that the sizzling sound of the machine at the rear was distinct and oppressive.

There was the blizzard, terrible in its biting realism. There was the old cow and calf, separated from the herd, fighting in the primal instinct to preserve themselves alive, - fighting and losing. There was that other, more terrible fight for existence, the fight of the Native Son against the snow and the cold. Men drew their breath sharply when he fell and did not rise again. They shivered when the snow began to drift against his quiet body, to lodge and shift and settle, and grow higher and higher until the bank was even with his shoulders, to drift over him and make of him a white mound - And then, when Andy staggered up through the swirl, leading his horse and shouting; when he stumbled against Miguel and tried to raise him and rouse him, a sound like a groan went through the crowd.

"Close a call as I ever had was in a blizzard like that," the old man at Luck's left whispered agitatedly to Luck behind his palm, when the lights snapped on while the operator was changing for the last reel.

There was Andy, haunted and haggard, at home again with his father. There were those dissolve scenes of the "phantom herd" drifting always across the skyline whenever Andy looked out into the night or rose startled from uneasy sleep. Weird, it was, - weird and real and very terrible. And, at last, there was that wonderful camp-fire scene of the Indian girl who prayed to her gods before she went to meet her lover who was dead and could not keep the tryst. There were heart-breaking scenes where the Indian girl wandered in wild places, looking, hoping, despairing - Luck had planned every little detail of those scenes, and yet they thrilled him as though he had come to them unawares.

He did not wait after the last scene faded out slowly. He slipped quietly into the aisle and went away, while the hands of the old-timers were stinging with applause. Halfway down the block he heard it still, and his steps quickened unconsciously. They were calling his name, back there in the hall. They were all talking at once and clapping their hands and, as an interlude, shouting the name of Luck Lindsay. But Luck did not heed. He wanted to get away by himself. He did not feel as though he could say anything at all to any one, just then. He had seen his Big Picture, and he had seen that it was as big and as perfect, almost, as he had dreamed it. To Luck, at that moment, words would have cheapened it, - even the words of the old cattlemen.

He went to his hotel and straight up to his room, regardless of the fact that it would have been to his advantage to mingle with his guests and to listen to their praise. He went to bed and lay there in the dark, reliving the scenes of his story. Then, after awhile, he drifted off into sleep, his first dreamless, untroubled slumber in many a night.

By the time the Convention was assembled the next day, however, he had recovered his old spirit of driving energy. The chairman had invited him by telephone to attend the afternoon meeting, and Luck went - to be greeted by a rousing applause when he walked down the aisle to the platform where the chairman was waiting for him.

Resolutions had already been passed, the Convention as a body thanking Luck Lindsay for the privilege of seeing what was in their judgment the greatest Western picture that had ever been produced. The chairman made a little speech about the pleasure and the privilege, and presented Luck with a letter of endorsement and signed with due formality by chairman and secretary and sealed with the official seal. Attached to the letter was a copy of the vote of thanks, and you may imagine how Luck smiled when he saw that!

He stayed a little while, and during the recess which presently was called he shook hands with many an old-timer whose name stood for a good deal in the great State of Texas. Then he left them, still smiling over what he called his good luck, and wired a copy of the letter of endorsement to all the trade journals, to be incorporated in his full-page advertising. By another stroke of luck he caught most of the trade journals before their forms closed for the next issue, so that *The Phantom Herd* was speedily heralded throughout the profession as the first really authentic Western drama ever produced. By still another stroke of what he called luck, an Associated Press man found him out, and was pleased to ask him many questions and to make a few notes; and Luck, wise to the value of publicity, answered the questions and saw to it that the notes recorded interesting facts.

That evening Luck, feeling that he had reached the last mile-post on the road to success, hunted up a few old-timers who appealed to him most as true types of the range, and gave them a dinner in a certain place which he knew was run by an old round-up cook. There was nothing about that dinner which would have appealed to a cabaret crowd. They talked of the old days when Luck was a lad, those old-timers; they talked of trail-herds and of droughts and of floods and blizzards and range wars and the market prices of beef "on the hoof." They called in the old round-up cook and cursed him companionably as one of themselves, and remembered that more than one of them had run when he pounded the bottom of a frying pan and hollered "Come and get it!" They ate and they smoked and they talked and talked and talked, until Luck had to indulge himself in a taxi if he would not miss the eleven o'clock train north. His only regret, in spite of the fact that he was practically and familiarly broke again, was that circumstances did not permit the Happy Family to sit with him at that table. Especially did he regret not having old Applehead and the dried little man with him that night to make his gathering complete.

B. M. Bower

CHAPTER TWENTY

"SHE'S SHAPING UP LIKE A BANK ROLL"

"Well," said Luck to the Happy Family, "we've come this far along the trail, and now I'm stuck again. Bank won't loan any more on the camera, and I've got a dollar and six bits to market *The Phantom Herd* with! Everything's fine so far; she's advertised, - or will be when the magazines come out, - and she's got some good press notices to back her up; but she ain't outa the woods yet. I've got to raise some money somehow. I hate to ask poor old Applehead - "

"Pore old Applehead, my granny!" bawled Big Medicine, laughing his big *haw-haw*. "Pore ole Applehead's sure steppin' high these days. He'd mortgage his ranch and feel like a millionaire, by cripes! His ole Come-Paddy cat jest natcherally walloped the tar outa Shunky Cheestely, and Applehead seen him doin' it. Come-Paddy, he's hangin' out in the house now, by cripes, 'cept when he takes a sashay down to the stable lookin' fer more. And Shunky, he's bedded down under the Ketch-all, when he ain't hittin' fer the tall timber with his tail clamped down between his legs. Honest to grandma, Luck, you couldn't hit Applehead at a better time. He'll borry money er do anything yuh care to ask, except shut up that there cat uh hisn."

"Well, luck may come my way; I'll just sit tight a few days and see," said Luck. "When that positive film comes, I'll have to rustle money somewhere to get it outa the express office, so we can make more prints. And - "

"And grind our daylights out again on that there drum that never does git wound up?" groaned Big Medicine, and felt his biceps tenderly.

"We won't rush the next job quite so hard," Luck soothed, perfectly amiable and easy to live with, now that the worst was over. "We made a darn good set of prints, just the same; boys, you oughta seen that picture! I've a good mind to get some house here in town to run it; say, I might raise some money that way, if I can't do it any other." And then his enthusiasm cooled. "Town isn't big enough for a long-enough run," he considered disgustedly. "I'm past the two-bit stage of the game now."

"Well, you ask Applehead to raise the money," advised Weary. "Or one of us will write to Chip for some. Mamma! The world's full of money! Seems like it ought to be easy to get hold of some."

"It is - but it ain't," Luck stated somewhat ambiguously, and turned the talk to his meeting with the old-timers, and prepared to "sit tight" and wait for his god Good Luck to smile upon him.

The smile arrived at noon the next day, in the form of a wire from Philadelphia. Luck read it and gave a whoop of joy quite at variance with his usual surface calm.

Can Offer You Fifteen Hundred Dollars for

B. M. Bower

Pennsylvania Rights The Phantom Herd Usual Ten Cents Per Foot Positive Prints if Accepted Wire at Once and Ship to This Point

RJ Crittenden

"I hollered too soon," groaned Luck, when he had read it the second time, pushing back his hair distractedly. "How the devil am I going to send him any positive prints at ten cents a foot or ten cents an inch or any other price? Till I get that shipment of positive, I can't fill any orders at all! And until I begin to fill orders, I can't realize on the film. Can you beat that? I'll have to wire him to wait, and that's two thousand dollars tied up!"

"Aw, gwan!" Happy Jack croaked argumentatively. "Why don't you send him what you took to the Convention?"

Luck stared at Happy stupefied before he said a word. "Say, Miguel, you saddle your ridge-runner while I get ready to take this wire hack to town and send it off," he snapped, preparing to write. "Sure, I'll send that set of prints! Happy, you can go to the head of the class. Now it's only a case of sit tight till the money comes. The prints are packed and in the bank vault, so I'll just get them out and send them C.O.D. to Mr. Crittenden, along with the states rights contract. How's that for luck, boys?"

"Pretty good - for Luck," grinned Andy meaningly. "Fly at it, you coming millionaire!"

"Just a case of sit tight, boys. *Adios!*" cried Luck jubilantly as he hurried away.

Once start along a smooth trail, and everything seems to conspire toward a pleasant trip. To prove it, Luck found another telegram waiting for him in Albuquerque. This was from Martinson, and might be interpreted as an apology more or less abject. Certainly it was an urgent request that he return immediately to Los Angeles and to his old place at the Acme, and produce Western pictures under no supervision whatever.

Luck gave a little chuckle when he pocketed that message, but he did not send any answer. He meant to wait and talk it over with the boys first. "Better proposition than before," Martinson said. Well, perhaps it would be best to look into it; Luck was too experienced to believe that one success means permanent success; there are too many risks for the free lance to run when a single failure means financial annihilation. If the Acme would come to his terms, it might be to his advantage to take his boys back and accept this peace-offering. At any rate, he appreciated to the full the triumph they had scored.

Next, by some twist of the red tape in the Philadelphia express office, - or perhaps R.J. Crittenden was a good fellow and asked them to do it, - the two thousand dollars came by wire, just three days after Luck had received notice that his shipment of positive film was being held for him at the express office in Albuquerque. Also came other offers, mostly by wire, for states rights to *The Phantom Herd.* And when the Happy Family realized what those offers meant, they didn't care how hard or how long Luck worked them in the little house which he had turned into a laboratory.

Being human, intensely so in some ways, the first set

of prints they turned out Luck sent to Los Angeles with a mental godspeed and a hope that Bently Brown and Martinson would see it and "get wise to what a *real* Western picture looked like." There were other orders ahead of Los Angeles in Luck's book, but they waited a little longer so that he might the sooner taste a little of the sweets of revenge.

Whether Bently Brown and Martinson saw *The Phantom Herd,* Luck was a long, long time finding out. But he learned that some one else did see it, and that right speedily. For among his many telegrams that came clicking into Albuquerque was this one which makes a fitting end to this story:

Luck Lindsay
Albuquerque
New Mexico

Congratulations on *The Phantom Herd* Wonderful Production New Proposition You to Produce Western Features with Your Present Company on Straight Salary and Bonus Basis Miss Jean Douglas to Play Your Leads if I Can Sign Her up Can You Come Here at Once to Close Deal Answer

Dewitt

"All right, boys, you can run and play." Luck handed them the telegram, looked at his watch, and began to roll down his sleeves. "I'll catch the next train for 'Los' and see Dewitt, - don't take any studying to know that's the thing to do, - and if you'll pack all this negative, Bill, I'll take that along and hire the rest of the prints made. Andy, you're riding herd on this bunch while I'm gone. Just hold yourselves ready for orders, because I don't know how things will shape up. But believe me, boys, she's shaping up like a bank-roll!"

B. M. Bower

Choose from Thousands of 1stWorldLibrary Classics By

Adolphus William Ward
Aesop
Agatha Christie
Alexander Aaronsohn
Alexander Kielland
Alexandre Dumas
Alfred Gatty
Alfred Ollivant
Alice Duer Miller
Alice Turner Curtis
Alice Dunbar
Ambrose Bierce
Amelia E. Barr
Andrew Lang
Andrew McFarland Davis
Anna Sewell
Annie Besant
Annie Hamilton Donnell
Annie Payson Call
Anton Chekhov
Arnold Bennett
Arthur Conan Doyle
Arthur Ransome
Atticus
B. M. Bower
Basil King
Bayard Taylor
Ben Macomber
Booth Tarkington
Bram Stoker
C. Collodi
C. E. Orr
C. M. Ingleby
Carolyn Wells
Catherine Parr Traill
Charles A. Eastman
Charles Dickens
Charles Dudley Warner
Charles Farrar Browne
Charles Ives
Charles Kingsley
Charles Lathrop Pack
Charles Whibley
Charles Willing Beale
Charlotte M. Braeme
Charlotte M.Yonge
Clair W. Hayes
Clarence Day Jr.
Clarence E. Mulford

Clemence Housman
Confucius
Cornelis DeWitt Wilcox
Cyril Burleigh
D. H. Lawrence
Daniel Defoe
David Garnett
Don Carlos Janes
Donald Keyhole
Dorothy Kilner
Dougan Clark
E. Nesbit
E.P.Roe
E. Phillips Oppenheim
Edgar Allan Poe
Edgar Rice Burroughs
Edith Wharton
Edward J. O'Biren
John Cournos
Edwin L. Arnold
Eleanor Atkins
Elizabeth Cleghorn
Gaskell
Elizabeth Von Arnim
Ellem Key
Emily Dickinson
Erasmus W. Jones
Ernie Howard Pie
Ethel Turner
Ethel Watts Mumford
Eugenie Foa
Eugene Wood
Evelyn Everett-Green
Everard Cotes
F. J. Cross
Federick Austin Ogg
Ferdinand Ossendowski
Francis Bacon
Francis Darwin
Frances Hodgson Burnett
Frank Gee Patchin
Frank Harris
Frank Jewett Mather
Frank L. Packard
Frederick Trevor Hill
Frederick Winslow Taylor
Friedrich Kerst
Friedrich Nietzsche
Fyodor Dostoyevsky

Gabrielle E. Jackson
Garrett P. Serviss
Gaston Leroux
George Ade
Geroge Bernard Shaw
George Ebers
George Eliot
George MacDonald
George Orwell
George Tucker
George W. Cable
George Wharton James
Gertrude Atherton
Grace E. King
Grant Allen
Guillermo A. Sherwell
Gulielma Zollinger
Gustav Flaubert
H. A. Cody
H. B. Irving
H. G. Wells
H. H. Munro
H. Irving Hancock
H. Rider Haggard
H. W. C. Davis
Hamilton Wright Mabie
Hans Christian Andersen
Harold Avery
Harold McGrath
Harriet Beecher Stowe
Harry Houidini
Helent Hunt Jackson
Helen Nicolay
Hendy David Thoreau
Henrik Ibsen
Henry Adams
Henry Ford
Henry Frost
Henry James
Henry Jones Ford
Henry Seton Merriman
Henry Wadsworth
Longfellow
Henry W Longfellow
Herbert A. Giles
Herbert N. Casson
Herman Hesse
Homer
Honore De Balzac

Horace Walpole
Horatio Alger, Jr.
Howard Pyle
Howard R. Garis
Hugh Lofting
Hugh Walpole
Humphry Ward
Ian Maclaren
Israel Abrahams
J.G.Austin
J. Henri Fabre
J. M. Barrie
J. Macdonald Oxley
J. S. Knowles
J. Storer Clouston
Jack London
Jacob Abbott
James Allen
James Lane Allen
James Andrews
James Baldwin
James DeMille
James Joyce
James Oliver Curwood
James Oppenheim
James Otis
Jane Austen
Jens Peter Jacobsen
Jerome K. Jerome
John Burroughs
John F. Kennedy
John Gay
John Glasworthy
John Habberton
John Joy Bell
John Milton
John Philip Sousa
Jonathan Swift
Joseph Carey
Joseph Conrad
Joseph Jacobs
Julian Hawthrone
Julies Vernes
Justin Huntly McCarthy
Kakuzo Okakura
Kenneth Grahame
Kate Langley Bosher
L. A. Abbot
L. T. Meade
L. Frank Baum
Laura Lee Hope

Laurence Housman
Leo Tolstoy
Leonid Andreyev
Lewis Carroll
Lilian Bell
Lloyd Osbourne
Louis Tracy
Louisa May Alcott
Lucy Fitch Perkins
Lucy Maud Montgomery
Lydia Miller Middleton
Lyndon Orr
M. H. Adams
Margaret E. Sangster
Margaret Vandercook
Maria Edgeworth
Maria Thompson Daviess
Mariano Azuela
Marion Polk Angellotti
Mark Overton
Mark Twain
Mary Austin
Mary Cole
Mary Rowlandson
Mary Wollstonecraft Shelley
Max Beerbohm
Myra Kelly
Nathaniel Hawthrone
O. F. Walton
Oscar Wilde
Owen Johnson
P.G.Wodehouse
Paul and Mable Thorn
Paul G. Tomlinson
Paul Severing
Peter B. Kyne
Plato
R. Derby Holmes
R. L. Stevenson
Rabindranath Tagore
Rahul Alvares
Ralph Waldo Emmerson
Rene Descartes
Rex E. Beach
Richard Harding Davis
Richard Jefferies
Robert Barr
Robert Frost
Robert Gordon Anderson
Robert L. Drake

Robert Lansing
Robert Michael Ballantyne
Robert W. Chambers
Rosa Nouchette Carey
Ross Kay
Rudyard Kipling
Samuel B. Allison
Samuel Hopkins Adams
Sarah Bernhardt
Selma Lagerlof
Sherwood Anderson
Sigmund Freud
Standish O'Grady
Stanley Weyman
Stella Benson
Stephen Crane
Stewart Edward White
Stijn Streuvels
Swami Abhedananda
Swami Parmananda
T. S. Ackland
The Princess Der Ling
Thomas A. Janvier
Thomas A Kempis
Thomas Anderton
Thomas Bailey Aldrich
Thomas Bulfinch
Thomas De Quincey
Thomas H. Huxley
Thomas Hardy
Thomas More
Thornton W. Burgess
U. S. Grant
Valentine Williams
Victor Appleton
Virginia Woolf
Walter Scott
Washington Irving
Wilbur Lawton
Wilkie Collins
Willa Cather
Willard F. Baker
William Makepeace Thackeray
William W. Walter
Winston Churchill
Yei Theodora Ozaki
Young E. Allison
Zane Grey